STOPPI

Victoria's gaze met his shyly before skittering away. "It's almost midnight. I've got to go."

"Don't."

Victoria licked her lips. "Don't what?"

Adrian opened his mouth and then closed it. He seemed to struggle with his words. A frown overtook him. "I...don't want you to go."

"What do you want me to do?"

He looked at her, so incredulous that Victoria wondered if her actual spoken question didn't match her thoughts at all. Adrian's low laughter made her take a step back. He immediately stopped and reached out.

"I'm sorry, Victoria. I'm not laughing at you. I'm laughing at me."

"Why?"

He shook his head. "It doesn't matter. Look, Victoria, I didn't plan for this. I plan everything but not this." His hand skated down her arm. Victoria felt the leashed power in it. "I planned to let you go. To do this slow. But I can't. I don't want to. Do you understand?"

ADRIAN

Anna Antonia

DelSin Publishing, LLC 2015

Published by:
DelSin Publishing, LLC
www.delsinpublishing.com

Cover Credits: ConnorE@depositphotos & George Meyer
Cover Design: CGM Web Designs

ADRIAN

ONE

Adrian Hawthorne was not a man prone to idleness. An early riser, he worked out like a professional athlete every day before showering and eating breakfast. Plugged into his mobile and laptop by seven a.m., he was generally the first to arrive at the office and the last to leave.

Work was his addiction of choice and Adrian had no desire to change that.

He was a child born with the proverbial silver spoon in his mouth, but Adrian fought his way to the top of a heap that cared exactly zero for his pedigree and Ivy League accomplishments. Never content with trading on his family name, Adrian had been determined to prove his mettle and change the world as a byproduct.

So he'd founded a company to do just that by the time he was twenty-one. The NYSE was just one of the markets to benefit from his digital prowess and excellent eye for finding and hiring the best programmers the world had to offer.

When his company went public every single hire, all the way down to the receptionist, was a millionaire. Scenting the winds were changing in tech, Adrian made the prudent decision to sell and walked away with nearly half a billion in his account.

Adrian could've retired to a sunny island and lived comfortably off the residuals for the rest of his life. Retirement wasn't even on the horizon for him because Adrian Hawthorne was just getting started.

Not the least bit complacent with his early success, Adrian left the tech field and entered the hospitality industry, boutique hotels in particular. Catering to the nouveau riche through thoughtful design and artisan detail did much to fatten his net worth, but Adrian soon found it to be dull work once he'd established his world-wide brand.

Hungry for a challenge, Adrian hurtled into the lucrative arena of data mining. When that didn't prove challenging enough, he turned his sights to the Arctic. Iron ore in particular. Partnering with an established firm, Adrian tackled the logistics and environmental nightmares with a laser focus that didn't leave room for failure.

Not surprisingly, the venture was an unequivocal success.

All Adrian's countless hours of unflagging work and predatory instincts left him in the enviable position of quadrupling the Hawthorne family wealth as well as his own.

A billionaire by age thirty, Adrian was confident there was little left to conquer—not in the business world and especially not in his personal life. A handsome face and staggering wealth were a potent combination to the women of his acquaintance. As a consequence, Adrian had sampled more than his fair share of models, actresses, and socialites throughout the years.

Even so, he'd yet to even come within spitting distance of a church. The only jewelry he bought were the colorful trinkets his latest paramour expected as her due. Never a stingy man in body or generosity, Adrian had showered his lovers with all the material possessions they could've desired. Trips around the world were commonplace in his courtships and he'd bought enough jewels, clothes, and cars to drive his personal accountant into apoplexy on a quarterly basis.

Still, none of those gorgeous women had stayed long enough to make an inevitable move towards the altar and matrimony.

Although once there was an actress who'd left a bridal magazine on his side of the bed, prompting Adrian to bid her adieu by the following evening. She'd gotten married to her costar six weeks later and Adrian had sent the blessed couple an all-expense paid stay at any of his exclusive hotels as a gift—which they'd politely accepted.

Adrian Hawthorne was in his prime and extremely happy with his life as it was. He went where he pleased, worked as often as he wanted, and never lacked for charming companionship.

The world was his and it was good.

Little did he know implosion was imminent to his carefully managed kingdom.

And that implosion's name was Victoria Montford.

***

Victoria Montford worked like a woman possessed. She had classes in the mornings and afternoons at the university five days a week. She worked at her first job Friday through Monday as a waitress at one of the many sports bars catering towards men who liked seeing the staff wearing as little as possible. The work was tiring but the great tips went a long way in easing her sore feet.

Monday night saw Victoria trading her miniscule kilt and barely-there top for gray coveralls when she went to her second job as an office cleaner. That work lasted through Wednesday, which left Thursday as her only day off.

Between homework, class, and work, Victoria didn't have much of a social life much less time for a boyfriend. Which suited her fine. Relationships, while nice, just didn't seem to be in the cards for her—at least for now.

A late bloomer, she'd had only one boyfriend in high school and he'd been a member of the Purity Club—which automatically made her a member by proxy. While she missed out on all the good stuff, Kevin had been a nice first boyfriend and Victoria looked back at her junior and senior year fondly mainly because of him.

They'd broken up before she went off to school and while Victoria had been sad at their parting, she'd been looking forward to the full college experience of partying, hookups, and eventually finding a serious boyfriend. Preferably in pre-med.

Instead, it was her senior year and not only had she'd not had the full college experience and hence was still a virgin, but more importantly, her father had passed away from a heart attack during her freshman year. His unexpected death had left Victoria, her stepmother, and her half-sisters reeling in grief at his loss.

Victoria had taken a leave of absence for a year, shocked by the turn her life had taken. She'd already lost her mother as a toddler, but she'd never expected to lose her father too. Victor Montford had been young, barely forty-five. Neither he nor his wife Kathy had even suspected he had issues with his heart until he dropped dead during an evening run at the local track.

Even now she could barely remember the funeral or the weeks that followed it. Victoria had eventually come out of the fog of grief more determined than ever to take the place of her father as provider for her family.

After paying off the house and outstanding bills, the life insurance policy would tide them over until the twins were out of high school, but only if Victoria took on the financial burden of paying her own way.

There was no question on what she would do. Although Kathy argued vehemently against it, saying that Victor wouldn't want that burden for his oldest daughter, Victoria couldn't be dissuaded from her decision.

She wouldn't rely on anyone's help—no matter how well-meaning.

So Victoria worked until she fell into an exhausted heap every night and usually woke up five hours later to start the cycle all over again. And even though she was running on empty more often than not, Victoria was confident that one day all her efforts would be rewarded.

She'd earn her degree in accounting, a solid position with the ability to become a licensed CPA, and the peace of mind knowing she'd done the best she could for her family.

But like all best-laid plans, hers were about to run aground when she met Mr. Adrian Hawthorne one late night at work.

TWO

T*wo more sections left to go and then I'm done for the night.*

Victoria liked the quietness of her job. No customers to serve, no smiles to fake, just the hum of her vacuum cleaner and the never-ending shuffle of her mp3 player.

Confident in the solitude of her space, Victoria turned up the volume and belted out her best rendition of Muddy Waters' "(I'm Your) Hoochie Coochie Man" while vacuuming a path in front of the break room door. While singing about being born for good luck, she did a little backwards slide and immediately stumbled into someone.

"Oh!"

Large hands reached out to steady her. Victoria whirled around, mouth open in shock and embarrassment painting twin stripes on her cheeks. Muddy Waters droned in her ears while she looked dumbly at the man still holding onto her shoulders.

Tall, broad-shouldered, dark hair, hazel eyes framed by thick lashes, and a perfect face to die for, the stranger stared at her as intently as she stared at him.

His mouth moved, the words lost to those of Muddy's. Victoria shook her head and he frowned. Belatedly, she took a step back and tried not to focus on the fact that his fingers had flexed, as if he hadn't wanted to let her go.

Victoria's fingers fumbled with the vacuum's power button. She managed to shut it off after two attempts. She then yanked the buds out of her ears and then turned to face the gorgeous man who still stood there.

"Sorry about that, Sir. I didn't know anyone was behind me." Victoria pushed a few loose strands of hair behind her ears, nervous the longer he went without speaking.

He simply remained silent, head cocked in apparent thought as he swept his gaze from the top of her dark hair to the tips of her sneakered toes.

I bet his smile has the power to knock a girl silly.

She pushed the wayward thought out of her mind. Victoria had never had trouble at her position, even after working there for the last two years, and hoped she hadn't just inadvertently invited it with her lack of awareness.

Maybe this was an executive who didn't appreciate the cleaning crew making their presence known with raucous singing? Maybe he took it as a sign of sloppy work or not caring about her job?

What if he complains? They might not just reprimand me.

Victoria's body tensed with nervousness. She really needed this position and hated to think that she'd just lost it over something so stupid.

When he didn't say anything or make a move to leave, Victoria decided it was best to act if nothing wrong had happened.

"Umm, okay. Sorry again for bumping into you. I'll be on my way."

She turned away and grabbed her vacuum cleaner. She could feel his stare bore into her back and while it may have been flattering under different circumstances, Victoria couldn't help but tremble beneath its intense regard this time.

Unplugging the machine, she carefully wound the cord around the neck and prayed he'd keep whatever thoughts he had about her to himself and let the whole thing slide.

Normally one would think this wasn't even close to a fireable offense, but Victoria had learned throughout the years that the high and mighty were quick to push the red button over offended dignity. It was infuriating for sure, but there was a time and a place for pride—having the rent due the upcoming week wasn't one of them.

Victoria's breathing evened out after she took a few steps in peace.

"Wait."

Oh God.

She could've pretended to not hear him, but her earbuds still dangled down by her legs—a fact she was sure he hadn't missed.

Victoria took a shallow breath and turned around. "Yes?" She took a reflexive step back when she realized how close he was to her. How had she not heard him?

He flashed a smile and it was even better than she imagined. She felt her lips forming one in return.

"I should be the one apologizing for startling you."

"No!" Victoria cut in reflexively. "I didn't know anyone was still here." He nodded, but his gaze was fixated on her mouth. Victoria's smile faded. "I'm sorry for disrupting you. I'll make sure to not do that again."

"Why ever not?"

"Pardon?"

He smiled again and this time it made Victoria's hand flutter about her waist. "You shouldn't stop. You have a lovely singing voice."

She smiled again, nervously this time. She wasn't sure if he was being polite or truthful. "Thank you."

"What's your name?"

"Victoria."

He said it slowly, as if savoring the feel of the syllables in his mouth. "That's a lovely name."

"Thank you." Victoria's gaze jumped to the floor and back up again. "Um, what's yours?"

He observed her for another second before answering. "Adrian. Adrian Hawthorne."

Victoria thought it seemed as if he was expecting her to know his name. She ran through her mental banks but came up blank. She'd never seen him before. Giving a shrug, she stuck her hand out and waited for him to take it.

A bemused crook of his lips and then he enfolded his large hand around her much smaller one. Victoria gave it a firm shake. "It's nice to meet you, Mr. Hawthorne."

"You too, Ms. ..."

"Montford."

"Ah. Is Ms. Montford appropriate then?"

Victoria bit the inside of her cheek to keep from smiling like a fool. Adrian Hawthorne was probably being polite and if he was a little flirtatious it was probably because it came second nature to him.

She wouldn't make the mistake of believing it to be more than it was. Nor would she make a total fool of herself by being gauche enough to let it show that while she knew how to handle rowdy men in a sports bar, she'd had far less experience with men who dressed and comported themselves like Adrian.

Even though it was almost two in the morning, Adrian's dark suit was completely free of lint and wrinkles. His perfectly-knotted tie remained in place. There wasn't even a hint of fatigue around his eyes, ones made even more beautiful by the fact that they seemed a shade greener than they were before.

The only thing betraying the late hour was the dark shadow of stubble on his sculpted cheeks, but that bit of imperfection only added to his delicious virility.

Victoria let her mouth curve into another soft smile. “Yes, it is.”

“Good.”

Even though her tummy tightened with marvelous appreciation, she didn’t allow herself the freedom to think behind what the one word could mean.

“How long have you been working here, Victoria?”

“About two years, Mr. Hawthorne.”

He held out a hand. “No, please. Mr. Hawthorne is for the regular workday and I hear enough of it. It’s Adrian.”

“But it’s still my workday.” She meant it as a point of fact, but Adrian seemed to take it another way.

He took a step closer to let his hand close gently over hers. Before she could react, Adrian took the vacuum cleaner away. “I’d like you to call me Adrian, but only if you don't mind. Would you mind, Victoria?"

The dulcet tones of his lowered voice slid over her like cashmere. It was so soft and light. Victoria's body swayed a fraction of an inch towards him, seemingly without thought. "Adrian."

"Lovely." Adrian beamed as if she'd granted him a priceless gift.

Victoria swallowed hard. The tension in her belly returned and it wasn't unpleasant in the least bit. It was the same feelings she felt when Kevin first asked her to be his girlfriend.

I feel smitten. What's happening to me?

She cleared her throat and then laughed. Instead of taking offense, Adrian joined her. Victoria's whole body seemed to come alive at the husky sounds of his pleasure.

The worries of her life disappeared. Victoria felt like the young woman she was instead of the older woman she lived like daily. Even if she never saw Adrian Hawthorne again, she wouldn't forget the magic he'd awakened in her tonight.

It was a reminder that life didn't have to be solely about existence and survival.

Once her laughter died down, Victoria said, "Sorry about that. I'm probably just tired."

Adrian nodded once. "What time do you get off work?"

Victoria looked at her wrist. "In about fifteen minutes. I just need to finish vacuuming this last part and the next hall."

He nodded again. "And then?"

She fought to keep her gaze on his. "And then I go home."

"I see." Adrian handed her the vacuum cleaner. "Well, I don't want to keep you any longer than I already have."

Victoria's hand tightened on the handle. She wasn't sure exactly what happened, but Adrian's demeanor changed. He pulled away from her and while she had promised herself she wouldn't look deeper into his words or demeanor, she'd found that it was too late.

She managed another smile, unable to force it to reflect in her eyes. "Okay. Bye."

Victoria made it down the hall when Adrian called out her name. She turned around quickly.

"Seeing that I'm going to be working late for the next two weeks, I imagine I'll see you again?"

Relief hit her harder than it should have. "I guess."

"See you tomorrow, Ms. Montford."

"See you." Victoria then rounded the corner, giddy smile in place, before it fell for two reasons. One—she wasn't going to be here tomorrow since it was Thursday. Two—she still hadn't finished vacuuming the hallway and had to go back, effectively ruining her exit.

Victoria turned around, sheepish grin forming on her lips, and walked back.

Adrian was gone.

***

Adrian cut through the break room and made his way back to his office five floors up. He rarely had to visit the customer service floor and only did it this time because his floor's break room was out of lemon-lime soda. So was theirs.

Impatient on the way down, he was in a much brighter mood on the way up—even without the drink. Victoria Montford was enough inducement for him to make the trek for the next couple of weeks, lemon-lime craving satisfied or not.

She was beyond adorable with her ponytail, shy smile, and large dark eyes. He hadn't been flattering her when he said she'd had a nice voice. He would love to hear her sing to him again, preferably those of different notes and while she was naked beneath him in bed.

If she was like the women of his set, Adrian would've proposed getting to know her intimately that very night. But Victoria wasn't. She was many interesting things wrapped in a small, curvaceous package but worldly she was not.

Fresh. Innocent. Sweet.

Adrian entered his office but instead of sitting back down, he paced in front of the enormous windows, eyes blind to the impressive city view glittering before him.

Impatience gnawed at him. It was much like the beginnings of his focused obsession every time he set his sights on a new goal.

Adrian was a man who trusted his instincts and his instincts demanded Victoria. It didn't matter to him at all that she was part of the cleaning crew and obviously a different social circle than him.

What he felt in her presence, and the way he became a live wire when he touched her, closed off any room for doubt as far as Adrian was concerned.

Now that his course was fixed, next came the planning for how to approach winning over Victoria to his way. Planning came as easy to him as breathing and as such, his brilliant mind ran through and discarded several scenarios on how best to approach Ms. Montford.

Admittedly, he was taken aback when she didn't betray any recognition of his name. It would've made things much easier if she had. They could've dispensed with the courtship and gotten on with the mating rituals deep into the night.

A wolfish smile appeared.

Challenges were what made life extraordinary and Adrian had yet to back down from one. Circle about and take a different tact—sure. Back down? Never.

Victoria Montford required a deft hand. She lacked guile but the intelligence shining brightly in her eyes proved she wouldn't be one to fall for flattery. Appreciate it? Yes. But she was the kind of woman who hungered for more and Adrian was bound and determined to give it to her.

The fatigue rolled off his back as if it never was. Striding to his wide desk, Adrian picked up the phone and dialed his head of security.

"Micah? It's me. Let me know when Victoria Montford from the cleaning crew leaves. No, there's not a problem with her and absolutely do not detain her for questioning or contact her employer. Got it? Thanks."

Adrian, always excellent at compartmentalization, placed the lovely Victoria in her personalized box and shifted gears to the present project at hand. Only he had to know that he pulled out her box often to replay the memories of the brief time he'd spent with her tonight.

Soon, Victoria. Sooner than you think.

***

Victoria spent her day off thinking about Adrian Hawthorne so much that her cheeks ached from smiling. Her roommates teased her about it, swearing that she had to finally, finally have found a boyfriend to be in that great of a mood.

She laughingly denied it. Even if she'd wanted to share about her encounter with a beautiful man like Adrian, Victoria would've kept it secret simply out of superstition. Better to keep quiet until...*if*...anything happened. Otherwise what was the point of explaining away the disappointment?

It was only after a long, hot shower that Victoria settled down long enough to pull out her planner and focus on the assignments for the upcoming week. An agile academic mind was the only reason how she'd been able to juggle so many balls in the air for so long.

If she didn't get the material so quickly there was no realistic way Victoria could've made it work.

Speaking of work…I can't wait until I go back on Monday.

She tapped her forehead and sternly reminded herself that Adrian Hawthorne was probably being polite and most likely wouldn't make it a point to cross her path again. The wind went out of her sails a bit at that thought. It was nice to be paid attention to by such a handsome and obviously successful man.

Although, Victoria was pretty confident that if she'd met him at the bar and he was dressed down in jeans and a t-shirt she'd be just as smitten.

There was definitely something about Adrian that made all her nerve endings come alive. Being in his presence was like a shot of adrenaline. She couldn't help but feel the urge to run, dance, and skip while being with him.

As the days passed she wondered if she'd merely imagined the connection she felt. Surely it couldn't have been as great as she remembered it?

Victoria asked herself that question countless times as she delivered pitchers of beer and plates of hot wings to the packed tables in her section. Dodging overly-friendly hands and seeing how quickly she was reduced to a body in a skimpy uniform, did much to try to chip away at Adrian's memory.

Besides, they'd only spent less than five minutes together. His hands couldn't have been on her shoulders for more than ten seconds. His hand touched hers for a fraction of that time.

Still, the scent of his cologne haunted her senses, doing much to crowd out the smells of fried foods, sweat, and beer. Victoria worried her brow, wondering if perhaps her fixation was a sign that maybe she'd spent too much time working and studying and not enough socializing with the opposite sex.

Sex.

What would sex with Adrian be like?

That was a dangerous question to have considering she didn't know him at all. It was even more dangerous because Adrian wasn't even in her dating pool. Never mind the age difference or the fact that he worked at the building she cleaned, he hadn't even asked her out on a date.

So why was Victoria even considering it as a topic of thought?

The more she tried not to think about it, the more it would sneak into her thoughts like a thief.

Would lovemaking with Adrian be like the movies—romantic and sweet? Or would it be like the videos her roommates passed via e-mail or laughingly pulled her into their room to watch on the computer—raw and impersonal?

Or better yet—romantic and raw. That would be the best kind.

Victoria enjoyed her time in the walk-in freezer whenever she had to pop in for a frozen bag of wings or fries. She truly needed to cool down from her carnal thoughts over Adrian.

She was as bad as a teenage girl with a crush on her teacher.

Still, Victoria had an extra bounce in her step when Monday came. She changed out of her revealing uniform and into the baggy coveralls faster than usual. Quick swipes of makeup remover, a splash of water to her face, an application of lip balm, and then she twisted her medium-length hair into a tight ponytail.

Victoria looked herself over in the mirror, satisfied that she looked bright-eyed and bushy-tailed. A chorus of goodbyes to the staff and then she was off to join the cleaning crew.

And hopefully see Adrian in the process.

THREE

Adrian hadn't expected to feel disappointment in not seeing Victoria so acutely. When he didn't see her the next night, he'd gotten Micah back on the line and asked him to find out her schedule.

Of course, this was after he'd had his people investigate her for good measure. While the thought originally crossed his mind that perhaps she was a clever social-climber who'd chosen working at his building all in the hopes of catching his attention, Adrian's instincts were confident that was a stretch.

Victoria genuinely didn't know who he was. For all she knew, he was just one of a hundred junior associates pegged for middle management. Once he got the report back on her he was even more convinced that she wasn't even close to being the kind of woman who'd trade on her looks.

Adrian already had her short but insightful dossier memorized.

- Mother deceased
- Father deceased
- Step-mother and two half-sisters currently living in the family home
- On track to graduating with a bachelors in Accounting, minor in Business Information Systems, in the Spring
- No police record
- No tickets, outstanding or otherwise
- No debt to include student loans
- No medical issues
- Currently living in an apartment with three other females
- Currently employed as a cleaner and a waitress

Ms. Victoria Montford was a clean-cut, honest girl just as he suspected. Nothing in her background check raised a red flag for him. She was as safe a possible companion as any he'd had in recent memory.

But would that last once she realized the 24 carat fish she had on her hook?

Adrian hoped so. It would be rather insulting to his sense of self-worth to think he brought nothing to the table beyond his bank account. Completely at ease with women and his effect on them, Adrian knew Victoria had fallen hard into like with him as he had for her.

Now it was up to him to make sure she stayed that way for as long as they had left.

And as cynical as it was, Adrian recognized the countdown to their end had already started. It was inevitable considering he was never interested in anything long term. Hopefully, the hard-working and ambitious Ms. Montford would feel the same way.

He truly did hope so. He'd hate for their end to be bitter.

Adrian's jaunty steps echoed in the stairwell as he made his way down to the Customer Service floor. Through security he knew Victoria had arrived promptly at ten and was due to be finished in less than five minutes.

His mouth broke into a grin when he spied her vacuuming away. Her jumpsuit, while utilitarian, did nothing to hide her delicious curves. Curves that were in no way hampered by her short stature. Adrian wondered what she looked like out of her uniform. He hoped to find out sooner than later.

Although she had her back turned to him and her earbuds in, Victoria suddenly straightened up as if she'd sensed his presence.

It was impossible really. She couldn't hear anything over the vacuum's dull roar, but nevertheless she turned around when he'd only taken a few steps towards her.

A strange sensation took root in Adrian's chest. His stride faltered slightly but he made up for it in speed. It was imperative to reach Victoria, to find any excuse to touch her. She was just as lovely as he remembered, more so after an absence of four days. Memory just didn't compare to the reality.

Victoria switched off the machine just as he reached her. Then she smiled. It was beautiful, full of sweetness and genuine pleasure.

Adrian felt regret punch him hard in the gut. The clock was ticking but strangely enough he wished he could stop it.

Just for a bit.

***

"Hello, Victoria."

"Hi, Adrian."

Victoria could barely hold back her happiness at seeing him again. Adrian had definitely sought her out and that made all the fatigue of her day slide away. Her gaze took him in, hungry for every detail just to see if he had been anywhere near as gorgeous as she remembered.

It was worse because he was even better looking than her memory gave him credit being.

The way Adrian fit his midnight blue suit, crisp white shirt, and black tie simply made Victoria's mouth water. As before, only the stubble on his cheeks betrayed the length of his day. She'd never met anyone who looked so good after being up for so long.

"How are you, Victoria?"

"Good. Thanks."

He gestured to the vacuum. "Almost done?"

Victoria nodded. She smiled, nervous and even more excited than she was the night she met him. There was so much she would've loved to say to him, but the words remained stuck awkwardly in her throat.

"Just a bit more until I'm finished."

"I see." Adrian thrust his hands into his pockets, projecting an easy image of quiet authority. "When you're done, would you mind meeting me in the break room back there?"

Victoria's instincts wanted to shout out "Yes!" without reservation. The other part of her, the supposedly smarter part, needed to keep her safety in mind. Her coworkers were spread out on the other floors and there was no one else around. Maybe it wasn't that much different than now, but she wasn't going to be closed into a small room with only two exits either.

Adrian picked up on her reticence. "Or we could meet in the lobby if you'd like."

Victoria hesitated and then said, "We don't have to go to the main lobby. The vestibule on this floor would work."

"I know where that is." He glanced at his watch. "Say in about ten minutes?"

"Sure."

"Okay, see you then." Adrian then touched her wrist before leaving her with another devastating smile.

Victoria watched him walk away, frozen in place until he rounded the corner. She then shook herself out of her stupor and then hauled tail to finish up her work, packed up her cart and vacuum, and took off to meet him after clocking out.

Belatedly conscious of her appearance, Victoria ducked into the bathroom. She never changed out of her work clothes because the hassle of being stopped by a security guard on her way out because he didn't recognize her wasn't worth it. But she could do some last-minute fiddling of her hair and since she was putting in the effort, Victoria dabbed a bit of color to her lips.

Satisfied, she practically skipped to the vestibule. Her steps slowed when she saw Adrian had beaten her there.

He immediately saw her and stood up. "I'm so glad you came, Victoria."

***

She reminded him of a startled kitten. The delightful shyness he observed in her the first night came back and just like then, it completely tugged at his heart strings.

Adrian had found himself in unfamiliar territory and was a bit taken aback when she didn't jump at the first venue he'd offered. The sexually adventurous women he'd been with recently would've taken the location as an invitation. Instead of being irritated at the unspoken implication that he could be a threat to her, Adrian was glad to see Victoria took care of herself.

Considering her jobs and the fact that she supported herself solely, it was probably naïve on his part to have assumed she wasn't street smart.

He directed her to the chair in front of him. "You must be tired, Victoria. Please sit down."

She nodded and came forward. Adrian caught the tremor that went through her frame and made note of it. He hoped it had to do with fatigue and not because she was nervous around him.

Adrian didn't want her nervous. He wanted her open and receptive to being close to him. He wanted her to think about him as much as he thought about her.

Once she sat down, he gestured to the utilitarian coffee table between them. "I assumed you might be thirsty but I didn't know what you'd like to drink." Adrian basked in her grateful and delighted smile.

"Thank you. That was very thoughtful of you, Adrian. I appreciate it."

He watched avidly as her slender fingers hovered over the bottled orange juice before taking the water. Adrian wondered why she didn't take what she so obviously wanted and filed away the observation for later.

To keep Victoria from feeling self-conscious, he took the soda can and opened it. She took a quick sip of water and shifted in the chair.

Too nervous.

As much as Adrian wanted to cut to the chase and ask her out on a date, his instincts warned him that moving too fast would scare Victoria off. Whether it would be because of logic or morality, the end result would leave him unhappy and without her.

He redirected the focus of his original request. "You're probably wondering why I asked you down here."

"I am." She blinked and then asked in a rush, "I'm not in trouble, am I?"

There went his protective sentiments again. He hated for her see them with the balance of power in his favor.

"Why would you be in trouble, Victoria? For the other night?"

"Yes. I know you said you didn't mind but then again maybe..."

"No." He leaned forward and linked his fingers together. "I know you don't know me very well right now, Victoria, but I hope to get to where you trust that I only say the things I mean." A dark thought entered his mind. "Has your supervisor or anyone on staff said otherwise to you?"

Victoria shook her head quickly. "No! I just...I...uh..." she continued to fumble for painfully long seconds before straightening up. "I just didn't want to presume why you asked me to see you after work. That's all."

"Ah. I understand." Which he did very well and it pleased him more than he could say. "I appreciate the kindness, Victoria, but in this case I hope your presumption matches up with mine."

Her lush mouth rounded. Delight danced in her dark eyes, alluring as anything he'd ever seen.

"Maybe."

"Just maybe?"

"I don't know. What do you think I presume?"

As far as flirting went it was pretty basic, but Adrian would take it all the same.

"I was disappointed when I didn't see you last Thursday or Friday."

"I'm sorry about that. I forgot that I was off the next day. I mean...I remembered I was off, but when you said you'd see me the next day I responded automatically."

Victoria's face took on an adorable tint of color. Adrian could've covered her in kisses just to see if he could make her flame several shades darker.

"I understand. So you work here part-time?"

"Yes. Monday through Wednesday."

"Ah."

"Yeah."

Adrian let her twitch for a bit before coming out with "I feel there's something here between us, Victoria. I hope you feel it too."

Her answer would tell him at least one important thing about her—was she a girl who liked to play games? Adrian didn't mind playing, but those based on denial and lies were tedious to the extreme.

"I do." Her shoulders rounded in apparent ease and she even leaned back in her chair a tiny bit. She rubbed her free hand down her thigh once. "I'm not sure if I even should be feeling anything but I do."

Adrian regarded her from beneath a steady gaze. He had to give her credit that she didn't squirm. "Why not?"

Victoria's impish grin and slight roll of her eyes charmed him further. "Because you work here."

"So do you."

"Correction. I do my work here but I don't *work* here."

"Well, that's even better. There's no HR stickiness to deal with."

"Maybe but I'm sure the cleaning service won't appreciate the help mixing with the non-help if you catch my drift."

"And that's important to you?"

"Well, yeah. I like my work here."

Adrian sidestepped the implication that he might not be worth jeopardizing that relationship. "You're a night owl then, Victoria. Like me."

She shook her head slightly. "Not really. Night work is just easier for me with my school schedule."

"I see. So what are you studying, Victoria?"

"Accounting."

He tossed out a friendly smile. "It's routine work."

"I like routine work. It's something I can count on as a career."

"You like stability?"

She cocked her head, eyes shining bright with secret mirth. His questions probably seemed silly to her, especially considering her background, but Adrian was extremely curious as to how she would answer them.

"I like it about as much as the next person. What about you, Adrian? Do you like working here?"

He didn't have to give it any thought. "Very much so. I love working. It's my passion."

Adrian expected her to ask him what he did. Instead, she said, "That's awesome to have found something you love doing so much."

"It is."

Victoria shared his smile for a long moment before breaking away to take a drink. Although Adrian would love to sit there with her for the rest of the night, he had to trust that the moment had come to part. Tomorrow would come soon enough.

"Thank you for spending this time with me, Victoria. I hope we can do it again tomorrow."

She rose to her feet, clutching her bottle to her waist. "Tomorrow?"

"Unless you'd rather not..."

Victoria bit her lip and then shook her head. She rolled her shoulders back, seemingly coming to a decision. He wondered at her thoughts.

"I'd love to see you. Maybe we can talk longer...unless I'm keeping you from something important."

Adrian liked that she respected his time and work. His head locked into agreement with what his instincts already confirmed. Victoria Montford would prove to be a delight to know and spend time with in and out of bed.

"Not at all. Do you need me to walk you down?"

"Thanks, but I'm okay." She let her hand rise a bit. "Thanks for the water. See you tomorrow, Adrian."

"You're very welcome, Victoria." Adrian watched her walk back towards the stairs. He purposely waited several beats before calling out her name. Only when she turned around did he walk over to her. "Here. You should take this with you."

Victoria looked down at the bottled juice he held out to her. "Oh no..." she demurred.

"If you don't take it, it's going to go to waste." There. That should get her to fold.

She glanced at his hand and then back to him. "Okay. Thank you."

A shy smile flirted with him in a way he couldn't even begin to comprehend. Startled by the unexpected pleasure he received in pleasing her, Adrian was tempted to tell her he'd buy her all the juice she could ever want if she'd just keep looking at him this way.

"Until tomorrow..."

"Until tomorrow..."

Adrian waited until Victoria disappeared out of view. He then pulled out his cell. "Micah? Let me know when she leaves the building and then send a detail over to make sure she gets home safe. Be discreet. Thanks."

He headed back to his office to wrap one last e-mail up. To say Adrian was going to be busy tomorrow was a severe understatement.

He had six meetings scheduled for tomorrow, along with a business lunch, dinner, and drinks. He also had to go through two reports and get back with his final decision regarding the efficiency of the new drill head being tested in the lab. Plus there were the thousand and one things that inevitably popped up every day.

Even so, tomorrow night really couldn't come quick enough.

***

Victoria quickly got used to seeing Adrian every night for the rest of the short week. She learned he had a taste for lemon-lime soda and made sure she brought one at their designated meeting spot. It was a little thing, but Victoria was sure Adrian appreciated it as much as he seemed to appreciate their chats.

They never shared anything too heavy which suited Victoria just fine. The past five years had been a grueling exercise in dealing with serious issues and situations. Being able to talk about TV shows, books, and the latest movie releases was a sincere pleasure on her side.

It was getting harder to part from Adrian. The first time he touched her hand in farewell, Victoria swore she felt the imprint last far into the next day. She squeezed his hand first the next night, more than a bit saddened that she wouldn't see Adrian until Monday.

But what about after that?

He had originally told her he was going to be working midnight hours only for two weeks. Would she never see him again? Or would he finally ask her out?

Maybe I can ask him?

Nope. Victoria wasn't on that level yet.

She hadn't developed her confidence yet regarding boys and Adrian Hawthorne wasn't even close to being a boy. He was a man in every sense of the word. As a man he probably was used to women wearing their hair in the latest style, not scraped into a tight ponytail. He was also used to them wearing slinky dresses and shoes with red bottoms or some other outrageously expensive label like the ones her roommate Shaundra wore.

Still, those were her insecurities because Adrian never acted as if it bothered him in the least bit that she wore her coveralls or that her shoes were off-brand sneakers.

Being with Adrian made Victoria feel good and she'd hate to lose that feeling come next Wednesday.

The days ticked by faster than ever and before she knew it the dreaded day had arrived.

Victoria dragged her feet, even though she knew she was eating into her precious time with him. Dread knotted in her stomach when she saw him waiting for her, achingly handsome as always.

Although she pasted a smile on her face, she instantly saw that she hadn't fooled him in the least.

Adrian stood up and came over to her. "Victoria, what's wrong?"

The feel of his hand on her arm was a pleasurable torment that Victoria didn't want to have to go without.

"It's nothing. Really."

"Victoria."

The curtness in his tone captured her attention. Her startled gaze flew to him. "What?"

"Tell me what's wrong. I don't like it when you keep things like that from me."

Adrian's strong words warmed her, making Victoria feel safe and cherished, even if he was being a little presumptuous. "Can we sit down?"

"Of course."

He led her past the club chairs they always sat in and moved them to the sofa. Victoria couldn't dismiss the significance. Adrian took both her hands in his and asked, "What's wrong and what can I do to help you?"

"It's nothing...really!"

"Victoria, I mean what I say. Now tell me."

She opened her mouth and nothing came out. Could she really share her sorrow at their probable parting?

I know he's been so nice to me but what if I'm really too much into his words? Maybe he's nice like this to everybody?

Victoria mentally shrieked in laughter. Even she couldn't be that naïve, could she? She thought back to his words from the week before.

"I feel there's something here between us, Victoria. I hope you feel it too."

She absolutely felt it. Was she brave enough to take a chance?

"I'm a little sad at the thought of not seeing you again."

***

Adrian's jaw clenched before he could stop it. Victoria was ending things with him before they even started. He didn't like that feeling at all.

"Why?" He'd done his best to modulate his tone but aggressiveness still managed to come through.

Victoria faltered. She tried to slip her hands from his. Adrian tightened his hold fractionally. When she didn't say anything further, he repeated his question and added, "Did I do something wrong to make you feel this way?"

Her mouth rounded again but this time Adrian didn't feel swayed towards the sweetness of it. He didn't want to lose her. Not yet. His plans for Victoria had changed from pure seduction to something else.

Adrian genuinely enjoyed spending time with this girl. Her sweetness was a balm he never knew he craved after a long day at work. It had become important to him to see her nearly every night. Besides, Adrian still had yet to learn anything intimate from her beyond the books she liked, her favorite classes, food, drinks, and movies.

It wasn't enough. He needed more time with her.

"Adrian, I'm not sure but I think there's been some kind of miscommunication."

His body tensed. He wasn't wrong about Victoria. He couldn't be, not with the way he felt every time he thought about her, saw her, heard her voice, and heard her laugh.

Adrian's instinct couldn't be wrong. Not about her.

The control cost him greatly, but he managed to keep his tone soft and even. "It would help if you told me plainly, Victoria."

"You haven't done anything to offend me. I was sad because today's my last night and this is your last week working so late."

Ah. I understand.

Relief roiled right through him. Adrian didn't try to hide it. "You're right. It was a total miscommunication. I thought you were dumping me."

This time her blushes affected him twice as much.

"I could never dump you, Adrian. We're not even dating."

"This is true." Adrian had originally expected he'd have Victoria in his bed by the end of the first week and had padded it with another week for good measure. He'd vastly underestimated his pleasure just speaking with her considering they hadn't even gone on a date.

Adrian made mistakes rarely, but he always rectified his error when he did. He took the plunge and hoped to meet her at the bottom.

"Victoria, I'd like to take you out on your next day off. Would that be okay?"

He'd barely finished speaking before she answered, "Yes!" and then clapped her hands over her mouth.

Adrian hugged her to him, enjoying the honesty and enthusiasm in her little yell. He allowed his nose to nuzzle the top of her head while he closed his eyes. Victoria felt so right in his arms, as if she'd been born solely to be hugged by him.

Reel yourself back there. It's not forever, remember?

Adrian loosened his arms reluctantly. Victoria, unaware of the warnings sounding off in his mind, apologized while she laughed. "I'm sorry. It's just that I haven't been on a date since...well...in a really long time. I let my excitement get the best of me."

I completely understand how you feel, Victoria.

Adrian's arms tightened a bit more. He took illicit pleasure in the fact that she seemed to not mind his touch in the slightest. "Where would you like to go?"

The joy dimmed a bit in her lovely eyes. She considered her answer. "I don't know. Maybe dinner?"

Adrian recognized and solved the problem immediately. "Would you like me to surprise you?"

Happiness returned back to Victoria's gaze. Adrian could become addicted to keeping it there far too easily. He'd worry about that later.

"Tell me what time you'd like me to pick you up."

"Maybe it would be better to meet you there instead?" Victoria didn't seem to be aware of woebegone lilt in her question.

"Would it make you feel safer, Victoria?"

She avoided his gaze for a split-second. “It’s just that I don’t want to inconvenience you since I don’t live in the city...”

Adrian already knew that and had made allowances for the commute time. Still, he didn’t want Victoria preoccupied and worried about her living conditions in the misguided belief that he cared about it at all.

“Okay, how about this? Why don’t we meet in front of this building? Is that good with you?”

Victoria gave him a relieved smile. “That works for me.”

“Then it’s settled. Does eight work for you?”

She nodded. “It works perfectly.”

Adrian squeezed her to him, completely enamored with how she felt against his body. “Good.”

He’d make it the most perfect date she could’ve ever imagined all in the hopes of keeping her just as happy as she was right now.

FOUR

Victoria woke up four hours later. She had a million things to get done if she was going to make her date with Adrian tonight. She had to finish her paper, do the homework for three classes, meet with her advisor, plus finish her laundry and complete her assigned chore of cleaning up the kitchen.

Then there was the tricky task of figuring out what to wear considering the near-barren selection of dresses she currently had in her closet. Between tips and savings, she had about $100 to spend to make herself up for her date. If she had any hopes of matching Adrian in wardrobe, that wouldn't even cover half the cost for a top.

Bummer.

Still, Victoria wasn't going to let something minor like a miniscule wardrobe get in her way. She already planned on going to a row of consignment shops in the neighborhood after returning from the university. She was bound to find something suitable there.

She got showered and dressed before tackling her laundry and the kitchen. Despite a few grumbles from one of her roommates, Jenny, the other two never even stirred. Victoria then buckled down on her school work, forcing her wayward thoughts to keep from lingering on Adrian for too long.

It was difficult, especially when she wondered if he was giving as much thought to her as she was him.

Focus!

By noon Victoria was all done. She'd e-mailed her assignments and received confirmation of receipt. Although fatigue tugged at her, Victoria made herself a quick snack and then left for her meeting. The subway wasn't packed so she had a seat for the whole ride there and back. And even though she caught her eyes closing and head bobbing forward, Victoria only had to think about Adrian to feel the familiar rush of adrenaline and excitement.

The consignment shops were a tougher nut to crack. Deciding to go safe with a little black dress, Victoria would either find one that was her size but out of her price range or in her range but not in her size. Finally, just when she despaired of ever finding something, the last shop came through for her. On sale, in her size, and most importantly in her budget, the sheath hugged her body in all the right places and made Victoria feel like a princess.

A sexy princess maybe but still royalty.

Victoria picked up a new pair of off-brand shoes, black naturally, and had just enough money to buy a new bra and matching panties before making her way back home. She felt victorious and couldn't wait for the upcoming night.

That enthusiasm carried her through to her second shower and careful grooming in prep for being smooth, soft, and alluring for the most exciting date of her life.

So when she lied on her bed to wait for her rollers to heat up, Victoria didn't expect to awaken two hours later and an hour too late to catch the train to the city.

Victoria snatched the clock off her night stand and stared at it in horror.

"Fuck! Fuck! Fuck!"

She jumped off her bed and scrambled to put on her new underclothing, yanking the tags instead of snipping them, while she frantically wondered what she should do next.

A knock sounded on the door before it opened to let her roommate's head to poke in. "Vickie, you okay in here?"

"No! I'm not okay!"

Jenny, a transplant from Minnesota, was tough as nails for a girl who looked like an angel come down to earth with her naturally blond hair, perfect oval face, and cornflower blue eyes. Working in security was a perfect fit for the girl whose ambition was to become a FBI agent.

She stepped in and closed the door. "First, calm your tits. Second, exactly what's the problem?"

Victoria explained in a panicked rush, nearly in tears as she outlined that even though she'd planned for everything to go right today, her plan had blown apart and it was completely her fault.

Jenny listened, arms crossed and face intent as she processed Victoria's wailing dilemma. She then walked out of the room and came right back with a box of tissues in hand. "Here. I'm going to fix this but you need to calm down. You're of no use to me if you're crying. Got it?"

Victoria took the box and giggled as she saw things from Jenny's point of view. Jenny would never get overwhelmed to meltdown mode just because she dropped the ball. She'd either pick it up and keep going or she'd kick it out of bounds and demand another one.

Victoria dried her tears and blew her nose. Letting out a cleansing breath, she declared, "My tits are officially calm."

"You sure?"

"Yes."

"All right. You need to go wash your face and when you get back I'm going to help you make that date."

Now that she was calm, Victoria felt more than a bit silly for flipping out. She'd just wanted everything to go perfectly on her end and when it didn't...

I need to work on improving that part of my personality for sure.

"I should call him and let him know I'll be late."

"Nope! You still got until 8:00. We've got about two hours left until you meet Mr. Cutie."

"Yeah, but I've already missed the train." Victoria belatedly realized she'd never even gotten Adrian's number and he hadn't asked for hers. She had no way of getting a hold of him. Her panic started rising degree by unhealthy degree.

"You're not going by train."

"I can't afford a cab, Jenny, but it looks like I don't have a choice." She was going to have to see if she could work a double on the weekend to make up the blow to her budget.

"I thought you said your tits were calm, Vickie."

"They are!"

"I beg to differ. I told you I was going to help fix this for you, right?"

"I know but you don't have a time machine, do you?"

Jenny shook her head and stood up. "She of little faith." Jenny then opened up the door and called out for Krista and Shaundra. "Girls, we got a situation here. We need your help."

Victoria sat there in her underwear, tissue clutched in her hand, while their two other roommates came over.

"What's up?" Shaundra, a fabulous Georgia peach, was only one semester away from graduating with her Masters in Education. She loved the city for its culture, fashions, and dining, but was planning on moving back to Hotlanta by the fall.

"Yeah?" Krista, another transplant like the three of them, came via I-95 all the way from Florida. She'd followed her boyfriend and his band but when they signed on for a tour in Japan, Krista decided on *Sayonara* to the boyfriend. She worked as a hairdresser in the Meatpacking District.

Jenny had Victoria recap her situation. Victoria blushed beneath their congratulations and gentle ribbings of "Finally!" and "I thought you were going to be a nun-in-training!"

Once their teasing died down, Shaundra got down to business. "So he's some kind of financial high-roller, right?"

"Actually, I'm not sure."

Three pairs of eyes looked at Victoria as if she'd lost her mind. "What? I never asked him what he did for a living."

"But he works at that building for sure?" Jenny asked.

"Well, yeah."

"Then we're going with he's a high-roller." Shaundra looked about. "Where's the dress?"

Victoria pointed to the bag hanging on the closet door. Shaundra opened it up. A quick inspection followed by “Not bad. We can work with this. Now what about a wrap?”

“I don’t have one.”

Krista raised her hand. “I got you covered. What about shoes?”

Victoria had a sinking suspicion the shoes weren’t going to pass inspection. At all. She sighed and waved a hand. “In that other bag.”

Since Krista was closer she picked it up and took a peek. “Victoria, you still have the receipt?”

Enough said.

“Guys, that’s the best I could come up with. I don’t have the cash for anything better.”

Shaundra bumped shoulders with her. “Don’t worry, girl. We got you covered, okay? What shoe size do you wear? A six? I’m only a half size up. You can borrow any one of my fabulous pairs.”

Victoria leaned her head on Shaundra’s shoulder, feeling all the pressure ease off now that she had help. “You guys have no idea what this means to me. Seriously. This date is so important to me and I don't want to do anything to ruin it."

"Yeah, we figured Mr. Cutie has to be very special to break you out of your routine and get you to freak out."

Victoria looked over at Jenny. "You're right and he is."

Krista grinned, her chic bob cut streaked the same red as her lipstick. "We'll do whatever it takes, Victoria, because we're just trying to get you laid before you turn twenty-four!"

Victoria laughed along with her roommates. Once the laugher died down, Victoria turned herself over to them. Her makeup was applied by Shaundra's deft hand, Krista curled and pinned her hair, and Jenny made several calls to take care of Victoria's transportation issue.

The girls then hustled her to Shaundra's room, and more importantly, her jaw-dropping shoe collection.

"I don't know what will go best with the dress. I'll let you decide, Shaundra."

The choice was made in a minute flat. Victoria slipped on the dangerously high heels. "Do I look okay?"

"Honey, are you kidding me? You can't go wrong with McQueen."

Jenny got off her phone. "Your ride's waiting for you, Vickie. You almost done?"

"I think so. I just need the wrap, right?" Once in Krista's room, Victoria waited while she brought out a small collection of shawls, wraps, overcoats, and jackets.

After quick changes and a few quicker debates, they moved away from wraps and all settled on a midnight-blue overcoat made of a lightweight material that shimmered under the right light.

Victoria rushed to her room and grabbed her small wallet, grateful that Krista's coat had roomy pockets. She gave herself a quick glance at the mirror, pleased by what she saw, and dashed out into the cramped living room.

The girls gave her their collective thumbs up and Victoria thanked them all for helping her out of a bind.

"I owe you all big time. Seriously. You need me to do chores for a month, anything, let me know."

Jenny waved her hand. "Normally this would go without saying but since you don't date—at all—here are the rules. Call or text one of us if you're not coming home. If things go bad and you have to bail, call or text us. If things go really bad, scream for help. I don't care where you are—just do it. Then call 911. You have your mace, right?"

"On my keychain."

Jenny waited until Victoria showed her. "All right. Other than that, have a great time."

"Okay, Mom!"

"Now that she had her say, let me have mine. Take care of my shoes, you hear?"

Victoria crossed her heart. "I'll protect them with my life and the coat too, Krista."

The lanky brunette shrugged. "It's cool."

Jenny clapped her hands once. “All right it’s time to hustle. The chariot is double-parked and won’t wait around forever.”

“Okay, okay! I’m gone, everyone. Bye!”

Jenny tugged her out of the apartment to the chorus of well-wishes and they went down the stairs. She waited during suitable intervals as Victoria got the hang of maneuvering while balancing on such a thin point. When they finally got outside, Jenny raised her hand in a wave.

“There he is.”

A luxury SUV in requisite black and chrome waited to whisk her away. “Wow. That’s nice.”

“I know.”

A young man got out. “Jenny! Girl, you know you owe me for this, right?”

“Put it on my tab, Anthony.”

“Yeah, like I always do.” He jogged around to the passenger side and addressed Victoria. “You want up front with me or in the back?”

Before she could answer, Jenny snapped, “Are you kidding me? You put her in the back like you're supposed to. Seriously, you just started working for Dominic or what?"

Anthony rolled his eyes and muttered as he opened the rear passenger door.

"What was that?"

"Nothing!"

"Yeah, I bet it was."

Victoria raised one recently-sculpted brow. Jenny snorted. "What? Just because he's doing me a solid doesn't mean you don't get the professional treatment."

She wisely kept her protests of "He doesn't have to go through that trouble" to herself and hugged Jenny instead. "Thanks for everything."

Jenny patted her lightly. "It was nothing. You'd do the same for me."

"I would."

The blond pulled back. "You better go if you want any chance of making it in time."

Those were exactly the words she needed to hear to get moving. Victoria hugged Jenny one last time and then walked over to Anthony. She smiled and thanked him before climbing in the back.

Anthony closed the door and then got in the driver's seat. He turned to her and asked for the address. Victoria gave it to him, already thinking of Adrian.

"Don't worry, Vickie. I know every shortcut between here and there. I'll get you where you gotta be before you know it."

And then just like that they were off.

Nervous butterflies danced in Victoria's tummy. To think she almost slept through her date! But with the help of her friends and Anthony, everything was going to work out beautifully.

I hope Adrian is looking forward to tonight as much as I am.

FIVE

Adrian cursed a streak as vile as it was long. Everything that could go wrong already had. His PA was on death's door with the flu. Her back-up was an inch closer with the same flu. The contracts that were supposed to land on his desk by 11:00am hadn't and couldn't be tracked by FedEx.

He had to skip lunch for a presentation with London that ran over into a video-conference with Vancouver. His partners, understandably, didn't care for the delay. By the time six rolled around he was starving, irritable, and itching for a fight.

As far as bad days went, it had to be in his Top 10.

Unfortunately, the day wasn't over. He still had a ton of work that had to be finished before he could leave his desk. The eye on his clock grew harder as it ticked ever closer to 7:30. He'd yet to shave or change, wanting to save that until the end.

Which wasn't coming any closer as more urgent e-mails arrived in his in-box.

The only thing that kept Adrian from flipping his desk over in fury was the reminder that Victoria waited at the long end of his hellish tunnel. That and the wry mental observation that these were the situations in which he usually thrived. Adrian just couldn't square away why he was so irritable over the off-chance of being late.

It happened and Victoria was sure to understand. She wouldn't take it as a slight against her or his commitment to going out with her tonight. She was too selfless for that.

But I want everything perfect for her. I don't want her to be understanding or have to sacrifice anything more than she already has in her life.

And that was that.

Adrian rolled up his sleeves and plowed through, refusing to let anything but success be the end result. His computer clocked showed 7:29 when he finally finished.

He shut down his computer before making use of his private bathroom. Every minute counted so he had to be quick. Finally showered, shaved, and changed, Adrian ran a critical eye over his appearance. Every strand of hair was in its place and his clothes were immaculate as ever.

There was absolutely nothing to betray the hectic day he'd just survived.

Running a hand over his smooth jaw, Adrian hoped to impress Victoria with the one thing that did go right—his plans for their date. He'd gone full out to entertain her, sensing that she wouldn't turn a jaded nose to drinks at an intimate jazz club, dinner at his favorite Moroccan restaurant, all finished off with a helicopter ride above the city.

And as much as he'd like to imagine taking things to his bedroom, Adrian knew he had to take things slowly with Victoria. Anything faster could potentially make her bolt and that was the very last thing he wanted.

Tonight was all about building on the foundation they'd already established.

No, he was going to be a good boy and do right by the very good Victoria. Later, well...there'd be the right time and place for the deliciousness of later.

Noting the time, Adrian grabbed his coat, turned off his lights, locked the door, and made his way downstairs. The elevator remained empty as it carried him quickly to the main floor. Standing there, lean body tense and impatience thrumming a tattoo in his heart, Adrian recognized the familiar mix of adrenaline and anticipation.

Except instead of feeling it because of an impending deal, he felt it for Victoria.

Slow down there. You'd think it was your first date ever.

Adrian shook his head, a wry smile making a brief appearance. He'd planned excursions like this a thousand times before. If he could impress a duchess, surely he could impress a sweet girl like Victoria?

The elevator doors opened and he stepped out. Although he wasn't close to the entrance yet, Adrian tried to spot her as he walked across the impressive lobby. Nothing, but then again he didn't have a complete vantage point. Once he stood outside, Adrian looked one way and down the other.

No Victoria.

He didn't have to look at his watch to know it was eight on the dot. Unease crawled down his spine. He had it on authority that Victoria Montford was punctual and had never been late to work or even missed a day.

She was also never late when meeting him after her shift. But she was late now. He reached for his phone but then realized that although he had her number, Victoria herself had never given it to him.

He couldn't call her.

Damn.

Being the city that never slept, the sidewalk teemed with people but not the one person he wanted to see more than anyone else. Unaccustomed nervousness dictated that Adrian pace back and forth.

Maybe she'd gotten hurt on the way over. His detail always reported Victoria's commute to her home as uneventful but what if this time was different?

I knew I should've sent a car for her!

Maybe there was an issue with the subway? A quick search showed no delays on any of the lines.

Maybe Victoria decided not to come.

That thought froze him in his tracks.

Was it possible that she had changed her mind? But why? Adrian thought back to their last meeting less than twenty-four hours before. Victoria had cuddled right into his arms, darling smile on her face, and pleasure gleaming beautifully in her eyes. There was nothing to indicate she didn't want to meet him.

But what if Adrian had read all the signs incorrectly? What if he had overestimated her attraction to him?

Not once had he ever been stood up before. In other circumstances, Adrian might've found twisted humor in the situation. This wasn't the time.

Just as he was about to work himself into a froth, a black SUV pulled up in front of the building. A young man in a smart suit jumped out and rushed around to catch a door already opening.

Adrian watched, transfixed, as an exquisite vision took the driver's hand and stepped out. It looked like a grownup version of Victoria from the top of her perfectly-curled hair, down past her nipped-in waist, and all the way to her sexy heels.

There was no doubt that this beautiful woman was the girl he had been waiting for. Even longer than tonight. Adrian, who had the envious experience of dating some of the most glamorous women in the world, had never, ever felt his heart tighten like this.

He took a step back.

Victoria turned to the young man and gave him a quick hug. Adrian's expression hardened immediately at the sight. He didn't like seeing her touching any man but him. Adrian wasn't a jealous man, and he couldn't be considering he never made a long-term claim on any of the women he'd ever seen, but this...

He didn't like it. At all.

Adrian's strides ate up the distance between them faster than a shot. She turned towards him before he reached her. His aggressive, animalistic instincts receded at the wide smile she gifted him.

"Adrian!" She spared another grateful look at the man next to her. "Thanks again for everything, Anthony. You saved me tonight."

"No problem. You got my number. Call me if you need me to take you home."

"That won't be necessary," Adrian broke in before Victoria could answer. "I'll send her home." He then reached into his wallet, folded a crisp bill, and shook the other man's hand. "For your troubles."

"Thank you, Sir." Anthony tipped his head at Adrian, closed the door, and then slid back into the luxury vehicle. Adrian didn't want to dwell on the relief he felt once the other man left. The foreign feelings of jealousy still ran hot and Adrian suspected it would take a while for him to calm down.

Victoria, unaware of his primal feelings said, "I'm so sorry to keep you waiting, Adrian."

He noted the breathless quality of her voice and wondered if it was the same excitement for him that he felt for her.

"I didn't have to wait long." Adrian opted to keep his previous worries to himself. It didn't matter anymore now that she was with him.

She touched his arm, relief heavy in her voice. "Thank goodness. Anthony drove like a champ to get here and he would've made it by eight, but one of the intersections was blocked. Still he did pretty well, don't you think?"

Adrian leaned down, unable to resist kissing her cheek for one second longer. "He got you to me and for that he deserves a trophy."

Victoria blushed. Adrian silently swore he'd never tire of seeing them color her cheeks so prettily. "Maybe that tip would suffice? Thank you by the way. I was so focused on getting here that I forgot to do it. How much did you give him? I can pay you back."

"Don't worry about it. It's my pleasure, Victoria, to take care of it for you." Adrian held out his arm and waited until she slid hers around it. "Ready to go, my lady?"

"Yes!"

***

Victoria didn't want the night to end. Ever. And they'd only just started.

Adrian didn't have them take a cab, but instead had a private driver shuttle them around. Being in a car made Victoria miss having hers.

Granted, she didn't have a Mercedes, but her green Mustang had been a fun car to drive.

Their conversation consisted of small talk.

"Tell me about your driver, Victoria."

She grinned. "Oh. I never met him until tonight. He's a friend of my roommate. Jenny. She really came through for me today."

Adrian raised a curious brow. "I sense a story here."

Victoria quickly recounted what happened, strategically leaving out the parts where she cursed a blue streak, had an emotional hissy, and had to borrow the coat and shoes because she didn't have the taste or the money for her own.

"And so thanks to her wonderful friends, Cinderella was able to go to the ball after all."

"That's one way of looking at it."

"I'll have to send them each a bouquet of roses as a token of my thanks." Adrian suddenly pulled out his phone. "I realized tonight I didn't have your number. Do you think you can give it to me or am I being too forward?"

"Not at all." Victoria told him her number and he told her his.

Adrian waited until she programmed it into her phone before saying, "Good. Now I know how to reach you." He eyed her, sparkle bright in his hazel orbs. "And you can call me too. Any time. You might have to leave a message, but I'll always call you back as soon as I can."

He said it with such sincerity that Victoria resisted the urge to put her hands on her cheeks. She was grateful for the darkened car interior because she already knew another infernal blush had taken over. Victoria eagerly looked forward to the day when she didn't give away her inexperience like this.

Conscious of the driver only a few feet away, Victoria kept their conversation light even though she would've liked to have asked Adrian more about his life. Thankfully, they arrived at their destination in no time at all which saved Victoria from increasingly awkward attempts to find impersonal topics to talk about.

Adrian helped her out of the car and kept his hand at the small of her back. He didn't remove it. All of her nerve endings seemed to center beneath his hand. So conscious of his touch, Victoria barely paid attention to her surroundings until they entered what looked to be a small ballroom.

She soon learned it was a jazz bar. Victoria had never been to one, didn't even think she'd like jazz, but found it to be a thrilling experience she hoped to have again. These were the kinds of places she dreamed of going to when she first moved to the city, before her father died. Victoria later learned a hand-to-mouth existence didn't really leave room for cultural events.

They sat at a table, off to the side but still close to the intimate stage. Once they were shown to their seats, Adrian helped Victoria take off her coat. He took one look at her and his brows raised high.

"Wow."

Victoria, used to wearing far less at her waitress job, blushed as Adrian appraised her form with appreciation. “Did I do well?” she asked while sitting down.

He pushed her chair in and whispered, “Perfect, Victoria. Absolutely perfect. “

Victoria floated on his compliment. A waiter came by and Adrian ordered a delicious plate of fruit, cheese, and desserts along with champagne. Before she could settle on a point of conversation, the lights went dim and the MC came out to introduce the group.

Victoria did her best to watch the performers on stage, but she found it difficult to concentrate because Adrian spent more time watching her than them. It thrilled her even as it made her feel self-conscious. When she tried a chocolate-covered strawberry, Adrian leaned close to ask in a drawling whisper, “Do you like it?”

“Yes.”

“Can I have a bite?”

“Sure.” Victoria went to put her strawberry down on her plate. Adrian stopped her by putting his large hand on her wrist.

Victoria watched, fascinated as his perfect white teeth bit into the plump fruit. He swallowed, never taking his gaze from hers.

"Delicious."

He's not talking about the strawberry, is he? He's talking about me. Please be talking about me.

She looked away, completely out of her depth and feeling as if she couldn't draw in enough breath. Should she act as if it wasn't a big deal? Could she be so blasé?

No.

How could she when Victoria obsessively wondered how his mouth would feel against hers? Would she get drunk just from one kiss?

Was she already drunk now?

Adrian brushed the back of his fingers against her flushed cheek and said her name in a sizzling croon. Victoria turned to him slowly, trying her best to keep her composure when all she wanted to do was melt into him. Her heartbeat quickened when he leaned close to her again.

"You're not watching the stage, Victoria."

Her trembling lips only inches away from his, she murmured, "No. Neither are you."

Adrian's hooded gaze zeroed in on her mouth. "No, I'm not."

He shifted even closer. Her heart was beating so loudly she was convinced everyone in the club had to hear it.

He's going to kiss me.

She ran the tip of her tongue across her lips, already tasting the sweetness of his lips on hers. Adrian murmured something that sounded like "...killing me!" and then pulled back.

Victoria would've been completely crestfallen if not for him slipping his hand in hers. Adrian lifted her hand to his lips and brushed a kiss across each knuckle. It was a sensuous promise of later.

Victoria tried to enjoy the rest of the performance but all she could think was "How will it be when I finally get to kiss him?"

Would he be tender? Would their first kiss be sweet and intoxicating? Would it be the kind of kiss that dropped Victoria to her knees?

She hoped to find out before the night was through.

It was hard to concentrate on the musicians because Adrian kept her hand in his, brushing his thumb against her palm slowly back and forth. Victoria did her best to pretend she was completely at ease being in this beautiful man's grip.

Like she did it all the time.

She fixed her gaze on the piano player, lips tipped in an appreciative smile, and while her ears tried to let the music sink into her, Victoria's lusty mind kept circling around the idea of *Adrian* sinking into her.

Lust hammered in time with each slow pass of his thumb.

When the performance ended, she looked at him and said, "This was really nice. I liked it a lot." The fact that was talking more about the feel of his hand in hers was going to be her secret.

"Did you? I'm glad to hear it." Adrian stood and held her coat open. Once he slipped it on, he placed his hands on her waist. "Are you hungry?"

Victoria licked her lips. "Y-Yes."

"Good."

Adrian brought her to a restaurant that served Moroccan food, which was her first time trying cuisine from that part of the world. It was delicious. She had chicken tagine along with chicken kabobs.

"Do you like chicken?" Adrian teased.

"It's my go-to food when I'm trying a new restaurant."

Adrian fed her bites of his lamb, wiping the corner of her mouth with his thumb before licking the pad. The tribal beats faded away. Victoria shifted in her chair, fists clenched around her utensils. Adrian seduced her so well and all seemingly without trying.

She clapped along with the rest of the diners when the belly dancers whirled skillfully throughout the crowded space. Adrian squeezed her hand several times and kissed her on the cheek many more times.

Victoria wished he'd kiss her on the mouth but wasn't bold enough to go for it. Yet.

Time paused long enough for her to recognize her life would never be the same after tonight—regardless of how she and Adrian dealt with one another.

Victoria could no longer deny that she needed more than she had allowed herself to have. She needed to fecl desired and to desire. Every touch, every whisper brought her back to life.

Adrian brought her back to life.

It was close to eleven when they finally left the restaurant. She had her leftovers packed up and bagged, which Adrian carried for her to the car. Victoria fully expected him to end the evening when they pulled up back in front of their starting point.

Instead, he kept her hand in his and said, "I've got a surprise for you!"

When they ended up on the building's roof, Victoria's legs trembled. Not in fear of heights but exhilaration. A sleek helicopter sat on the pad. She had to raise her voice because of the wind. "Is that for us?"

Adrian took the opportunity to draw her close. He leaned down and spoke in her ear. "Yes, ma'am."

"You're kidding!"

Adrian laughed and guided her to the waiting helicopter. He handed Victoria into the plush seat, making sure to buckle her in himself. She looked out the window, seeing the older gentleman still standing by the door. "Can you fly, Adrian?"

"Not a chance. That's why we've got the best pilot in the city."

He climbed in next to her. A few minutes later and they were off. Victoria reached out for his hand first and held it the entire time, squeezing it tightly when they first rose up in the air.

The city unfolded. Darkness and diamond lights scattered beneath hid all the pollution and decay Victoria knew existed. They flew over the water, flying by all the popular tourist sites that looked so breathtaking from above. Victoria turned to Adrian several times to say, “Did you see that?”

Maybe he already had, but each time Adrian leaned close to her side of the seat and verbalized as much enthusiasm as she did. Time slipped away in the air. It was thrilling. Exciting.

It was Adrian.

Soon they landed back down. Once the helicopter powered down, Victoria turned to Adrian and spontaneously kissed him on the cheek.

“I’m so happy! I’ll never forget this night!”

***

One look at Victoria’s face proved his meticulous planning had been a success. He had enchanted her. He had dazzled her. He didn’t doubt that Victoria would ever forget tonight. However, Adrian enjoyed and disliked their date all at once. He enjoyed make her happy. That objective had been paramount to anything and everything else.

So where was the lack? How had he failed in pleasing himself?

Adrian missed talking to her. Every event had seriously curtailed the ability to share more than a few words. Even when they were alone in the car, Victoria had been extremely conscious of his driver.

If he could've done it over again, Adrian would've invited her to dinner in his penthouse. Not to seduce her, but to simply enjoy conversation.

The last week had shown him how much he didn't converse with anyone just for the sake of sharing words. Every conversation had an agenda in his regular life. Lunches, dinners, drinks, golfing, vacations—they all served a purpose for business.

Adrian's pleasure had to be orchestrated as well. Different venues perhaps, but the words were merely a means to an end on both parts.

Victoria wasn't anything like that.

She spoke to him and he spoke to her just to know a bit more about each other. It was easy in a way he had quickly come to depend on, but the rub of it was that while she had been honest in her interactions with him, Adrian hadn't. At least not at first. His primary purpose had been to find a way to bring her to this point.

Now that he had, Adrian suffered dissatisfaction. He didn't want the night to end. He craved conversation with her. The elevator, while not their usual vestibule, would have to serve to create connection.

"Did you enjoy tonight, Victoria?"

Her brilliant smile lit her from within. "I did so very much. I don't think I've ever had this much fun."

A rueful smile crossed his lips. "It was my pleasure." He rooted for an appropriate bridge to maneuver this lovely girl across. "Are you tired?"

Victoria shook her head. "Not yet. I'm used to having to function on little sleep."

"Me too."

Words failed Adrian. He watched the numbers count down with dread. He needed more time with her. Just a bit. The elevator doors opened. Adrian kept pace with Victoria as she walked towards the exit.

She stopped suddenly. "Are you still going to take me home? Because you don't have to. I know how late it is and I can make my own way."

Adrian blurted out, "I don't want you to go yet."

Victoria's gaze met his shyly before skittering away. "It's almost midnight. I've got to go."

"Don't."

***

Victoria licked her lips. "Don't what?"

Adrian opened his mouth and then closed it. He seemed to struggle with his words. A frown overtook him. "I...don't want you to go."

"What do you want me to do?"

He looked at her, so incredulous that Victoria wondered if her actual spoken question didn't match her thoughts at all. Adrian's low laughter made her take a step back. He immediately stopped and reached out.

"I'm sorry, Victoria. I'm not laughing at you. I'm laughing at me."

"Why?"

He shook his head. "It doesn't matter. Look, Victoria, I didn't plan for this. I plan everything but not this." His hand skated down her arm. Victoria felt the leashed power in it. "I planned to let you go. To do this slow. But I can't. I don't want to. Do you understand?"

Victoria understood she was at the precipice between the life she had and the shadowed one waiting for her. Everything would change if she responded to him, especially in this way.

"What are you saying? Say it straight."

Adrian tipped her chin with one finger. "I want you to come home with me tonight. I want to make love to you all night long."

Her pulse sped up. She closed her eyes and let the dulcet notes of his voice bend her to his will.

"I want you, Victoria, but if you say no then I'll understand. I'll still ask you to come home with me and I'll promise to be a perfect gentleman even if it kills me. I'll have dessert sent up to us. I'll talk to you about anything and everything you want. I'll watch the sunrise with you. I just want to be with you."

Logic told Victoria all the reasons why she shouldn't even entertain his request. Despite their time spent together, she still didn't really know him. Adrian didn't know her. Then there was the tricky bit of her moral code and why she was still a virgin while closing in on her mid-twenties.

And yet...

Adrian fascinated Victoria. She felt ecstatically alive in his presence. All her fatigue and worries about her future, her little family back home, all of it disappeared when she sat down in that leather chair and spoke to Adrian.

The way he completely focused on her, making Victoria feel that she had his undivided attention, captivated her. During those fifteen to twenty minutes she wasn't an overworked drudge dressed in an unflattering jumpsuit, but rather a young woman who had everything to look forward to.

She was alive and he was the man who brought that out in her.

So could she go with him? Could she take that chance? There was no question about it.

"Yes, Adrian."

"Yes?"

"Yes, I'll go with you."

SIX

Adrian held Victoria's hand. He felt the slight trembling.

"Here we are."

She looked at him, gaze gone adorably shy, before crossing the threshold. Normally he would've shoved his companion against the wall as soon as the door slammed shut. Victoria required finesse. Kindness. Gentleness.

All the things that didn't come naturally to Adrian, therefore, putting him in the rare position of feeling inept and unsure.

Logically, this state of affairs would be absolutely unacceptable to him and cause enough to terminate the situation.

It was the last thing he wanted to do.

Adrian would simply do as he always did—trust his instincts. No matter how many cold showers he might be forced to take as a result.

"May I take your coat?"

Her gaze widened. She licked her lips with a furtive swipe of her tongue. "Ah, okay."

Adrian bit the inside of his cheek to keep from smiling. He'd already made the decision he wouldn't pounce on her. Too bad she didn't realize it. Adrian took her coat and then seriously rethought his decision.

The way Victoria's dress hugged all her delicious curves...he groaned silently. It positively made him ache. Adrian wanted to unzip her dress right now.

But he couldn't.

Damnit.

Adrian took her coat and hung it up in the closet alongside his.

"Living room?" He held his arm out and directed her to walk in front of him. Adrian needed to readjust himself but couldn't take the chance of her looking back. He'd have to deal with the discomfort.

Seems like I'm going to have to make friends with that feeling for a while.

She sat down on the couch, bottom at the edge and legs together primly. It aroused him as nothing else because it was the exact posture she took when they met in the vestibule.

"Would you like a drink, Victoria?"

"Yes, please."

He smiled, a brief, tight thing, and hoped she didn't study it too closely.

"Here. I can take your leftovers and put them in the fridge." Victoria looked down at her bag in surprise, as if she'd forgotten she still carried the bag with her.

"Thank you."

Satisfied that he wasn't the only one affected, Adrian took her food and promised he'd be back in just a bit. He went into the sleek, modern kitchen, deposited her food, and then leaned against the island.

What was he thinking? Having Victoria here was like bringing Red into the Wolf's den. How could he possibly believe he could sit next to her and have a conversation while the lure of his bed sang its siren song?

Suck it up. You're not going back on your word. You never *go back on your word.*

Exhaling heavily, Adrian pushed away from the counter. He opened up his fully-stocked fridge and pulled out a bottle of orange juice and a can of his favorite soda. Adrian grabbed a couple of glasses and filled them with ice. He then arranged them neatly on a serving tray, complete with a plate of petite fours and napkins.

She'd pulled her phone out of her little purse and had a half-smile on her face.

"Everything okay?"

Victoria nodded with a small grin. "Yes. I just needed to text my roommate that I was probably going to be home late."

"You have good friends to be worried about you."

"I guess you can say that."

Her smile tempted him to kiss her secrets out of her. Instead, he set the tray down on the coffee table.

"Here you go, Ms. Victoria."

"Thank you, Mr. Adrian."

"It's absolutely my pleasure," he murmured while sitting down next to her.

They both took a sip of their respective drinks while looking away from the other. Adrian mentally shook his head. Conversation was his gift. How could he possibly be so nervous?

Because Victoria is different.

"You have a lovely home, Adrian."

He looked about him. "I suppose I do. Thank you."

"You suppose?" she asked with a wry smile. Victoria pointed behind her. "I bet the view is gorgeous."

"It is. That I know for sure." Adrian waited for her to ask him how he could afford the view, especially in the city where square footage was some of the most expensive in the world.

Victoria just nodded. “I’ve always wondered what things look like in the day. I only see out the windows at night because in the day my feet are firmly on the ground. At school. I mean...ah...I’m not in any skyscrapers until the night...at my job.”

This time Adrian couldn’t bite back his smile. She sounded so adorably flustered. “I completely understand, Victoria. Although I would say you have the best views when you see them at night. Want to see what I mean?”

“Sure.”

Adrian stood up and held out his hand. She took it without hesitation. It thrilled him more and more how easily she was getting used to his touch. He led her to the window. “See. Look at all the lights, Victoria.”

She sighed in appreciation. “It’s so beautiful. I can hardly miss the stars in the sky when the lights are spread out all around us like this.”

Adrian let go of her hand to slip his arm around her waist. He caught the ragged inhale of breath and smiled.

"Where did you live before this?"

"Further down south."

Adrian paused. "Is it a secret?"

She laughed and shook her head. "No. I was just feeling a little embarrassed to admit to a big, fine city-boy like yourself that I'm from North Carolina."

Victoria had let her voice lapse into a delightfully sexy Southern drawl. Adrian tightened his hold around her waist and whispered in her ear, "Now how did you mask that accent so well and more importantly, why?"

She giggled and leaned into his side. "It's my thing. Accents, I mean. I can pick them up easily."

"Hmm...well, I've just discovered that I happen to love your Carolina accent." Adrian ached to nuzzle the sweet spot of where her neck met her shoulder. He wanted to taste it and let his tongue make her moan for him.

She looked up at him and Adrian raised his head, putting distance between himself and temptation.

"Now you're just saying that to be sweet." Victoria laid it on thick with a saucy grin.

"Is that so?" Adrian's cheeks hollowed. She lost her smile and stared at him, dark gaze serious and watchful. There were a million questions that she obviously could've asked him but Victoria remained silent.

Adrian suspected the only reason she came with him was because he had practically sworn that he would be a perfect gentleman.

He couldn't betray her trust.

He wouldn't betray it.

He could control himself.

He *had* to.

Adrian released her even though it physically hurt him to do. Desire to strip her naked, to taste every part of her body, especially the honey between her thighs, pounded relentlessly.

"Don't."

He froze.

Victoria reached out. "Please don't."

Adrian didn't move an inch.

***

His eyes gleamed amber in the half-light. It was the gaze of a half-tame predator. Victoria didn't have to keep touching him to know the tension in his body reflected the one running through hers.

It hurt.

Victoria didn't have to wonder what the pain was because she knew. The pain that dug velvet talons into the underbelly of her will was desire. Pure animalistic desire. She wanted Adrian more than she'd ever wanted anyone or anything before in her life.

"Please don't leave me."

"I'm not going to leave you," Adrian answered immediately in a hoarse voice unlike any she'd ever heard from him before. "That's the farthest thing in my mind right now, Victoria."

Right now.

Those were the words that should've pushed her away. It was the visceral reminder that right now might be all she'd ever have with him. After all, Victoria couldn't trust that anything between them might continue after tonight.

Adrian might find her infinitely less interesting once they slept together.

Victoria might feel that way about him herself.

However, right now was all anybody ever had.

Right now.

"I came here tonight because I wanted to." Victoria cleared her throat. "I wanted to be with you, Adrian."

"Be with me?"

"Yes. Be with you." She took a step closer so she could touch his arm. "I want you, Adrian. I want you to make love to me—"

Adrian yanked her to him and buried his hands in her upswept hair. His mouth crashed against Victoria's. She whimpered. When he softened the pressure she moaned and pushed her body hard against his. Her small hands reached for a fistful of his hair as well and she nipped his bottom lip.

He responded to her primal command beautifully. Adrian pressed Victoria against the window and devoured her mouth. His tongue expertly slid against hers, coaxing it to play with him. It was everything she'd ever imagined and more.

Much, much more.

Victoria couldn't draw enough breath into her lungs. She wanted Adrian more than she wanted air.

When he placed his hands on either side of her breasts, Victoria ripped her lips away from his and moaned one word.

"Please."

"God yes!" Adrian bent down and kissed circles around her breasts, getting achingly close to her nipples before starting back again. She dug her fingertips into his shoulders but it didn't hurry his pace at all.

Victoria reached behind her. Her fingers fumbled with the zipper, desperate to pull it down.

Adrian's hands stayed her. "Not yet." His beguiling lips kissed away her protests. A long minute later he looked into her eyes. His heavy-lidded gaze reflected the lust pounding throughout her body. "Let me do it. Turn around for me, Victoria."

She did as he asked, eyes staring blindly at the view. Victoria felt his hands slide across her back as if memorizing the shape of her body. She shivered and held back a hungry moan when he finally undid her zipper. Her dress fell to her feet.

More than ever Victoria was so glad she bought new underwear. Practical thoughts evaporated when Adrian's lips made contact with the base of her spine. His tongue tasted her and his kisses followed. Victoria leaned against the window with both palms against the window. It was cold but she was so heated that she barely noticed.

"Spread your legs."

The command was a thing of beauty. Victoria widened her stance, excited beyond words at what Adrian would do next. She heard him murmur something unintelligible and then his tongue laved her mound. The satin clung to her wetly as he did it again and again.

Victoria's legs trembled. She leaned against the window and pushed her backside out, needing to open herself further for Adrian's erotic onslaught. He squeezed her bottom while he rhythmically rasped his tongue against her.

She gasped loudly, feeling the drugging-sweet tightening in her belly. "Oh God!"

Adrian growled, "Don't hold back, kitten. Let go for me."

His words threw her over the edge. A snap and then pleasure waves crashed over Victoria. She reached behind her, needing to touch Adrian. His fingers entwined with hers, keeping her in his hold even while his tongue never slowed its wonderful rhythm. Except when he stopped long enough to whisper, "I want you to do it again for me."

Victoria closed her eyes and slid right back into desire as if she hadn't come hard already.

She was hyper-focused when Adrian slowly pressed butterfly kisses all along her slit. After many minutes of playing with her, he let go of her hands and tugged her panties down.

Imagination couldn't prepare Victoria for how good his mouth felt on her bare skin. He tongued her slippery folds, probing them with a hungry thoroughness that had her straining harder against Adrian. She whimpered his name, falling ever-faster down into a sensual world where Adrian created and controlled every one of her sensitized nerve endings.

Then everything ratcheted up when his fingertips carefully slipped inside her just a fraction of an inch.

Victoria arched up with a strangled cry. She wanted more and said so. Adrian lightly tapped her aching bud with the tip of his tongue as he slid one finger deep inside.

She exploded.

Adrian immediately rose to his feet and yanked her bra down as he kissed her passionately. Victoria tasted herself on his lips as she thrust her tongue into his mouth. It was so incredibly erotic, especially because Adrian seemed to take so much pleasure in her taste.

Victoria's thoughts hazily drifted about how glad she was to have taken a chance on him when Adrian suddenly lifted her with one arm.

"I got you. I won't let you go...promise."

Victoria sighed in bliss as his lips traveled down the column of her neck. Her hands roamed over his wide shoulders. Greedy to feel his skin beneath her fingertips, she pushed at his suit jacket and then roughly unknotted his tie. Victoria's fingers fumbled with the shirt buttons, stoking her impatience and lust for this beautiful man.

Finally her hands met warm flesh. Victoria purred in pure pleasure. His muscles flexed beneath her questing fingers when Victoria pressed her lips against his throat. Adrian felt so perfect, warm...alive. She craved to sink her teeth deeper and to leave her mark.

"Victoria, look at me."

She tore her mouth away. The heat in his gaze melted her completely.

He smiled wolfishly while adjusting her easily in his arms. “Don’t close your eyes. I want to see them as I come inside you.”

Victoria’s breath caught in her throat. Excitement throbbed as she felt his shaft enter her inch by exquisite inch. The incredible fullness would’ve stretched her to the near-point of pain if Adrian wasn’t going so slowly.

Then he was completely inside.

She let out a ragged breath. It was done. She wasn’t a virgin anymore. Spontaneous happiness possessed her. She laughed out loud. Adrian grinned.

“Good?”

“Better than good.”

He closed his eyes and moaned. “Are you ready for more?”

“More? I want it all!”

Adrian grinned feral and raw while squeezing her bottom in his large hands. He then rocked into her, hips increasingly pounding faster and faster, until all Victoria could do was hold on and cry out loudly in appreciation.

He was so hot and hard and she was so wet for him. It was decadent and delirious. Adrian kisses drew her pants into him. In no time at all, Victoria felt the stirrings of another orgasm.

“Adrian! Oh God, I’m about to come again!”

He groaned loudly and bent his head so he could tongue her stiff nipples. Victoria instantly shattered in his arms. Adrian then became ravenous. He kissed every part of her he could reach. Victoria barely came down from her carnal high when Adrian stiffened.

One arm wrapped around her, pulling Victoria into him. She felt her name as a sensual whisper against her neck. She could feel the hot spurts and shuddered erotically. Dimly, she was aware that she’d broken the rules but it didn’t matter as it should’ve.

Held in his arms, her back against the cold window and her front pressed tightly against her lover’s naked chest, Victoria tasted happiness.

She didn't know, couldn't even imagine, this feeling of pure joy.

"That was incredible, Victoria." He exhaled heavily. "It felt so perfect being inside you. This is...words fail me."

She laughed, ecstatic and happy beyond recent memory by the feeling his words inspired. "I know it felt incredible to me too. Is this normal?"

Adrian kissed her, softly and sweetly. "You're stroking my ego, Victoria."

She linked her arms around his neck. "Really. I don't know."

His sleepy smile curled her toes. "What do you mean you don't know, kitten?"

"You're my first."

***

Shock hit Adrian like a fist low in his gut. Of all the words he could've guessed she'd say, those weren't anywhere on the list.

"When you say 'first' you mean..." He let his words lapse into silence.

The pure joy in Victoria's beautiful face faded away. Adrian immediately felt guilty.

"I mean what you think it means. I'm or at least I was a virgin." She raised her chin, gaze glistening with vulnerable defiance. "Is that a problem for you, Adrian?"

"Actually it is."

Victoria looked away. "Put me down please."

Adrian cursed softly under his breath. He bungled it completely. He had to make it right. "Victoria, don't misunderstand me. If I had known that this was your first time I would've done it right."

Her mouth pursed into a precious moue. "What do you mean?"

Adrian dared to kiss her gently. She responded to him and he felt relieved that he hadn't lost her. "I wouldn't have taken you against a window for your first time. I would've made love to you in the bed like you deserved."

Victoria caressed the side of his face. "I like how you did it. It was perfect and better than anything I could've ever imagined."

“God, I didn’t hurt you, did I?”

A sweet blush appeared. She looked down and shook her head.

“Look at me, kitten,” Adrian commanded softly. “Tell me the truth. Did I hurt you at all?”

“Only a little. Not really.” She bit her lip. “I thought you knew. I thought that’s why you were taking it so slow.”

He hadn’t suspected a thing. Past experience had shown Adrian that because he was rather endowed, it was best for his partners that he take his time. He wisely kept his explanation to himself.

“I didn’t.”

Adrian felt a bit of a fool. He wanted to ask her how it was possible that she’d remained untouched for this long. Instinct warned him to keep his questions to himself. Victoria would tell him if and when she desired. Still, the mind boggled.

“Oh.”

Unwilling to leave himself open to unsavory speculation, Adrian nuzzled her mouth. “Let me redeem myself?”

“There’s no need.” Victoria’s tongue teased his with soft strokes.

“Maybe not, but it’ll be fun for both of us if I try.”

Victoria sighed against his mouth. “Very well. If you insist.” She winked audaciously and wiggled her hips.

Adrian was still hard inside her. He didn’t need a second invitation. He strode towards his bedroom and her laughter echoed like a thousand delicate bells.

SEVEN

Victoria awoke in the predawn hours. She looked over at the sleeping man beside her and experienced a curious rush of awe and shyness. Awe that she'd experienced an unforgettable night with such a beautiful man and shyness because she was naked beneath the sheet.

"Adrian?"

"Mmm?"

"I have to go home." Although she'd whispered it, his eyes flew open as if she'd shouted it.

"Home?"

"Yes. I have a 9:00am class today."

Adrian rolled over and looked at the clock. He sat up with a confused frown on his face.

"I slept through my alarm?"

Victoria reached out and ran her hand down his bare arm. "I never heard it go off."

Adrian's gaze met hers. His smoldered with hunger. "I'll get my workout another way then..."

Even though they'd just fallen asleep a couple of hours before, Adrian immediately rolled her underneath him. They made love urgently without words, letting their hands and moans speak for them. They shuddered together, mouths open and eyes wide with bemusement at how much more pleasurable it was to come simultaneously. They showered together the same way, even when Adrian had Victoria bent forward at the waist as he pounded her into keening submission.

Adrian rained kisses all over her face afterwards, murmuring, "It's never been this good, kitten. Never."

Breathless and feeling as if she could barely stand up, Victoria couldn't ever imagine experiencing this with anyone else. All she could do was smile.

He cupped her face and kissed her hard. His gaze penetrated. “Never. Do you understand?”

“Y-Yes.”

His feral smile melted into a possessive kiss that had Victoria scrabbling for more of him—which he was generous enough to give her again right there on the bathroom counter.

Eventually, Adrian left her to get dressed in peace. Victoria pulled a new toothbrush out of its container and wondered why seeing a drawer full of them made her uneasy. She blow-dried her hair, doing her best to finger-comb her long locks because she didn’t want to be presumptuous by using Adrian’s hairbrush.

What’s happening to me? Why am I feeling so weird about him...us?

Victoria’s unease increased when Adrian joined her fifteen minutes later in the kitchen.

Attired in a dark suit, hair perfectly in place, Adrian was a gorgeous sight to behold. Victoria’s body responded as if they hadn’t spent half the night making love in his bed...and on the floor...and in the shower...and the bathroom.

“You look quite handsome.” Victoria hoped that the distance she sensed was one being created on her side. It went without saying that she’d never had a “morning after” so she didn’t know what was considered normal.

He smiled. “And you’re as beautiful as always.”

Victoria didn’t mistake the tightness of his smile. He seemed distracted, nothing like he usually was when with her. She clenched and unclenched her fists with nervous rhythm.

Things had changed.

Adrian offered her a light breakfast but she passed. Victoria didn’t want to watch him break away from her completely. If one night was all they really had, then she wanted to remember that night and not the morning.

“Thanks for the offer, Adrian. I really need to get home if I’m going to have enough time to change before going to class. So...”

He stood there with an impassive expression as she explained. Victoria found her voice trailing off softly the longer he stared at her.

After a night of passion, to see Adrian be so self-contained was like a dunk in cold water.

Unpleasant and bordering on pain.

“I see.” Adrian pulled out his phone and then ordered the person on the other end to “Be here in ten minutes.” Once he disconnected the call he said, “I’ve called for a driver. He can take you wherever you wish to go.”

“Thank you.”

“Don’t mention it. Please have a seat wherever you’d like.”

Victoria thought the phrasing odd. It only made her feel even less comfortable. “I can sit here,” she said while gesturing at the breakfast bar. “If you don’t mind.”

“Of course not.” He then moved about the kitchen before sitting down next to her and eating a meager meal of toast and fruit. His attention remained firmly on his phone. Victoria’s stomach tied itself into knots the longer the minutes ticked by.

It was as if she was already gone.

When she couldn't bear the silence one second longer Victoria turned to him. "You can go if you want. I can wait here until the driver comes."

It was only after she said the words that she realized the fallacy of her suggestion. She was a stranger in his home. How could he trust a stranger having free rein with his personal possessions?

Undoubtedly Adrian thought the same but was too polite to give voice to it. "No need, Victoria. It will be my pleasure to see you out."

The words didn't make her feel the least bit better. Victoria itched with the need to leave, to not continue to feel like an intruder in Adrian's life. After the intimacies they had shared, it stung to think of herself as an intruder.

She couldn't be angry with him because he never made her any promises comc morning. She had made the decision to be here last night and now that it was over, it was increasingly obvious Adrian had already moved on.

Victoria blinked back an embarrassing rush of tears. She may not be angry with him, but it didn't mean she wasn't hurt.

As she lied by his side and watched him sleep, Victoria couldn't deny the dreams she'd built with every draw of his breath. She wanted to see him tomorrow, and the day after that, and the month after that.

Victoria let herself imagine that maybe all her waiting throughout the years, all her lonely nights, all the dates she didn't take, was for this man. And now...right now she learned the hard lesson that dreams were meant for the night.

Right now there could be no hiding the changes taking place between them. The magic binding them in the night disintegrated in the cold light of day. Just as she should've already known if she'd let herself really think about it.

Minutes ago she'd taken pleasure in seeing him dressed for his day. Now the difference in their clothing was more salt on the wound. Victoria's clothes had made her feel like a princess the night before. Now they simply made her feel like a piece of the past that needed to be forgotten.

Adrian's phone rang. He looked at it and then strode into the living room. Victoria debated on whether she should take the opportunity to leave and make her way to the subway. Adrian's politeness and her dignity didn't have to take a beating this way. She could slip out in a few seconds. Victoria was halfway to the front door when Adrian joined her.

"Going somewhere?"

"Ah...well," she stammered before giving him a tight nod.

He merely reached into the entry closet, pulled out her coat, and held it open for her. Victoria slipped her arms through and tried not to think about what happened the last time he was behind her like this.

Adrian put on his overcoat, black like his suit and dress shirt, and then escorted Victoria out of his home. The hand at the small of her back burned like a coal. She had a masochistic craving for that piece of coal masquerading as a brand on her flesh.

Their ride down to the underground garage passed in silence. Adrian deposited her by the sleek Mercedes.

"Mr. Jordan will take you wherever you need to go, Victoria."

She summoned a polite smile to match his tone. "Thank you."

Adrian opened his mouth and then abruptly closed it. Whatever he was going to say had softened his gaze just the tiniest bit. "I'll call you."

Victoria looked away. She didn't have to have tons of dating experience to know those three words meant the exact opposite. It was probably a good thing that he wasn't going to be crossing her path at work now that his late nights had come to an end.

There was nothing left to salvage the rest of her dignity. She may not regret having slept with Adrian and the ecstasy he'd given her time and time again, but she did regret how dirty this parting made her feel. Pain shot through her.

So this is what it feels like to be discarded.

Victoria's gaze met his unflinchingly. "Goodbye, Adrian."

***

Victoria got home, showered again, and then went through the rest of her day as if nothing momentous had happened in the last 24 hours. The only way she made it was by keeping her mind blank. One foot in front of the other. Only the present moment mattered.

When she made it home for the second time that day, Shaundra was the first person she saw. Victoria knew her coping technique was about to be tested big time.

Reclining on the couch, she gave Victoria a saucy wink. "How'd it go, baby? Everything you hoped it would be?"

Victoria forced a nonchalant shrug she didn't feel in the slightest. "It was...fine."

Shaundra sat up and cocked a skeptical brow. "Fine? Fine isn't the first word of choice

I'd use when rolling around in the sheets—if you know what I mean."

Neither did Victoria. Sex with Adrian had been criminally exciting. A dream come true. Too bad the rest of it didn't hold up.

"It was good and that's all I'm going to say about it."

Shaundra let out a mournful sigh. "You're too shy, you know that?"

"I guess."

"If you're not going to give up deets on the goodies, tell me about what you did on your date. That should be PG enough. Where'd you go?"

Another jolt of pain shot through her. Reliving the beauty of last night would be so hard now that it was over. Victoria sat down on the other end of the couch. "Where's Jenny and Krista?"

"At work and don't change the subject."

Seeing no other way out of it, Victoria briefly outlined her date with Adrian. She took care to keep her voice upbeat but it was hard going.

"He took you on a helicopter ride? Girl, he must've really wanted to get into those panties!"

Victoria fervently hoped she'd get to the point where she didn't feel so raw about having what turned out to be a one-night stand. She'd love to be able to say something like "It was fun for a night and only for a night. Now I'm ready to see what else is out there."

She was far from that.

"So when are you going to see Mr. Lover Man again?"

Never.

Victoria dreaded having to say it out loud. "I'm not sure. Actually, I don't know."

"Why not?"

"I don't know. I'm just not sure. That's all."

Shaundra considered her for a moment. Whatever she saw in Victoria's face made her say softly, "Understood. It happens, Vickie."

The sympathy in her roommate's voice brought a rush of embarrassing tears. She turned her attention to the television and pretended to watch the reality show rerun.

ADRIAN

"All right, you're crossing this..."

"Adrian."

"Adrian off your list. Disconnect completely."

I never connected at all. Not like I thought I did.

"If that's what happens it's not a problem. I won't see him again at work. At least, I don't think I will."

"You only think?"

Victoria shrugged, gaze glued to the TV. "He never told me what he did. Just that he was only going to be working late nights until this week. I guess he's some kind of manager or something."

"Girl, do you even know who this man is?"

Victoria turned to see her incredulous expression. "Well, I've just gotten to know to him. I mean, we talked a lot and he never tried to do anything until last night. Even then he pulled back but I was the one...I was the one who...you know."

Shaundra pursed her lips. "Have you Googled him yet?"

"No."

"Why not?"

"You know how I feel about prying into people's lives via social media. It's not my way." Victoria would hate for someone to do it to her which was why she wasn't on any of the sites.

Her roommate shook her head in disbelief. "Vickie, you have got to join the rest of us in the 21st century, okay? It's a tool and tools are meant to be used." Shaundra pulled out her phone. "What's his name again? Adrian what?"

"Don't do it. I don't want to know."

"Well, I do. Name?"

Victoria sighed. "Adrian Hawthorne."

Shaundra's thumbs quickly tapped across her screen. A minute later she looked up. "Victoria."

Uh oh. She never calls me that.

Victoria squirmed in her seat, worried that Shaundra discovered something heinous.

Oh God, he's not married, is he? Don't tell me I gave my virginity to a married man? I never saw a ring! Ever!

“What?” Victoria dreaded hearing whatever awful thing Shaundra found out about Adrian.

“He took you on a helicopter ride last night and it took off from the building you clean. Right?”

“Yeah...”

Shaundra blew out a long breath. “He owns that building.”

Victoria’s current worldview collapsed. That couldn’t be right. “Come again?”

“He owns that building and a whole bunch of other stuff too. He’s a billionaire, Vickie. A real-life, under-the-age-of-ancient, *gorgeous* billionaire.”

Shaundra rattled off several stats but they went in one ear and right out the other. Victoria drew her legs up, trying to wrap her mind around the outrageous news.

“You scored big, Vickie. I mean, really, really big.”

Victoria broke out of her stupor. “I didn’t like him or go out with him because of his financial situation. I wasn't trying to land anyone, Shaundra."

"Well, you did."

Victoria just couldn't process this stunning bit of information. Not now. "I'm running late." She shot up to her feet. "I have to get ready for work."

Shaundra raised her brow. "Don't shoot the messenger."

"I'm not! I'm just...I don't know." Victoria stalked to her room. She stopped and turned back. "Is he married or engaged?"

Her roommate didn't bat an eye. "100% single." She scrolled through her phone. "He has dated a lot of famous women though—"

"Stop." Victoria raised her hand. "I don't want to know."

Shaundra put her phone down. "I don't blame you."

Victoria took a quick shower, but she couldn't run away from her thoughts. Every brush against her skin reminded her of Adrian. Of how he kissed her collar bones, her breasts, her belly, and lower. Her body didn't feel her own anymore. The tenderness between her thighs made her want him even more.

What she didn't want was the feeling that all this couldn't possibly mean the same to him as it did her.

Why was a billionaire wasting time with the cleaning lady? Even if she worked ten lifetimes as a senior CPA, Victoria wouldn't come close to touching his personal wealth.

So why her?

The question haunted Victoria all the way to work. And even though it was busy and Victoria practically ran her feet off, she couldn't outrun the fear that Adrian was only playing with her feelings.

What if it was all a game to him? What if last night meant nothing to him because he did it all the time?

Victoria had to remind herself that Adrian never pledged his heart to her. He never lied to get her into bed with him. It was her decision to have sex with him. He never promised her forever.

So why did Victoria feel so cold? Why did she feel sick at the thought of Adrian using her because she'd been so gullible? Why did she want to cry at the thought that he would replace her with someone else tonight? That she'd never had a chance to be anything more than a lay?

Victoria's eyes burned with sudden tears. She bit the inside of her cheek and sternly commanded herself to get it together. She had five orders to get out and no time to waste on her personal life.

You should be used to that already.

Besides, she was a big girl. If Adrian turned out to be a womanizing jerk, well, she'd have to get over it, wouldn't she? This kind of thing happened all the time to people all over the world.

She wasn't special in that regard. She would get over it and she would eventually find someone else who was able to see past her current circumstances and appreciate the good person she was inside.

Her pep talk lasted all of a few minutes because just as she finished delivering a final plate of wings, she turned around and ran right into Adrian.

EIGHT

Adrian could hardly believe what he was looking at. Victoria, *his Victoria,* was dressed in a tiny skirt and shirt, her dark hair in two saucy pigtails. A light sheen of perspiration dotted her forehead and the mouthwatering planes of her bare stomach.

She was sexy. Painfully so.

He'd watched her for a long minute, seeing how fluidly Victoria glided across the floor. She moved as gracefully here in this darkened, overly-loud sports bar as she did in his bed.

Before he knew it, Adrian had walked past the cheerful server and straight towards the woman who'd skillfully tied him into knots from the first moment he'd woken up today.

Although it wasn't the first time he'd had a lover sleep over, it was the first time that he'd disrupted his entire routine for one. Adrian never overslept. He never missed his workout. And he positively, absolutely never felt disappointment when his lovely lady bid adieu.

Adrian didn't know what to do with those emotions rocking through him like a chaotic freight train. He'd thought the sex would be enough to set him straight. It wasn't. The strained minutes before his driver arrived should've been the impetus to prove his fascination with Victoria had come to an end.

Not even close.

When she'd entered his car, he had to kill the impulse to jump right in with her. Adrian had seriously considered cancelling all his appointments and seducing Victoria into cancelling hers. In those seconds before Mr. Jordan had closed the door, Adrian had to tighten his fist to keep from hauling her out of the car and over his shoulder.

He always trusted his instincts. For the first time in forever, Adrian didn't trust them at all. How could he when they urged him to make decisions that didn't compliment his structured life?

Adrian hadn't planned on calling her tonight. He hadn't planned on seeing her either. Not until the fever eased. And yet here he was...

He stopped a few feet away and waited for her to turn, to see him and prove that she felt the same madness he did.

Come on, kitten. Don't let me be alone in this.

And much like the first time they met, Victoria turned around and ran right into him.

"Oh!"

He reached out and steadied her. The feel of her arms beneath his palms reminded Adrian of how he held them as he pounded into her from behind last night. Victoria had responded wildly to that position, especially when he let go of one arm and slid his hand around her hip to slide across her slippery folds...

Adrian's shaft filled. He ached to bring her close, to run his hands beneath her short skirt and feel her as he did the night before.

Victoria's mouth had been fixed in a friendly smile until she saw it was him. The smile disappeared. An array of emotions sped across her flushed face, too quickly to decipher.

"What are you doing here?"

He felt his brows snap together in a frown. She didn't sound happy to see him at all. He thought about her distance from him this morning and didn't like the conclusion his agile mind drew.

"Can we talk?"

He watched as she scanned the restaurant. Adrian wanted to just focus on Victoria, but he was acutely aware of the men appraising her. Some discreetly while others were blatant in their looking. Adrian immediately wanted to wrap her up in his coat, to hide her from the imagined leers surrounding them.

The rush of possessiveness and anger he felt took him aback. Adrian didn't lose his cool. Ever.

"Okay. Follow me."

Victoria asked another skimpily clad waitress if she could cover her tables for five minutes. Adrian wanted more but wisely kept his silence. She didn't seem happy to see him and perhaps she had every reason to be unhappy. His presence pushed an unspoken boundary. Being on her turf put Adrian at a disadvantage versus being at his building and he didn't care for the tactical error.

They exited through the back door and into the empty alley. Silence wrapped them close the whole time. Now they faced one another, her on one side of the alley and him on the other.

"Adrian, what you doing here?"

He searched for a ready-made excuse. "You forgot your leftovers."

"Oh. Thank you. You didn't have to worry about it. You could've just thrown them out."

Adrian didn't like her response. At all. Especially because she seemed so polite and sincere about it. He went next for humor. "I was hungry for some wings."

Victoria looked at him skeptically. “This is far from your neighborhood. Really far.”

Adrian tried for casual, summoning his charm and gambling it would be enough to draw her attention away from how he knew where to find her.

“So this is where you waitress?”

“Yes. How did you even know?”

“Well, my driver did take you home and I remembered that this was where you said you worked.”

“Ah.”

She had mentioned it once. Thankfully, she apparently remembered. An awkward silence passed. It was long enough for Adrian to realize Victoria wasn’t bothered by his unexpected appearance as he’d thought.

“What’s wrong?”

Victoria looked down, mouth pursed tight. She still held her tray against her chest like a shield. She kicked at the ground with her boot, drawing attention to the lean muscles of her thigh. Adrian clenched his jaw at the fresh surge of possessiveness he felt knowing scores of men got to see her like this.

Bastards.

Adrian blew out a sharp breath. He didn't understand where this insane jealousy was coming from. Adrian was far from a prude. His previous girlfriends had walked runways wearing far less and had taken more than one pictorial completely nude.

That had never bothered him. Their body, their choice.

So why did this bother him now?

It wasn't like Adrian felt Victoria was doing anything wrong. It was her job and he already knew how hard she worked for her independence. He didn't doubt her character, especially after last night.

Yet, the jealousy itched. He didn't enjoy the way it made him feel. For a man who accepted control as his birthright, the lack of it in any way was completely unacceptable.

He'd keep away from the source if he was sane.

Adrian focused on her. He could self-analyze later. Victoria was the only thing that mattered.

“What is it, kitten? Tell me”

The pet name, so passionate and from the night before, apparently didn’t have the same reaction today in a filthy alley. Victoria straightened. Her face, curiously blank, unnerved him.

“I found out about you today.”

Adrian shrugged. “What specifically?” He instantly had a strong suspicion what it was, but his business instincts came into play. Adrian wouldn’t show his hand. Instead, he’d wait for Victoria to show hers.

“That you’ve done very well for yourself.”

“That’s one way of putting it.” His breezy smile didn’t have an effect on her other than to make Victoria even more remote.

“You’re a billionaire.”

He shrugged and remained silent. What was there to say?

Victoria apparently felt differently. “What are you doing here, Adrian?”

"Seeing my girlfriend is what I thought." Adrian felt the beginnings of a flush. He wasn't generally fond of that word and rarely ever used it. Especially after one day.

But it felt right.

And because it felt right to him Adrian experienced a touch of arrogance in assuming it would feel the same for Victoria. Unease gripped him when she frowned.

What if last night wasn't as earth shattering for her as it was for him? What if it was just him? What if she'd left this morning the way she did because she didn't want to be with him at all?

What if Adrian had gotten it all wrong?

"I'm not your girlfriend. You're a billionaire. Billionaires don't date cleaning ladies or girls who wear uniforms like this at their other jobs. Billionaires like you date other rich and famous people. You *have* dated other rich and famous people."

Ah. He could fix this. Relief pounded blood-thick. She wasn't rejecting him at all, at least not for the reasons he feared.

“Well, I am dating you. At least, I hope I am.” When she didn’t say anything to refute it, Adrian stated, “I’d like to date you, Victoria. Exclusively.”

Vulnerability flashed across her face. Doubt chased it. “You knew I didn’t know, right? You knew I didn’t want you for money, right? Being with you was never about money.”

“I wasn’t entirely sure at first, but yes, I knew.”

She inhaled sharply, her mouth opening and closing several times. “Maybe I’m wrong in feeling this way, but I feel stupid.”

“Why?”

“Because I thought... I thought we were friends. I thought we could be more. But we can’t.”

“Hold on.” Adrian took a step closer. “Nothing has changed between us, Victoria. I haven’t changed. *This* doesn’t have to change.”

She closed her eyes. “I don’t want you because of your money. I haven’t spent all this time with you because of money. I didn’t go out with you because of money. I liked being with you because of *you*."

She's reassuring me. Me.

Adrian's heart seemingly slowed before trying to beat right out of his chest. He knew what was happening between them was unlike anything he'd ever had. He knew and accepted it.

"I know, kitten. I have to tell you something and if you laugh at me...I'll die." The lighthearted chuckle he meant to release came out strangled instead. "I want you badly, more than I've ever wanted anyone else. I've wanted you from the first moment I saw you. That hasn't changed except I want you more. Do you still want me, Victoria?"

She didn't answer his question but the flush on her lovely face proved to Adrian she had most definitely heard him.

"You know no one in your world will ever believe any of that. They'll all think I'm a gold digger. They'll laugh at you behind your back. They'll think less of you for being with someone like me. Eventually, you'll hate that. Eventually, you'll end it and I'll be trapped because..."

She looked away but not before he saw the glitter of tears. Adrian didn't want her unhappy, not with him. Not ever.

Restrained emotion throbbed in the low tones of his voice. "That doesn't matter to me now and it won't matter later. Do you still want me, Victoria?"

She crossed her arms, looking incredibly helpless and so very young. Adrian balanced on the edge. He wanted to take away all the burdens she carried. He wanted to be the man to make her world right.

Her answer meant more to him than anything in recent memory.

"Do you still want me, Victoria?"

Pain rippled across her face. Her shoulders slumped as if the burden of her thoughts was too much to bear. Panic quickened his heart.

Kitten...Victoria...please.

She closed her eyes and whispered, "Yes."

Adrian immediately pulled her to him. Her tray clattered to the ground. The tenseness melted away when she didn't pull back. He had her and he knew it. The emotions rocketing through Adrian weren't victory and domination. They were euphoria and peace.

He was going to take her home tonight. He didn't doubt it for a moment. First, Adrian had to soothe her fears.

"I haven't spent my adult years letting other people's opinions influence me until right now. Victoria, no one else's opinion matters to me about us except for yours."

"Really?"

"Yes, really. I like you. A lot. I hope you like me too."

She laughed. Adrian's heart took off on wings. "I do like you a lot, Adrian. Last night would never have happened if I didn't."

His hands slow danced on her waist. Memories of her sizzled across his mind. "Last night was beyond incredible, kitten. I loved every minute of it."

"Did you?"

"Definitely."

"Then why did you act so cold towards me this morning?"

***

Adrian's lengthy silence told her a tale that made her miserable to hear.

Her happiness disintegrated into ash. Victoria tried to take a step back but he tightened his arms. He sounded bemused as he asked, "Was I cold to you?"

"Yes!"

"I'm sorry. I thought...never mind."

"What?"

"I thought distance was what you wanted."

Victoria shook her head. "That's not what I wanted at all. It seemed that was what you wanted."

"Kitten, I'm so sorry. Let me make it up to you."

"That's the second time you've said that to me."

Adrian's flashed a naughty grin. "I followed through on my promises last night, didn't I?"

"You did."

He leaned down and pressed a kiss on her throat. "Do you get off soon?"

I'll never hear or say that again without thinking about this man.

"Not for about four more hours." It felt like an eternity to her when all she wanted was to stay in his arms.

Adrian's tongue pressed against her pulse. "Oh, that's too bad. For me. I guess I'll just have to wait that long then."

Victoria found it difficult to concentrate with each sensual stroke of his tongue. "Do you want to try to get together tomorrow? I can shuffle my free time around and meet you late morning."

Adrian's teeth nipped the side of her neck. Victoria let out a ragged cry that turned into a breathy sigh when he soothed the sting with butterfly kisses.

"Not good enough for me, kitten. I want to sleep with you in my arms tonight."

“Oh.” She bit her lip but the pleased grin broke free anyways.

“Will you come with me if I pick you up?”

Yes!

“Do you mean spend the night? All night?”

“Yes.”

Adrian’s fingertips played with the bottom of her skirt. Victoria’s excitement grew with each brush against her bare thigh. She didn’t need to think about her answer at all.

“I’ll come with you, Adrian, wherever.”

He chuckled. “That you will, kitten. That you will.”

Victoria thought he would kiss her right then and there, but all he did next was say, “I don’t want to keep you any longer, especially if it means it’ll keep you later. Call me when you’re ready for me. I’ll be here.”

“Won’t a text be easier?”

“I want to hear your voice, kitten. Call me.”

“Okay.” Victoria watched Adrian walk out of the alley and onto the sidewalk. He raised his hand in farewell. She spontaneously blew him a kiss. Adrian caught it and brought it to his mouth sweetly.

Quitting time can't come fast enough.

***

Adrian held Victoria in his arms as he dreamed of doing since the moment he had to let her go. He couldn't get over how perfectly she fit there. It exhilarated him as much as it unsettled him. He kissed the top of her fragrant head and smiled.

The night had unfolded beautifully from the time Adrian picked her up until now. Victoria had him stop at her cozy apartment where she quickly packed an overnight bag for herself. While waiting for her, he'd met two of her roommates, Jenny and Krista, and apparently passed the first inspection even if they'd been a little cooler towards him at first.

When they arrived at his penthouse, Victoria looked around and shook her head. "I can't believe I still thought you were some kind of middle-manager after seeing this place."

“To be fair, kitten, I didn’t give you the tour. I simply ravished you right…about…here.”

Adrian then gave Victoria an encore presentation with a couple of carnal twists. It was even better than the night before.

Later after a bubble bath and another slippery round of lovemaking, Adrian had a couple of burgers sent over. He’d wrapped Victoria up in one of his robes and had her sit on his lap while he fed her a simple dessert of chocolate chip cookies.

“I’m so happy!” Victoria hugged him tightly and he didn’t have to tell her he felt the same. Adrian showed her exactly how happy she made him right there on the couch. Making love to her in that position gave Adrian access to all of her, but especially the expression on Victoria’s face when she came with a soft moan.

Much later they got ready for bed but ended up lying on their sides and talking for an hour. He told her about the Arctic and she told him about her summers at the Outer Banks. Adrian shared his experience of running with the bulls in Pamplona. Victoria shared her experience about how to make the perfect burger.

Adrian couldn't remember the last time he actually had a casual conversation with a woman besides Victoria that didn't involve sex, flirting, or shopping.

It soothed him. The normalcy of being with her brought Adrian a sense of peace he didn't even know was missing.

But now that he had it, Adrian didn't want to ever lose this feeling of rightness. He couldn't even fathom that things between them would alter and change for the worse. Maybe that was why he suddenly blurted out, "Victoria, I want you to stay with me. Permanently."

The life-altering words were spoken but Adrian didn't feel sick to his stomach as he might've felt had it been said to someone else. He felt happy. Free. His instincts approved.

Now all he needed was for Victoria to feel the same way.

His gorgeous lover blinked rapidly. "What?"

"I want you to move in with me. Now. Tonight."

Victoria pulled back from him far away enough to look at him fully. Her face was wary but not closed off. "Isn't this going kind of fast?"

Now that his mind was made up, Adrian's sole focus was getting her to see things his way. "No, it isn't. I want you here. You want to be here."

"What makes you say that?"

Adrian smirked. His hand reached down and cupped her damp mound. "This sweet part of you tells me that."

Victoria's eyes closed and her hips arched up. "Maybe it does."

"There's no maybe about it, kitten." One finger slipped in to rub teasingly over her pearl. Adrian brought his hand to her mouth and painted Victoria's parted lips with her honey.

She looked up at him, gaze heavy with desire.

"Taste."

Obedient to his command, Victoria delicately licked her lips. Adrian swooped down to kiss her. He longed for the feeling of her lips along his body just as she'd done for him a few short hours before.

Adrian groaned just remembering the erotic image of seeing her full lips fastened around his thick shaft. It was heaven the way she'd trailed her fingers up and down his sack before grabbing the base as she swallowed as much of him as she could.

She's a fast learner. I can't wait to teach her other things. Just as she's taught me.

He broke their kiss. She'd stolen his heart and his breath with each passing minute. Adrian brushed a hand over her silky hair. The words spilled from him.

"I want you with me every day, Victoria. I want to wake up seeing your face every morning. I want to hold you in my arms every night. I want to spoil you. I want to take care of you. I want to make you happy. I want to take away all of your worries. I want you, kitten, and I want you to say you want to be with me too."

***

Victoria couldn't believe Adrian wanted her so much. All the dreams she constructed the night before instantly sprang back to life. Caution should've stopped her dead. Instead, the wheels of madness rolled in a blur. She already knew her answer but whether she would speak it aloud would depend on him.

"Moving in this fast would be crazy. You know that, right?"

"I can do crazy."

"Obviously!" She cupped the side of his face. "What if you change your mind?"

"I won't."

"You don't know that."

"I do."

"How can you be so sure?"

"Because I've never lived with anyone else before. I've never wanted to, Victoria. Not until you."

Her heartbeat quickened. Still, caution threw a wrench in the wheels of madness. Victoria's insecurities made themselves known again. "You can have anyone you want. What's so special about me?"

Adrian traced the shape of her brow. His tenderness devastated her doubt. "I wish I could say, Victoria. I can't really explain it in a way that would satisfy either of us. Every time I touch you...every time I hear your voice...every time I see you...I just want time to stop."

Victoria's eyes filled with tears.

"Kitten, don't cry." Adrian gently kissed each eyelid. "I don't ever want to make you cry."

"I'm not crying because I'm sad. I'm crying because I understand what you're telling me. I understand because I feel it too."

"You do?"

"Yes."

Adrian pushed her back down onto the bed. "Tell me the one word I want to hear, Victoria. Tell me."

She stood at the precipice between her old life and a new one. Victoria leapt without hesitation. “Yes.”

Adrian’s smile rivaled that of the sun. “Say it again.”

“Yes.”

“Again.”

“Yes.”

Adrian kissed her breath away. “You won’t regret this, kitten. I swear you won’t. We’re going to be so happy together.”

Victoria wrapped her legs around his waist and soon was chanting his name as he gave her a taste of what their future held.

NINE

"Kitten! I'm home!"

Victoria uncurled herself off the couch. She met Adrian at the foyer with a sweet kiss. It had become their traditional greeting over the past five months. He lifted his head up long enough to whisper, "How was your day?"

Victoria answered breathlessly after another deeper more intimate kiss, "Busy but I still found time to miss you."

"And you know I missed you." Adrian wrapped his arm around her waist and walked them into the cavernous living room. He sat down on the dark leather couch with her in his lap. His hand stroked her leg. Adrian audibly relished in the simple joy he felt in touching her. They sat there like that for several minutes, just long enough for Adrian to decompress from his day and for Victoria to soak in his embrace.

This was undoubtedly the favorite part of her day.

She loved hearing his heart beat steadily beneath her ear. She loved the delicious scent of his cologne teasing her nostrils. She loved the way he trailed his hand up and down her leg.

Victoria loved *everything* about her life with Adrian.

There were the weekend trips across the ocean that he surprised her with regularly. Paris, London, and Rome were her favorites. There were the charity benefits he took her to in the city and the social events they traveled across the country in his private plane.

As wonderful and exciting as those experiences were, Victoria's favorite times were the ones like this. She loved when it was just the two of them and no designer gown or fabulous trip could ever compare to being in his arms.

Adrian let out a peaceful sigh, signaling the end of his decompression. “You said you were busy today. Tons of homework?”

“Yep. Lots of papers and study guides, but I got them done. Barely, but they’re done.”

“Barely? Hmm, that doesn’t sound like my studious, little Victoria.”

She nipped his chin. “Studious, little Victoria was kept up rather late last night and the night before that.”

“What’s for dinner?”

Victoria linked an arm around his neck and laughed. “Smooth move there, Adrian.”

He winked and whistled innocently. “What?”

“I’m making roast chicken, mashed potatoes and gravy, green beans, and rolls.”

Adrian nuzzled the tip of her nose with his. “I love your Southern cooking, you know that?”

“It’s faux-Southern. True Southern cooking would have me frying the chicken instead of roasting it.” Victoria tried to pinch a nonexistent inch of fat on his lean waist. “I’m saving you from having to double your workouts in the morning."

He ducked in close to her neck and kissed the sensitive spot beneath her ear. "Just admit you're doing it to keep me in bed with you longer."

"I won't deny that," answered with a delicate shudder.

Adrian stood up with her in his arms. He kissed her mouth, only letting his lips part for the barest of moments. "Let me get changed, kitten. I'll be back, okay?"

"Sure. Hurry."

"Always."

Adrian set her down and Victoria watched him walk away. She didn't have to look in a mirror to see her face was wreathed in what felt like a mile-wide smile. Victoria sometimes couldn't believe a person could be this happy all the time. It just didn't seem possible, but it was her life.

It's perfect.

Victoria's decision to move into Adrian's place sent a shockwave throughout her little world. Her roommates were completely against it, logically saying she didn't know Adrian well enough to put her entire life in his hands.

"What if he ends up dumping you next week? What are you going to do then?" That came from Jenny.

"Have you lost your mind? You didn't even know Adrian's background as of yesterday and now you're moving in with him? Please." That came from Shaundra.

"Not the best plan." And that final tidbit came from Krista.

Her stepmother's words were more robust.

"Victoria, I know these past five years have been hard on you. No, really. You've been so supportive of the girls, and I'll always appreciate it, but you can't deny that it's been hard. I also know it must seem like since you've got this chance at happiness you've got to take it now. I just don't want you rushing into anything this drastic without giving it thought."

Victoria had appreciated all their warnings and would've been saying the same thing if it had been any one of them making the same decision.

She really did understand.

Moving in with Adrian after one day *wasn't* logical. It wasn't within eye-view of logical. She recognized that.

However, logic couldn't always be the deciding factor in life.

Victoria's instincts dared her to listen to them for a change instead of always going with her head. So she packed up her few possessions and moved in with Adrian.

She didn't allow herself to think about the possibility that they might implode within a week. She refused to consider that he might decide she was more trouble than she was worth and replace her with someone who came from his world.

Victoria took a chance and the chance, so far, had been more than worth it.

Even when she'd had to quit her jobs in order for Adrian not to lose face. Granted, he hadn't asked her to do it and it'd been her choice, but how could she have continued to clean offices in his building? And then how could she continue waitressing when she ran into one of his acquaintances and a woman who was obviously not his wife?

"I won't tell if you won't," the middle-aged banker had said with a faint leer on the way to the bathroom. Later the jerk went out of his way to find her, standing too closely behind Victoria at the bar, and whispered, "Are you working tomorrow? I've got the taste for...wings...and would love to see you again."

Victoria had quit immediately. She also avoided doing more than saying "Hello" whenever she came across him and his wife at the occasional social event.

Unease batted about her mind like a moth at a brightly-lit window. Had she'd been too quick to give up her financial independence? Adrian set aside an account in her name and funded it generously, but Victoria didn't see it as her money.

Not really.

Why am I thinking about this now? Everything is fine between us and besides, I'm about to graduate in less than a month. Once I start working 60 hours a week, I'll be wishing I appreciated this little vacation more.

Mind firmly at ease again, Victoria hummed and headed to the kitchen to check on dinner.

***

Adrian quickly changed his clothes. His pleasure at being home again with Victoria dimmed as he wondered if she was as happy with him as was with her.

She's had to sacrifice more for me than I have for her. It's not right.

Aware of the upheaval in her life, Adrian tried his best to smooth her way and preserve her independence. Of course, his way dealt with money.

Adrian paid her rent for a full year so she'd have her room to go back to if she decided he was, as he put it, "A total pain in the ass to live with." This went a long way in easing any lingering worries and hostilities her former roommates might've had towards him and her judgment in moving in with him.

That and the flowers he had sent to each of them weekly.

Adrian also set up a bank account solely in Victoria's name with enough money to support her for several years if she lived modestly—in the city. It would be plenty of money to last two decades if she ever went back to North Carolina.

Victoria had no intention of touching that money and told him so quite clearly.

Adrian wasn't surprised. Victoria was a sweet girl but prideful. She was also the most stubborn person he'd ever met. He learned very quickly to not push when she made up her mind.

A case in point was her jobs. Victoria kept working for the first two months, despite Adrian's assurances that all she had to do was concentrate on finishing her last semester in school.

"Working makes me feel good."

How could he argue with that? Adrian learned the hard way that there was no moving her when Victoria made up her mind. All it had taken was one argument which Adrian had lost—a rarity for him to be sure.

Victoria replaced her cleaning job with extra shifts on the restaurant. She never explained why, but it didn't take any thought as to why she ended her employment. She didn't want to put him in the position of having to explain her connection to him.

Adrian appreciated her caring about him that way, even if it didn't matter to him what others thought about him or their relationship. What he did care about, however, was what others thought about her.

Especially, if they were lustful, disrespectful thoughts.

The possessiveness Adrian felt whenever his driver ferried Victoria over to her waitressing job didn't die down as he assumed it would. Not by expression or tone would he let it slip that he hated her job. He dutifully accepted her goodbye kiss and told her, "Have a good night. I can't wait to see you when you come home."

Adrian then spent those miserable nights immersed in his never-ending paperwork. When that failed to keep his simmering frustration in check, he got physical. Sometimes it was at the boxing club. Other times he played pickup games at a nearby basketball court. Adrian ran for miles at an indoor track when either of those options weren't available.

He'd do anything to distract himself from thinking about all those strangers looking at the curves of Victoria's beautiful body.

Abruptly, she ended her waitress position one night. Victoria didn't tell him why and Adrian didn't press, but he couldn't deny he was secretly glad for it. Adrian had immediately offered to help her find another position, especially because he felt guilty at taking pleasure in a situation that made her so obviously unhappy.

"Kitten, with your qualifications I can get you an internship at the best accounting firms in the city. Let me do this for you. It's no hardship."

She merely patted his hand. "Adrian, babe, I appreciate it. Really I do, but I have to do this on my own. It has to be *my* accomplishment. Do you understand?"

He did.

Her independence was just one of the many things he loved about Victoria. That was why he felt so conflicted in feeling pleasure over something that aided in keeping her dependent on him.

Adrian loved taking care of Victoria. He loved that his position afforded to give her the world and not only that, but it made him feel for the first time that all his work *meant* something. It wasn't just to build up his company stock or personal portfolio, it was to take care of Victoria.

And yet...

Victoria needed to work just like he did. She'd been independent ever since her father had died. It wasn't something she wanted to give up easily.

Not one given to that much waffling back and forth on an issue, Adrian decided not to let it bother him more than it already had. He put it out of his mind and every time guilt crept back in, he would look at their growing life together. The uncomfortable feeling usually left then, especially when Victoria lay curled up next to him, a beautiful smile for him at the ready.

All those moments of happiness deserved material acts of appreciation in Adrian's mind, so he took immense pleasure in showering Victoria with presents. He especially loved draping jewels around her neck. Sapphires were his favorite. And even though Victoria appreciated his largesse, she made it a point to let him know that he didn't need to buy her affection with emeralds, rubies, and sapphires.

"I just want to be with you, Adrian. That's all."

"I know. Thank you for indulging me."

And it was a beautiful indulgence. Adrian fancied having a diamond collar commissioned for his kitten, but he didn't want her to get the wrong idea about his appetites. Still, a collar would be lovely to mark her as his...

And more than anything, Adrian wanted Victoria to be his. He wanted her to be as mad about him as he was about her. She was everything he never knew he wanted. Being with her was the best drug he'd ever taken. Everything was heightened—especially his emotions. The thought of losing Victoria made him wake up in the middle of the night and reach for her to make sure she was still there.

Victoria never knew the irrational fear gnawing him for the inside and that was the way it was going to stay.

So instead he threw more money at it. Adrian supplied Victoria with her own credit cards. She rarely used them, but when she did it was usually to take a friend out to dinner on celebratory occasions. He was sure there had been a problem with the statement the first month he received it because there had been no purchases.

So while he respected her need for autonomy, Adrian took advantage of it by indulging in his ever-growing need to take care of Victoria. He constantly took her shopping for clothes. Already there were whispers about the Cinderella he'd taken under his wing, and while Adrian couldn't control their snide tongues, he could at least make sure no one could look down on Victoria because of her lack of labels.

She took the purchases in stride, but Adrian noticed she preferred to wear her pre-relationship clothes when at home.

Just like now.

He leaned against the doorway and watched her. Victoria had a little green apron wrapped around her trim waist. Her jeans pulled across her lush bottom when she bent over to check the oven and her little black t-shirt rode up her back. Adrian's lips itched with the urge to kiss that strip of exposed skin.

Victoria took that moment to look over her shoulder. Her full mouth opened slightly. The familiar look of desire stamped her pretty features. Adrian padded over to her. His finger hooked into her waistband and pulled Victoria close.

"Stop looking at me like that, Adrian."

"Like how?"

His playful denial coupled with one hand innocently brushing across the front of her thighs made Victoria lean close. Her stance widened. He slipped his hand closer. The heat of her inspired him to cup her before squeezing rhythmically.

"The last time you did this, Adrian, I burned dinner."

He remembered. Smoke filled the kitchen and made the whole place smell pungent for hours. He bared his teeth in a smug grin anyways.

"So? That's what take-out is for, kitten."

Adrian licked a path down her neck. He loved hearing the breathy little moans she always made when he reached the juncture of her neck and shoulder.

Victoria untied her apron and threw it on the floor. She snatched her shirt off and undid her lacy bra. Adrian smiled and took what she so prettily offered with her hands. His mouth tugged on her pert nipples, tonguing them thoroughly before giving them each a playful bite.

Her moans grew louder and he became a beast, stripping her quickly so he could play with his kitten. Adrian had Victoria stand over him while he pleasured her with his lips, tongue, and fingers. The scent and delicate taste of her intoxicated him. Victoria's cries filled his ears with beauty. When she bent down and unbuttoned his pants, Adrian's tongue drove deep inside. He then went wild when her mouth traced a line around his shaft.

Nothing could ever feel better.

It wasn't the sex, or rather it wasn't *just* the sex. It was their cozy domesticity. Victoria fit him. She truly was his everything...

Adrian's thoughts disintegrated when she fisted him. He zeroed in on her honeyed cleft, keeping in time with her strokes. His tongue teased the sweet pearl while Victoria's mouth fastened around his thick, overly sensitized head.

They ended up on the floor before he could spill. Victoria straddled him, churning her hips while he pumped into her madly. His hands roamed from her thighs, to her slick mound, up to her full breasts, and then further up. Victoria nipped his fingers before sucking them deep into her mouth.

Adrian truly couldn't get enough of Victoria and apparently neither could she get enough of him. It was always like this between them. A beautiful, perfect storm of desire and need.

When they finally collapsed against each other the timer began beeping.

"Perfect timing," she sighed against his neck before giving it a quick kiss. "You couldn't have planned it better, Adrian."

Indeed.

TEN

Time passed and Victoria's graduation was upon her before she knew it. Her family had flown in on Adrian's private jet. He'd also booked them the presidential suite at one of the city's most luxurious hotels.

Victoria's sisters had declared themselves princesses as they ran throughout the well-appointed rooms. Her stepmother and step-grandmother seemed to be impressed with the space too.

Adrian had done his best to rearrange his schedule, but unfortunately only had enough time to pick them all up from the airport and bring them to the hotel. Still, he'd managed to be his charming best to them all. When he left he kissed her on the cheek in deference to their small audience.

"I look forward to seeing you all tonight at dinner. Goodbye, kitten."

Victoria didn't have to look in a mirror to see the besotted grin stretching her mouth wide. As soon as the door closed her stepmother said, "I don't have to ask if you're happy, do I?"

"Nope."

Megan and Reagan skipped over to her, one on each side to tug at her hand, and asked in unison, "Mommy says you live with Mr. Adrian. Does that mean he's going to be your husband?"

Victoria looked up for help. Both of the women waited with curiosity for her answer, one more intently than the other. "Uh, I'm not sure."

"Why? Don't you love each other?"

Victoria squirmed mentally. Adrian hadn't said the words to her yet, but to be fair, she hadn't said it to him either. It wasn't strange, was it? Of course, they had really strong feelings for each other. Adrian spent nearly all of his free time with her and not just in bed. They talked, laughed, and shared their innermost selves with one another.

That had to be love.

"We like each other *very, very* much." Victoria looked up in time to see the oldest member of their party tighten her lips in disapproval.

Rose McKinnon was of a different era and Victoria didn't have to ask her stepmother if her mother approved of living together before marriage. The answer was written all over her face. Victoria thought it better to change the subject. Fast.

"So how was your flight—"

"Can we be your bridesmaids at the wedding? Can we wear pink tutus? Ones that go all the way to the floor?"

"Megan! I like purple. You *know* I hate pink."

The girls squabbled as usual, saving Victoria from having to answer any more questions. Conversation moved to safer topics of school, plans for a job, and whether she was going to go to the Outer Banks with them during the summer.

It reminded her of being home in the family kitchen. All that was missing was the family cat Cedric circling the table for an indulgent hand to pet his sleek back.

Still Victoria was grateful when it was time for her to go home an hour later. Leaving her little family in their luxurious rooms with plans to pick them up for dinner at eight, Victoria wondered why she was so glad to go. Normally, she loved visiting them.

Instead, Victoria kept mentally replaying the image of Rose McKinnon's mouth pursing in distaste. It seemed like a portent for disaster but she couldn't understand why.

Victoria shook her head. She wouldn't dwell on the fact that neither of the other women asked her questions about Adrian or her relationship with him. She wouldn't allow herself to wonder if they were respecting her privacy or if the lack of questions meant they didn't really approve.

Everything was fine. How could it not be? She was graduating tomorrow. All her years of hard work, sleepless nights, and sacrifices were going to be coming to an end. Victoria's real life was about to begin and Adrian was going to be a part of it.

***

Adrian stood up and clapped when Victoria walked across the stage. He barely held any attachment to his own graduation but hers was different. Adrian burst with pride, especially knowing how hard she'd worked to earn her degree. When the ceremony was over, Victoria made a beeline straight towards him. Adrian picked her up and rained kisses all over her flushed face.

"You did it, kitten!"

She laughed and wrapped her arms around his neck. "I know! I can barely believe it!"

Adrian set her down and wrapped his arm around her waist. Victoria's stepmother smiled and took several pictures of them, even one when she kissed him on the cheek. He then let her go so he could play cameraman. Victoria's smile never dimmed even while Adrian took dozens of pictures with her and her little family.

It was different from his experience. Both of Adrian's parents had come to his graduation, but there were no giddy displays of pride and happiness. There'd been one obligatory picture and dinner at the club, but then nothing.

Adrian never knew he'd been missing something until today.

Victoria's stepmother had to take the twins to find a restroom just as several of Victoria's classmates swooped in and took her away for even more pictures. Adrian was so focused on watching her that he almost didn't hear Mrs. McKinnon's words.

"I take it you're making plans to marry our Victoria."

Adrian froze. He kept his expression friendly and open but his mind whirled like a dervish. He hadn't expected Victoria's step-grandmother to say something so personal. It never dawned on him and Adrian didn't care for the unprepared position.

"I care very much for Victoria, Mrs. McKinnon."

"Yes, you do care. You care enough to have kept her in your home for going on half a year. That should be plenty of time to know whether or not you feel she suits you."

"She suits me very well, Mrs. James."

"Well enough to put a ring on her finger?"

Adrian found himself at a rare loss of words. He cleared his throat. Although he kept his tone respectful, steel lightly scored each syllable. "Please excuse me, Mrs. McKinnon, but that is between Victoria and me."

"Hmph." She fixed a bright blue eye on him. "You know her daddy's dead, but let me tell you something. I knew the man well. There'd be no way he'd stand for you playing house with his daughter. That girl deserves to have a man who isn't afraid to make it right in front of the church. If you're not him then don't waste her time."

Adrian saw Victoria's stepmother approaching. He hoped it wasn't reinforcements for this particular conversation. "I appreciate your candor, Mrs. McKinnon."

"I bet you do. Here's some more candor. She expects it. Her family expects it. Our patience is coming to an end."

Mrs. Montford joined them with her twins on either side of her. Although they'd been chattering nonstop, they'd suddenly quieted when in front of him. They looked up shyly at Adrian with eyes as dark as their older sister. It instantly made him wonder if his children with Victoria would also have her eyes.

A pit in Adrian's stomach tightened as caution finally ground him to a halt.

Children? This is going too fast. Much too fast.

Victoria crashed into his side with a gleeful smile on her beautiful face. "Are you ready?"

"No." At her frown, he shook his head and pasted on a smile. It felt heavy, false, especially while he burned beneath the disapproving glare of her step-grandmother. "I'm sorry, kitten. Ready for what?"

Adrian could've kicked himself when her grin dimmed. Guilt made for a poor companion when all he should've been feeling was joy and pride in the immense accomplishment Victoria had achieved today.

After years of working two jobs, struggling and sacrifice, she'd earned her degree. Nothing could come in the way of that. Not his fear. Not her relative's disapproval. Nothing.

I'm not going to lose her. Victoria would never leave me. We feel the same way about each other. I know we do.

Adrian held her close to him with one arm around her waist and kissed her warm cheek. "Ready for what?" he prompted.

"Ready for dinner?"

"Of course, I am. We can go whenever you're ready, Victoria."

The happiness in her gaze returned tenfold. "I'm ready now."

Adrian escorted all the ladies to his limousine, smiling indulgently at the excitement of Victoria's little sisters when they entered. He'd made sure the bar was stocked with water and juice boxes for them as well as the champagne for the grownups.

Unfortunately, he wasn't surprised when Mrs. McKinnon passed on the champagne and took water instead.

Dinner was an elegant affair and every detail he'd planned had gone off without a hitch. Victoria had loved her roses and her sisters had worn their little corsages all throughout dinner.

Mrs. Montford had appreciated her flower arrangement while Mrs. McKinnon had given him a polite "Thank you" and simply set her flowers aside and didn't look at them again except to carry them out of the restaurant.

Victoria didn't seem to notice the elderly woman's disapproval but Adrian noticed it all too well. He didn't like it. He didn't like the threat it represented to his relationship.

After they dropped off Victoria's family at their suite and arrived home, Victoria hugged him as hard as she could.

"Thank you so much for today. It was perfect."

Perfect. The word lashed at him because Adrian now knew it wasn't perfect. Not anymore.

Seemingly unaware of the turmoil raging inside his calm exterior, Victoria slept peacefully against his chest later that night. He stroked his hand down her silky back, marveling once again at how perfectly she fit against his side.

How perfectly she fit in his life.

Adrian always assumed life had to be boring for those men who rushed home right after work, but now he understood. He hadn't felt a hint of confinement during all their months together. He loved coming home to Victoria every night. When he had to leave her for a business meeting, it was all he could do to wrap things up as fast as possible.

Looking back on his past relationships, Adrian always sensed the clock ticking. No matter how charming, how much fun they had jetting around the world, the sound ticked away relentlessly.

Adrian never wanted to be tied down. He'd always needed his freedom, regardless of what capacity it came in.

Adrian had fought to be free of his inherited privilege. He'd demanded freedom from the old structures of wealth and embraced technological equalizers. Adrian hadn't allowed himself to be tied down to one woman until now.

It would be logical that Victoria was obviously the one woman he hadn't even known he'd been waiting for all this time. So why did he hear his internal clock ticking when he hadn't for so long?

Time was running out. He had to stop it. He had to figure out what to do to keep Victoria. The thought of her leaving...

Sickness rose. He couldn't draw in a proper breath. Adrian kissed the top of her head. She snuggled closer to him and he closed his eyes in pain.

Victoria deserved the best life had to offer. She didn't deserve to be with a man who didn't know how to...

What? Love her more than he loved anyone else? Who respected her above all others? Why isn't that enough?

The answer came to Adrian, cold like a surgical knife slicing away his joy. He'd become too attached to her. He'd become too dependent on her for his happiness. He'd thought that just because he was happy it meant she was too.

"She expects it. Her family expects it."

Was Mrs. McKinnon right? Did Victoria expect marriage? Was he letting her down?

He let his fingers trail through her dark locks. Marriage had never been on his horizon before. Could it be time for him to see it now?

Adrian imagined a wedding. He saw Victoria in a fluffy white dress, trailing veil, and diamond-bright smile. He saw kids, preschool interviews, birthdays, family vacations, and college. Adrian saw Victoria and their family depending on him for everything, especially happiness.

He saw them disappointed.

I know how to build, manage, and maintain a company. I don't know the first thing about doing the same for a family.

Adrian needed time. He needed time to figure out the next move for them. He needed time to get past the fear eating him alive that he might lose Victoria.

Adrian never backed down from a challenge. He refused to allow fear to have any influence in his life.

Until now.

***

Victoria couldn't put her finger on it but something between them had changed.

Adrian worked longer hours, coming home later and later until there were some nights she didn't remember him coming home at all. The only sign he'd been there was the indention on his pillow because he'd be gone before she woke up.

Whenever she tried to talk to him about it...well, that was another problem.

Victoria couldn't seem to make the words come out. She didn't ask him why he was working so hard or why he didn't ask her to come with him on the inevitable trips that he took each week. All her interviewing prior to graduation paid off because she'd secured an entry-level position at a midsize firm. It wouldn't start until July 1 so she was free to go anywhere with him.

All which meant that she was lonely for the next month.

Adrian wasn't unkind to her. If anything he seemed to be even sweeter towards her on the weekends, as if to make up for not being plugged in during the week. And once night fell, Adrian became insatiable. He devoured her body and soul, as if he couldn't get enough of her.

It was easy to believe there weren't any problems when she was pinned beneath him. When Adrian's hand held her wrists above her head and when his thick shaft slowly slid in and out of her, Victoria knew their connection was real.

Come Monday though, Adrian was back to a polite distance.

Victoria didn't know what to make of it. She only knew it hurt and when she hurt, Victoria withdrew. She pretended she was okay. She acted as if nothing was amiss, but the longer it went on the more it drained her to pretend.

Victoria's tummy was upset at least once a day and her appetite waned. Adrian didn't notice because he was never there anymore. His business trips stretched over into the weekends. Adrian used to call her every day when away. He stopped calling for the first time.

Victoria couldn't keep pretending anymore when the clock turned to midnight.

Her roommates' warnings went from ghostly whispers in her mind to full blown shrieks.

What's happening to us? We were fine, weren't we?

Wrapped up in a thick blanket on the couch, Victoria stared blindly at the TV. She let the fear out in a threaded whisper.

"He's cheating on me. He's found someone else. He's tired of me..."

Victoria rushed off the couch and headed straight for the nearest bathroom. She emptied up the contents of her stomach before retching on bile. A long minute passed before the spasms stopped. Exhausted, Victoria wiped her mouth and then lied on the cold tile.

He's already left me. He just hasn't told me yet.

Victoria's face crumpled into tears. She sobbed as the grief roared out of her. Adrian had never said he loved her for a reason. But she loved him and now she was forced to know why she never said the words.

It was because Victoria always knew deep down that someone like Adrian could never have loved her. He could've loved her body or the sexual chemistry between them, but not *her*. If

Adrian did then he couldn't have pulled away so drastically.

He wouldn't have left her like this, one slow day at a time.

Victoria's mind whirled about. She dissected each part of their lives from the beginning until the present. Was the sex between them no longer good? Was she boring? Hadn't she been supportive? Did she not show him enough appreciation for what he did for her? Was she not what he wanted anymore?

He'd always said I was unlike anyone he'd ever met. Maybe that's not true anymore.

The idea that she lost her novelty, that all she had *ever* been was a novelty, gutted Victoria. Her fears presented nightmare-black. The questions became fact in her fevered brain.

He'd tried slumming and maybe now he was ready to go back to the familiar. Victoria knew what that would be because she'd finally broken down and Googled him.

I regret it so much.

Like a kamikaze masochist, Victoria had looked the night before at the numerous images of Adrian and his glamorous exes. Fashion Week in Paris, Cannes, and Hollywood premieres weren't unknown to him. Sunning on a yacht moored in the Mediterranean with pop stars and A-Listers hadn't been a rare event. Ignorance *was* bliss because how could Victoria ever hope to compete with that world?

She was just a girl who grew up middle-class. She was a girl whose biggest ambition was to be a CPA like her father. Important, yes, but not the kind of position one chose to set the world on fire.

Her goals were solid. Ordinary. Regular.

Adrian and everyone who visited his sphere were extraordinary on their off-days. They were gods and world-changers and she was just a mortal visiting their world. There were no happy endings for people like them. They were too different and they always would be.

Dawn broke before Victoria got up off the floor. She felt old as she shuffled out of the bathroom and into the cavernous bedroom. Victoria couldn't keep hiding in silence. She had to confront him. Depending on the answer, Victoria was going to either stay or leave.

And in doing so she had to be ready to see their fairytale romance crumble into ash.

ELEVEN

Adrian knew as soon as he crossed the threshold that something was terribly wrong. The apartment was too still. Its familiarity to how life was before Victoria moved in with him wasn't comforting.

At all.

Adrian left his suitcase, laptop bag, and coat in the foyer. "Victoria?" She didn't answer. A sense of panic cut his breath when he called out for her again. Adrian knew he should've contacted her while he was gone.

He wanted to call her. He craved the sound of her voice.

So what stopped him?

It was the insidious belief he had to keep his distance until he knew what to do next about their future. He wasn't ready to take that final step but he didn't want to let her go either. Adrian had spent the past month weighing options, analyzing their living situation from every angle just so he'd know what to say to her.

Would he make her dreams come true or be cast in the abyss of her scorn?

Even after a month Adrian still didn't have a suitable strategy. There was too many variables. He prayed his indecision hadn't forced a decision to be made anyways.

How much longer is she going to wait for me? Not long. I'm sure of it.

Adrian strode into the living room only to find it empty. His hurried steps headed straight for the bedroom. Relief crashed into him when he saw Victoria sitting at the end of the bed. Only when he saw her did he allow himself to acknowledge that he'd been so afraid she had simply packed her things on moved out.

Which was obviously paranoid on his part. She would never do that to him. Victoria wasn't like that kind of girl. She was fair, thoughtful, reasonable, lovable, and far too good for an indecisive bastard like himself. Why couldn't he have thought like that over the weekend?

"Kitten...Victoria...didn't you hear me? Why didn't you say anything? You had me worried."

Adrian's instincts called a warning. She wouldn't look up at him. Instead, her pink ballerina flats held her undivided attention. He vaguely noted she was dressed in a flowered, fluttery skirt and an ivory sweater. She looked sweet like candy.

"Hello, Adrian. We need to talk."

He didn't approach her. He remained by the door.

"What about?"

The corner of her mouth creased in a parody of a smile. "Everything."

Not good. "Okay. Do you want to talk here?"

She looked about as if she didn't quite know where she was. Worry wormed through him. Adrian's instincts bade him to keep his thoughts to himself, to let her show hers first so he could render the appropriate plan of defense.

Victoria stood up. “No.” She walked past him. He noted how she didn’t even brush her hand across his arm as she usually did. Victoria just left, head held high and arms stiff by her side. He didn’t have to wonder if she was upset. The tension running through Victoria was obvious.

As he followed her into the living room, Adrian would’ve bet his fortune she was furious with him for not calling.

Damnit, I should’ve called. I know I should’ve called.

Adrian waited until she sat down. He frowned at her choice. A club chair. Her distance was too much like when they first talked, but not nearly enough. Then was the beginning of their chase. The now didn’t bear thinking

He seated himself across from her and waited. The minutes rolled by while she simply stared at her hands. The delicate fingers brought to mind of the marital blade hanging over them. More than ever Adrian was convinced that her step-grandmother’s words were true and that

Victoria indeed was already disappointed in him for not giving her the only ring that counted.

He positively itched with impatience from not knowing the thoughts coursing through her mind. Still he kept quiet.

Keep your thoughts clear. Wait for her to speak. Don't rush it.

"This isn't working anymore, is it?"

Adrian let out grunt because it was all he was capable of considering the agony those softly-spoken words detonated. He must've taken too long to reply because she looked at him with such intense sadness.

He mentally weighed his options before settling on innocent enough words. "Why do you say that, kitten?"

Victoria winced. Adrian clearly saw his reply wasn't the one she'd wanted. He wished he could've denied it instead of assessing her. It was too late to undo the damage.

"Because of you. You've changed, Adrian, and I don't understand why. Please help me understand."

Adrian winced. He couldn't deny it as much as he would've wanted to. Yet, he still didn't know what exactly to say to keep her. Their simple happiness seemed like such a long time ago.

"It's been really busy at work." Adrian just gave up serious ground and put his entire position at a severe disadvantage. It was a pitiful excuse and it was obvious they both knew it.

"It's always been busy at work, but you *always* made time for me. You don't anymore. Not since my graduation."

Adrian winced. "I still make time for you."

"No you don't," Victoria contradicted softly. "You're avoiding me. It's like I'm not even here for you anymore. I'm a house plant for all the attention you show me. It hurts me when we lie in bed together and you're fixated on your phone. It hurts worse when you stay locked up in your office until I can't wait up for you any longer. It's not work. It's not you being busy. God knows I understand busy. But that's not it with you. I feel it's purposeful. Is it?"

Yes.

Adrian wasn't fool enough to say it out loud. Somehow Victoria heard him anyways.

Her voice choked on a sob. "What's wrong, Adrian? What did I do wrong? I can change—" She bit her lip as if to take back the words.

Guilt scorched right through him. He had to make it right with her. Adrian would do and say anything to take them back to the way they were before. Anything to freeze time to the instance when Victoria looked at him as if he was her dream come true.

"Kitten, you didn't do anything wrong. Never."

His answer apparently didn't soothe her worries. If anything she grew more agitated. "Then why did you change? Why are you so far away from me?"

Adrian had always known how to hide his reactions and discomforts. It was imperative in his world where even the slightest hint of emotion could affect a man's bottom line.

He couldn't do it this time.

Raking a hand through his hair, Adrian fought to find the correct words. He didn't want to lie to her, but he wasn't ready to share his fears about their unmapped future. He couldn't tell her that the idea of marriage made his veins turn to ice.

He'd seen firsthand how hellish marriage could be for two people. A commitment to keeping appearances had doomed his parents and by extension, him and his brother. Never would Adrian want that for himself. Just the thought that one day Victoria would look at him the way his mother looked at his father...it was enough to send a shudder right through him.

"It's been difficult for me, Victoria. Life is changing for us, for you, and I don't want to stand in the way of your future. I want it to be right for us both."

A frown knitted itself across her brow. "I don't understand. How would you be in the way of my future? You *are* my future."

His stomach dropped. He felt the dampness of his palms when he clenched his fists.

"Victoria, don't think that way. For your own sake, don't put me in such a place of importance. I don't deserve it."

As soon as he spoke the words Adrian knew he had spoken his heart's truth. How could he be that important when the idea of marriage, of making that permanent decision, scared him as nothing had ever before?

The color drained from Victoria's face. She looked like a beautiful, broken doll. Her eyes condemned him yet her voice remained as soft as ever. "Tell me what I do deserve then. I'm curious. Obviously, it's not your presence. It's not your conversation. It's not your body. It's not your respect."

"Victoria..."

She leaned forward. "Do I deserve a life without you? Is that what you have been preparing me for?"

Adrian dropped his gaze. He heard the quick intake of her breath. It was in that awful, lonely sound that he knew he had to make a decision. The only decision left to him.

***

Victoria studied the painfully quiet man across from her. She knew exactly how his dark hair fell across his brow at the end of a long day. She knew the bridge of his perfect nose. She knew the shape of his mouth. She knew every inch of his beautifully masculine body and had tasted much of it.

Yet, she didn't know this man at all.

This stranger inhabited Adrian Hawthorne's body. He carried the same timbre of voice. His eyes even gleamed the same beguiling shade of hazel. But this man wasn't the one who had seen her as something special, something to be treasured. This man saw her as a burden. One he wanted out of his life.

Victoria found a way to be grateful for the night before. She'd cried all her tears then. Numb and drained enough to hold it together, she could at least keep a sense of dignity as her entire world unraveled.

"You don't have to say anything else. I understand, Adrian."

He looked at her blankly. Victoria's lips curled into a bittersweet smile. It had been a beautiful dream. A fairytale is even. Now it was time to return to the real world.

In the real world, moms died of cancer before their twenty-third birthday and left their daughters with hazy memories of their hugs and kisses.

In the real world, dads died of heart attacks while their daughters still needed them to love and protect them.

In the real world, billionaire boyfriends didn't love their working-class girlfriends forever.

"I guess there's nothing left to say." Victoria stood up. She smoothed her hands down her skirt. "I guess I'll be on my way then."

Adrian broke out of his stupor. He frowned in confusion. "Where?"

She bit the inside of her cheek to keep from spewing spite. Her numb façade cracked. Pain oozed where there should only have been quiet dignity. Clearing her throat, she answered simply, "Away."

"Away where?"

Why was he making this harder for her? Did he want to see her break down? Was he truly that pitiless?

"Away from here. Just as you want."

"No. That is not what I want. You're misunderstanding me."

"I'm not."

"Kitten..."

"Don't call me that. My name is Victoria." She swallowed hard when she saw stunned rejection speed across his handsome face. She felt petty for saying it, but if Adrian didn't want her he couldn't call her that anymore.

It hurt too much.

"*Victoria*, I don't want you to go anywhere. I want you to stay with me. Really, I do." Adrian swallowed hard. His words came out halting and slow. "I know what you want. I know what you're expecting. And I... I...Christ!"

He raked both of his hands through his hair and hung his head.

"It's probably past time for me to do this anyways. It's not like I can say that I haven't lived well before now. I mean, no one could ever accuse me of living like a monk. So there's nothing for me to miss, right? I like you well enough and I know you like me. Successful partnerships have been formed on a lot less. And we do like each other as people. Not just as lovers. Friends. We're friends. I know we are."

The beginnings of a headache formed. Adrian barely made any sense but she feared she knew where he was going. She prayed she was wrong, that it was going to be anything but a proposal. Any other time Victoria would've been ecstatic to say "yes" and be his wife forever.

But not now and not like this.

Victoria tried to save the situation. "Maybe now isn't the—"

"No! Now is the only time." Adrian flung his head back. "All right. I agree."

"Agree to what?"

Please, please don't say it. Please, Adrian.

He stared at her. "I agree. I'll give you what you want."

Victoria trembled with the beginnings of supreme humiliation. How could he pin this whole debacle on her?

"Just *exactly* what do you think I want?"

Irritation edged his tone. "Come on, kitten. Pardon me. I mean, *Victoria*. I'm giving in as gracefully as I can. This is hard for me but I'm willing to go through it for you. Only for you." He sighed when she remained silent. "You're going to make me say it out loud, aren't you?"

Victoria shook her head, not in answer, but in shock. This couldn't be happening.

A crooked smile broke through his frown. It was the one she'd never been able to resist until now. "Thank you. At least you're not that insensitive. God, I hope to never have to go through this again." He stood up and walked over to her. Adrian reached for her hands. "I'm so glad it's over. Now we can go back to our lives like normal, right?"

Victoria could barely feel his touch. No one had ever proposed to her before and it would appear that even now no one still had.

"Would you like to pick out your ring today? Price is no object, kitten. I can call you that again since you're my fiancée, right?" he asked wryly.

She looked up. Her brittle words wiped off his smirk. "No. I'm not your fiancée and I'm not your kitten."

Adrian frowned. He searched her gaze as if expecting to find she was joking with him. Whatever he saw made him angry enough to tighten his jaw. "What kind of game are you playing with me?"

Victoria knew her words were going to be hurtful, spiteful even, but she couldn't rein herself in.

"That's what I'm asking you. What makes you think this is what I want? What kind of ego do you have to even think that this was remotely close to what I want? A proposal from you is the *last* thing I want. Oh and trust me, the next time you propose to a girl make sure you don't say the words that you've just said to me. You won't get the results you're looking for."

"There won't be a next time."

Agony flared throughout her body. Some shameful part of her begged that she apologize to him. Victoria ruthlessly crushed it.

Adrian wasn't finished. "How could you throw that back in my face? Do you have any idea how hard it was for me to say those words to you?"

I'm not going to feel guilty about this. I'm not.

Victoria silently repeated the words over and over to herself. "And do you know how difficult it was for me to hear it? I imagine a man on the way to his execution would sound far more cheerful than you just did."

Adrian let go of her hands and took several steps away from her, as if he couldn't bear to touch her one second longer. Victoria had never seen him so enraged. She would've been nervous if she wasn't so flaming mad herself.

“Pardon me for not following a Hollywood script. I didn’t know there was a right way and a wrong way to ask someone to be with you forever.”

She didn’t know what hurt worse—his anger to her reaction or that he gave his ‘proposal’ so little thought. Victoria wrapped her arms around her waist. “I never wanted this. I just wanted you.”

“Then what’s the problem, Victoria? You’ve got me. I’m yours. Shouldn’t this be cause for celebration?”

Perhaps it was wrong of her to think, but Victoria couldn’t help but wonder if she had a different station in life would Adrian have still delivered his proposal this way? If she had been a supermodel like the last one, would Adrian have arranged a private visit to the Eiffel Tower along with the release of a dozen doves instead?

Even now does he still see me as some poor cleaning lady? No. He never stopped seeing me that way. That’s what all the clothes and jewelry have been about. He’s just tried to hide my background and dress me up like someone of his social class because he's been ashamed of me all this time.

Even this...proposal...was done quietly, without fanfare, like something for him to check off his list. Or something to hide because he has no intention of keeping it.

Why now?

The genuine confusion in Adrian's face made Victoria so very sad. "You really don't understand what you've done to me by saying this, do you?"

"Done to you? No, I don't. I've given you what you want. I've gone against my entire way of life to do this for you. Why can't you just be grateful?"

Victoria blinked back a hot rush of tears. "I thought you really understood me, Adrian, but you don't. On one hand, you don't treat me as someone from your world. But on the other hand, you think I'm like everyone else in your world."

"What does that even mean? Make some kind of sense, please."

His contempt made Victoria feel an inch tall. "You think I should be grateful for the chance of marrying a man like you. You think so *little* of me that you can come in here and practically tell me you're sacrificing yourself to the burden of marrying me. You think so little of me that you honestly believe that I shouldn't take offense at the insult you've just given me. The only way that can be square in your mind is if you think the promise of your money is all I would focus on."

"Don't be ridiculous! I know you're not a gold digger. If you were, I would've never let you stay the night much less move in with me."

His vehemence should've heartened her. At the very least he didn't think that badly of her. But he still didn't treasure her enough to put his heart and soul into asking her to marry him. Adrian just flung it at her, as if she just needed to be appreciative for his great sacrifice.

Maybe for him it was a sacrifice. Maybe she should've been grateful. Maybe.

But Victoria didn't want a man to feel that marrying her was a detriment. She wanted someone who was ecstatic with the thought of joining his life to hers. What had just happened here was so far from that and Victoria couldn't accept it.

Mournful, she focused her gaze back on his. "I thought you knew me, Adrian. You don't know me at all and I don't know you like I thought I did."

Adrian fisted his hands. His jaw worked from the effort of keeping his voice calm. "I thought we always told each other the truth, Victoria. I thought honesty was something we both held as important."

"There's honesty and then there's this," Victoria pointed out tightly.

"What?" he spat. "What 'this' are you talking about?"

She turned away, unable to look at him for one second longer. "Why'd you offer to marry me, Adrian? I don't think you really want to do it."

Adrian growled in frustration. "Of course, I don't! I'm doing it because it's what you expect. You expect it and I want to keep you. If this is the price I have to pay then so be it. Besides, I don't understand why you're complaining. I'm the one giving up my freedom for a lifetime. I'm the one who should be complaining about this. I'm not so why are you?"

Victoria mentally staggered. She knew it was bad, but she never suspected it was this bad. Victoria felt as if Adrian had scooped out all of her insides and left her as a hollowed and broken shell.

"You jerk!" She dashed tears off her cheeks. "You're so cruel, Adrian. I never knew that until today."

"I'm a jerk? How can you even say that to me? I've never been cruel to you, Victoria. Not once have I ever treated you with anything less than full respect. And today I've tried to give you the highest respect possible and you've thrown it back in my face. If anyone's cruel it's you."

Victoria's shoulders slumped. She didn't know what else to say or how else to say it. Madly, she wished she could've wound back time to right before he came home. Victoria wished she could've shared her fears about his growing distance in another way.

Maybe she could've said something after dinner. Or maybe she could've wrote it down for him in a card or on pretty stationery. Everything they said to each other today had become twisted and malignant. It especially hurt deep in her soul because talking had always been easy for them and a way to bring them closer.

How do I stop this? Can I stop this or is it too late for us?

Adrian stalked over to her. His fingers, while gentle, refused to let go of her chin as he tipped it up. His gaze penetrated. Whatever he saw in her eyes caused his to go flat with disappointment and anger.

"Tell me your answer clearly. Are you marrying me or not? And remember—make sure you mean what you say to me. I won't ask you again and I won't beg you."

Her heart hammered painfully. Victoria felt as if she could barely draw in enough breath. There would be no going back after this, but her conscience was clear.

She couldn't keep him and despite what he said, Adrian was obviously ready to let her go. The love she couldn't speak or even share demanded this of her. No matter how much it shredded her heart to say it.

She'd rather lose him than force Adrian to be with her out of some sense of misplaced loyalty. She loved him too much to ever do that to him. She'd never trap him.

Never.

Victoria reached out. Her palm cupped his cheek. His heat thawed her enough to remind her of all the beautiful memories he had created with her before this terrible month.

She thought back to the wonder of first bumping into this man. How excited she had been to see him for those first couple of weeks and every night since! Adrian had fulfilled her in every way imaginable.

He'd laughed with her, made love with her, and shown her a glittering world she never would've had hopes in seeing otherwise. Adrian had been everything to her and even though she'd never told him she loved him, Victoria had loved him every day with all of her heart.

"Not. I won't marry you, Adrian."

***

The penthouse was quiet. It was the silence of a time before Victoria. It was a silence that once soothed Adrian. He didn't know it then, but it was the silence of privacy, of not having to hear the incessant chattering of a self-involved, shallow, and pampered companion.

He hated it now that he knew better.

This sound wasn't silence. It was oppression.

Wandering around his home, Adrian searched for the ghost of his kitten. All of her things were gone except for the designer clothes filling her walk-in closet and the cases of jewelry he'd bought her. He didn't know that until much later after she left.

Maybe things would've unfolded differently if he had realized it earlier.

Hours ago Adrian had assumed that Victoria would definitely be back when she walked to the door empty-handed. Mistakenly he'd thought that she just needed time to cool off. He knew he did. When Victoria came back he would ask her to explain why she'd gotten so upset with him for doing as she and her family wished.

He had assumed the next minutes of his life wrongly.

"I've already moved all my stuff out. Not that there was much of it. I thought I was overreacting, but I guess I wasn't. Better prepared than sorry." She looked away from him, but he could see her eyes blinking rapidly. She cleared her throat. "You don't have to worry about me coming back here again."

Adrian threw his hand up in the air, thinking her words were a ploy to get him to capitulate to her will. He'd had others manipulate him like that before. He had the same level of patience for it now as he did then.

Zero.

Betrayal burned him to know Victoria wasn't above playing the same dirty tricks. "Whatever you say. Whatever. You. Say."

Her face crumpled for too brief a moment. "Wow. After all these months, this is all we have left to say to each other?"

"Sure. Why not?"

She whispered his name, but Adrian looked at her in disgust before stalking out of the room. Not once did he take her words seriously. It was only when he came back to the living room an hour later did he see the house keys she left on the coffee table.

Fear sluiced through his resentment.

Until that point, Adrian had stewed in his self-righteousness. He'd focused on his side of their argument, bitter with the repeating question of how could Victoria have behaved that way towards him?

She had been completely thoughtless towards his feelings. He had agreed to marry her to make her happy and she had acted as if he had dumped a bucket of dirty water over her head.

Adrian paused. He hadn't exactly asked her to marry him, had he? He replayed the scene in his mind. Unease settled in his gut. Was it the lack of a planned proposal that offended her so?

Perhaps Victoria saw it as a sign of disrespect. The more Adrian thought about it the more confident he was about why she had gotten so angry with him. Then he would think about how much it had personally cost him to capitulate to her wishes. Resentment built up and the repeating question would appear again.

Now all his justifications died.

The keys changed everything. They brought into focus just how much time he'd wasted nursing his resentments instead of seeing things from Victoria's point of view.

She wanted marriage but she wanted marriage to *him*. And just because she wanted to get married didn't mean that she didn't expect or deserve a proposal befitting that of a princess.

Adrian thought of each night he had stayed away from her in the hopes of slipping into bed unnoticed. He thought of each wounded glance she gave him over dinner when she thought he wasn't looking. Each additional memory brought a wince. He couldn't believe at how poorly he had treated Victoria over the past month.

In his growing panic over what to do, Adrian had pushed away the only woman he had ever loved.

Adrian walked over to the coffee table in disbelief.

I love her. I love Victoria.

He picked up the keys and stared at them with horror.

Adrian loved Victoria and didn't realize it until right at this very moment.

How could I be so stupid? So fucking, ridiculously, colossally stupid?

She was right. He had treated her like a houseplant. Worse—an unwanted pet. He'd treated her as a creature who had no other power but to stay at his whim and curry his favor.

Adrian closed his fist over the keys. The metal dug into his palm.

Victoria had shown her power. She wouldn't accept anything less than what she deserved.

My kitten wasn't playing a game with me. She wasn't trying to manipulate me. She had been trying to talk to me and I blew her off.

Adrian dialed her number. It rang until her voicemail picked up. He dialed it again. And again. And again. He kept doing it for ten minutes straight.

Finally, Victoria answered. Her voice was hoarse, as if she'd been crying for hours.

"Hello?"

"Victoria! Don't hang up. I'm so sorry for tonight." Adrian heard a muffled sob. "Kitten, I didn't understand. I'm sorry."

"It can't be undone."

Panic grew in sickening waves. Adrian couldn't have destroyed everything without knowing it. He just couldn't have.

"Don't say that."

"I'm sorry, Adrian. I'm sorry but I can't go back again. Not after knowing how you really feel about me."

"Victoria, you don't know because I never told you. I love you. I love you so much."

She gasped and then "Oh, Adrian. I love you too."

Relief beat a tattoo. He wasn't going to lose her after all. Everything was going to be okay. He had said the right thing after all. Everything would go back to the way it was. They could be happy again, happier than before.

Victoria then let out a shuddering sob. "It's because I love you that I can never go back."

Adrian's fist tightened around the phone. "You don't mean that. Victoria, we both know you don't mean that."

"I do. Adrian, what we had between us was better than I could've ever dreamed. Thank you."

"No!"

She sobbed again. The sound was like a repeated punch to his gut. Adrian never wanted to make her cry or let her down. He never wanted to hurt her. Ever.

"Victoria, this isn't how it has to be. We can work this out. We can fix this. I can fix this—"

"Remember how you said you wouldn't beg me?"

He slashed a hand through the air. "I shouldn't have said that. I was wrong."

"Keep your promise. Goodbye, Adrian. Please don't call me again. And please, please be happy."

The phone went dead. He looked at the screen in disbelief.

Midnight.

Adrian wished he could stop all the clocks in the world just so he wouldn't have to suffer a new life without Victoria.

TWELVE

Adrian didn't listen to Victoria.

He called every day for two weeks. When she wouldn't return his calls after the first week, he'd taken to coming to the apartment. Jenny put a stop to it after two days.

"Come here again and she'll put a restraining order on you. I'm sure the papers will *love* to splash that all over town. Can't you just see the headlines? 'Billionaire Stalker!'"

Apparently what she'd threatened had been enough. Adrian stayed away after that. His calls came to an end too.

Victoria was inconsolable when she heard what had happened. "How could have said that to him?" she screamed at a stone-faced Jenny. "I would never do that to Adrian! He didn't deserve to be treated that way!"

"Is it over or is not? If not, then talk to him. If it is, dragging it out will only make things worse for both of you. Are you going back to him or not?"

Victoria's answer was a warbled "Not," even as her heart screamed otherwise.

It wasn't because she didn't want to, but how could she? Adrian's secret thoughts about love and commitment had come out. Even if she went back, Victoria would dread the march of days. She'd feel like she had an expiration date and she couldn't live like that. Victoria couldn't take the chance Adrian would come to his senses and toss her out the next time.

So she sobbed herself sick everyday while listening to Muddy Waters over and over again. She wanted to go back to that time when she'd first met him. If only she'd known that her days with him were so limited she wouldn't have spent so much time letting "I love you" go unsaid.

Shaundra took to bringing her washcloths and sitting with Victoria in her darkened room. Just having her rub the cool cloth across her face made Victoria feel slightly better. The tears wouldn't stop though.

"I know it hurts, baby girl. I know. But it will come to an end. No, don't shake your head. One day it will hurt a little less. And the day after that will be better. And the one after that. Trust me. We've all been there."

Victoria accepted the comfort but she couldn't ever imagine this rawness ever going away. She'd lost a huge part of herself. Her rage visited her most strongly then. Victoria wished she'd never laid eyes on Adrian Hawthorne. If she hadn't she wouldn't know this kind of agony. Then her tears would give way and she'd sob uncontrollably for even thinking it.

The months she spent with him were the best months of her life. Nothing could take that away.

As she tossed and turned, Victoria would remember the tender way he held her as they drifted off to sleep. She believed she'd never be able to sleep again without remembering him.

Victoria would often hold her left hand up on the nights when infomercials dominated the television landscape. Her watery eyes would focus on her bare ring finger.

If he was going to ask me to marry him, why couldn't it be because he wanted me that much?

Knowing the answer was because he didn't want her at all, not really, would cause Victoria to then turn and scream into her pillow. If only that day wouldn't have happened. If only it had turned out differently.

If only he'd had more faith in her...or she had less faith in him.

Victoria had put Adrian on a pedestal and now she was paying for it.

The girls took turns bringing Victoria food, but she could barely keep any of it down. She continued to drop weight until she'd lost about ten pounds. It wasn't until the third week after the breakup that Krista came into her room after work, sat down, and then asked quietly, “When was your last period?”

“What?” she croaked from under the blankets.

“Think about it.”

Victoria shoved herself up against the headboard. She mentally counted the weeks and then stopped. Her wide gaze met Krista’s. She didn’t have to say it out loud. Krista patted her hand and got up from the foot of the bed.

“You need to take a test to know for sure.”

Victoria immediately cleaned herself up and headed down to the closest drugstore. She thought of taking the small box home, but didn’t want to wait. Ten minutes later she left the ladies restroom a changed woman. Victoria would have to verify the results with a doctor, but she already knew in her heart it was true.

She came back home to find her three roommates gathered in the living room. They turned as one to look at her expectantly.

“I’m pregnant.”

Only the sound of the TV interrupted the collective silence that had descended upon them.

Jenny spoke first. “What are you going to do?”

“Do?” Victoria felt clear-headed for the first time since she left Adrian. She had a purpose and a goal now. “I’m going back home to North Carolina.”

“What about your job? Don’t you start in a week or so?”

Victoria had already decided on her course of action as soon as she’d left the pharmacy. “I’m not going to have my baby here, Jenny. It’s too much for me here. I’m moving back permanently and I’ll find a job there. I’m sure the Research Triangle Park has plenty of positions for me to take.”

No one tried to talk her out of it.

Shaundra asked softly, “What are you going to tell Adrian?”

“Adrian? I can’t even think about him.”

Her eyes widened. “You mean not now but later. He has to know, right?”

Victoria smiled in answer. It was the kind of smile that meant whatever the recipient wanted it to be. At this minute, the only person she cared about was the unborn baby nestled safely in her tummy.

Which meant the time for grieving over Adrian had to come to an end.

She had to figure out what to do and how to do it first before she could include Adrian. Her hand hovered over her belly. It seemed fantastical to believe that they had made a little baby together.

A part of him is inside me. What's going to happen when I tell him?

Her wondrous grin faded. Adrian had only asked her to marry him because he thought it was what she wanted, strange as it was. Even if she'd said yes, he would've eventually regretted that decision. If she came to him now he'd probably muster the strength to throw himself on the marital sword, but Victoria didn't want him in those circumstances.

She didn't want to trap him and this wouldn't seem to be anything other than a way to force him down the aisle.

Still, it's his baby. He has a right to know.

Victoria definitely would tell him soon but only after she settled things in North Carolina. Maybe if he saw that she was being independent then he'd understand that she wasn't trying to get married or trying to force him by her side.

Maybe then things would work out for them in the future. Victoria definitely wasn't going to pretend that she wouldn't want that.

First things first, she needed to develop a plan and then she'd come to him.

When Victoria went to bed that night she lied with both hands over her stomach. How did this miracle happen? Except for that first night, Adrian had used condoms all the way until she went on the pill and it was safe to abandon them.

But we all know abstinence is the only thing that's 100%. Even though at the end there I qualified for the Immaculate Conception, it definitely had to have been before that.

ADRIAN

Truthfully, it didn't matter to Victoria. All that mattered was that she was going to be a mother.

I can't wait until I can tell him. I wonder if he'll be as happy as me. I hope so. I wonder what we'll be having—a boy or a girl? Will he or she look like me or like him? If we have a boy I hope he looks like Adrian. If we have a girl I hope she gets to be tall like her daddy.

For the first time in weeks, Victoria went to sleep without tears staining her pillow.

***

After Adrian got the report that Victoria had left for North Carolina his whole world went dark. She was gone and there wasn't a damned thing he could do about it.

Everything about Adrian sharpened with that realization. If he wasn't working in the office until well past midnight, then he was working out in the evenings and then again in the mornings until exhaustion overtook him. Adrian kept his focus on the next deal so that he wouldn't have to focus on the fact that Victoria wasn't in his life anymore.

Nothing helped him on that front. Everything was a reminder of his kitten. A burst of feminine laughter in the hallways, a head of glossy dark hair ahead of him on the sidewalk, the scent of vanilla—all of it was Victoria.

Adrian was going mad with longing.

So he redoubled his efforts. More work, more physical punishment, more money, Adrian did it all just to numb the pain in his heart.

And like beautiful sharks drawn to blood, females of his past acquaintance circled about. The more he ignored them, the faster they chased him.

Adrian wasn't the slightest bit tempted.

He wanted the impossible. He wanted Victoria back. Anything less didn't bear contemplating.

But she's never coming back. We broke up. Breaking up is always permanent. I never go back to my exes. Why would she make an exception for me?

Even though he logically understood why she wouldn't take his calls or see him, Adrian couldn't deny that it hurt that she wouldn't tell him herself. Having her roommate threaten him with a restraining order had been humiliating. Every time he thought of it Adrian felt as if his head was going to explode.

He had never, ever chased after anyone that way. He had never *cared* enough about anyone to chase after them that way.

Despite the burn of humiliation, Adrian saw the threat as a necessary wakeup call. So he withdrew and didn't allow himself to think of Victoria until he was safe from doing anything stupid like going to her apartment again.

For all his flaws, Adrian was *not* a stalker or someone to be feared.

Late at night, on the cusp of passing out from sheer exhaustion, only then was it safe to think about Victoria. And if the agony of missing her was too much, it was still better than the numbness Adrian felt the other twenty hours of the day.

Even so compartmentalizing became increasingly difficult to perform about a month after their breakup. Victoria couldn't be dropped in her labeled box and dealt with later. She dominated his mind until he could barely function. He finally stopped running so much when his fitted shirts became too loose and his pants hung too low on his hips.

Adrian absolutely refused to stop working his punishing hours, even when he had to take to carrying around handkerchiefs because of sporadic nosebleeds. Instead, he took to haunting the halls of his office when he couldn't sleep.

Even though he knew Victoria was in North Carolina, Adrian couldn't help but feel his heart jump in his chest every single time he saw a cleaner in a grey jumpsuit. He sat in their lounge and replayed the thousands of memories he had of Victoria. What he wouldn't give to relive those months again! Adrian wouldn't change a thing...well, except for two things.

He would've called her that fateful business trip and he wouldn't have asked her to marry him.

Then everything could've stayed like it was.

Adrian even went to her old restaurant weekly just in the pitiful off-chance that he'd overhear someone mention her name or gossip about how she was doing.

And as always—nothing. Still, he kept going.

It was no way to live but what else could he do?

***

"Victoria, are you sure you don't want to stay here? You know there's plenty of room and it's not a bother. Honest."

"Thanks so much, Kathy, but I've already been here a month. I need my own place, especially for when the baby gets here."

Kathy lifted her coffee cup. "I still can't believe you're going to have a *baby*. I still remember when you were a little girl like it was only yesterday."

Victoria smiled. "Time flies, doesn't it?"

"Yes, it does. I guess it's something you'll learn for yourself." She sighed. "I wish your father was here. He'd be so tickled to be a grandpa."

Victoria took a sip from her water bottle. She wasn't quite as sure that her father would've been happy about her current circumstances. In fact, she was pretty sure he would've been livid that Adrian got her pregnant.

"So have you decided what you're going to do about work? It's going to be harder to find a job in your condition."

Victoria shrugged. "No harder than it's ever been, but even with my qualifications—small as they may be—I've already been on several interviews. I'm hopeful about two of them actually."

"Really?" Kathy shook her head with a rueful smile. "What am I saying? It's you we're talking about. Of course, you'd find a way. You always do." Victoria barely had time to form a reply when her stepmother asked, "So when are you going to tell Adrian that he's going to be a daddy?"

Kathy only knew the sketchiest of details about their breakup and seemed inclined to believe that it was only a bump in the road of their love. If only Victoria was as convinced that they were just on a break.

"I'm going to fly back once I accept a job offer. I've already had second interviews on the two I'm hopeful about."

"When do you think you'll hear something?"

"This week if all goes well."

"So where do you want to live?"

"It'll depend on where I end up working. I want to be within fifteen to twenty minutes of daycare."

"Victoria, you know I'll watch the baby every chance I get."

She smiled. "You're home but you're working."

"Freelancing has its perks and having a flexible schedule is one of them."

"I know, but—"

"But you have to do this on your own. I know." Kathy pursed her lips in a mock-pout. "You're so bullheaded, Victoria. Really. You always have to do everything on your own."

Victoria winked and laughed when her stepmother turned her head with a sniff. "It's in my DNA. Dad was the same way."

"I know. You two were a pair when it came to being bullheaded." Kathy gestured to her stepdaughter's tummy. "Just watch. Your baby will be worse and then you'll know my pain."

Victoria got up and stretched. "I'm sure it'll happen. You can babysit on those days."

"Gee. Thanks."

She leaned down and kissed Kathy on the head. "I'm so sleepy I can barely keep my eyes open. I'm going to go take a nap."

"Okay. I'll wake you up for dinner if you're not up by then."

Victoria waved and made her way upstairs. She yawned widely. Pregnancy hadn't given her much morning sickness, but it definitely made her exhausted. Soon she changed into her pajamas and crawled under the covers. And although she did her best to control her emotions, she couldn't help but wish Adrian was with her.

If her fantasies could come true he'd sit up against the headboard and hold her in his arms. She'd be able to hear his heartbeat and the soothing sound of his breathing. Victoria imagined Adrian would run his fingers through her hair and tell her a story about his travels.

It hasn't gotten any better. I still miss him as much, no, more than ever before.

Victoria arranged one pillow the long way so she could wrap her arms around it and lay her head. It was a poor substitute for Adrian but it would have to do. Just like she did before sleep every time, Victoria prayed.

"Please let this all work out. If we can't be together, please let Adrian accept this baby and be a good father to it like mine. But please, please let this all work out. I want us to be a family. We don't have to be married, but please let it work out."

***

Adrian tossed and turned. Against his better judgment he'd had his people check on Victoria. The news wasn't good. Victoria was still in North Carolina. His fears that she'd moved there permanently ate away at him. He resisted the demented urge to hop on a plane and fly down there.

That'll go real well. She'd most likely spit on me before calling the police.

Adrian knew he was going down a dark road. He hated everything around him. His thoughts strayed to Victoria over and over again. Adrian was disgusted by his unhealthy attachment. He was pitiful, a creature of embarrassment because he couldn't let go of her.

And Victoria obviously had let go of him the night she left. He'd waited for one sign of her, one phone call, *anything* to prove his affection wasn't so lopsided.

Nothing.

Work no longer provided solace. He began to wonder what was the point of all his labors.

Those were treasonous thoughts for a man in his position. Those were the kind of thoughts that led to companies going under, people getting laid off, and corporate bankruptcy being declared.

In other words those thoughts were unacceptable.

Adrian got up from the bed. Naked, he walked to the floor-to-ceiling window and surveyed the city. There were millions of people surrounding him day in and day out and yet, he was so alone. It pressed on him, suffocating Adrian until he feared he was going mad.

I miss her every minute of every damned day. Is that ever going to stop? Will I die with her name carved in my heart?

Adrian turned away and shrugged on a robe. He hadn't left to tour his holdings in a while. Perhaps a trip to the Artic was what he needed. Maybe the isolation would be enough to refocus his attention to the here and now.

Victoria isn't coming back. Ever.

He dismissed the tightness in his chest. This was a hell of his own making. He should've just been straightforward with Victoria instead of trying to be a ridiculous Prince Charming.

Which I failed spectacularly at that.

All Adrian really knew was that the next time he got entangled with a woman, he'd know better than to think a permanent attachment was wanted or needed.

I just need to find women like I used to—unattached and looking to stay that way. And then maybe I'll...what? Go back to how I was? No, not that.

Grabbing a robe, Adrian slipped it on and headed towards his home office. Even while he thought of the million things he needed to take care of before leaving town, he couldn't help but think "What if?"

What if things had turned out differently? What if Victoria had said yes or, at the very least, hadn't stormed out in disgust? What if instead of planning a trip to the Arctic, Adrian was planning a honeymoon trip to Fiji?

He couldn't deny that he'd rather plan that than the current alternate.

By the time the sun rose, Adrian was all set to leave in a week. He wouldn't be back for at least a month. Hopefully, he'd come back in a different frame of mind. Adrian knew he could never go back to how he was before Victoria, but at least he could be wiser.

The hope was empty consolation in comparison to his true wish of having the woman he loved back in his life, but it was the best he could expect now. Loving Victoria had cost him everything—his dignity, his self-respect, and his precious freedom.

Most of all, it cost him the peace of knowing that he lost her because of his own damned fear.

Never again.

THIRTEEN

Victoria's heart sped up the closer she got to Adrian's building. She tried not to imagine his reaction to her news, but fear choked her. What if he didn't believe her? Or worse, what if he did and told her to get rid of the baby?

That's not going to happen. I'll kill him *first.*

Victoria's bloodthirstiness receded long enough to remember the man who'd taken her heart wasn't that cruel. In fact, he'd never been hurtful to her except for that last night. Even then his crime was proposing to her for the wrong reason.

In reality, Adrian had just been honest with her about his true feelings. It wasn't his fault that he felt the way he did. And that was why she had to leave, not because he'd mistreated her.

He needed to be free from me. I needed to be free too. I couldn't stay and force him to feel about me the way I wanted. I just wish that it could've turned out differently. I wish I could've been telling him about our baby when we were together. Maybe I was too rash to end things?

And maybe I've gone about this all the wrong way?

She let out an internal scream. Rehashing their end and all the circular thinking that came along with it wasn't going to help her now.

I should've called him first. Maybe I should do that now? He might not even be home for all I know.

Victoria wondered about it too late. The taxi pulled up to the curb, right behind a limousine. She paid for her fare and exited. Steel butterflies swarmed in her belly and her heart seemed to rise up to lodge itself in her throat.

"You can do this. It's going to turn out well. It really will."

And she believed that all for less than a minute.

***

"Adrian, I'm not the least bit hungry."

His skin itched with distaste when his unwanted and intrusive companion put her hand on his arm. "That's too bad, Cynthia. I'm starving and you're not. Seems we're at an impasse." Adrian shifted his arm neatly away from his ex-girlfriend's grasp. "Why don't you go back to your hotel?"

She pouted in a way that many found adorable, considering it was her signature look and had landed her in the "Top 10 Kissable Lips of All Time" according to the latest poll. That little fact was only known by Adrian because she shared it with him not even an hour before when she arrived unannounced at his office. Cynthia had also been brazen enough to hitch a ride, even though he'd made it more than clear that he wasn't looking for company.

"Why are you being such a beast, Adrian? One would think you weren't happy to see me."

"One would think right." His driver opened the door for him. Cynthia strode forward, completely confident that Adrian wouldn't turn her out. He clenched his jaw and neatly blocked the way. "Why are you here?"

She flicked her long blond hair over her shoulder. "A little birdie told me that you're going away for a month. I thought you might want some company before then."

"You thought wrong."

Her brown eyes hardened. "Why are you being such a bastard, Adrian? I thought we parted nicely or was it just me?"

Adrian sighed. It wasn't her fault that Victoria had dumped him like last night's trash. It also wasn't her fault he wasn't over it. Adrian straightened and sketched a quick bow. "You're right. I am being a jerk. Start over?"

Cynthia sauntered over to him, forgiving smile becoming on her full, pink lips. She kissed him lightly on the mouth. "Sounds good to me." Her slim hands skated down his chest. "You had me thinking the rumors were true."

Adrian had the urge to wipe the back of his hand against his lips. “Rumors? Why don’t you enlighten me?”

“I heard that you were serious with a girl. Marriage and 2.5 kids kind of serious. I got a little jealous when I heard.”

Adrian’s face hardened. “Marriage? Family? Are you insane? I’m as single as they come and plan on staying that way, Cynthia, so if you came to see if you could be the one to change me—forget it. It’s not possible.”

A choked cry cut through the ever-present noise of traffic and people. Adrian looked to his left. His gaze strained to see who had made that cry of heartbreak. The crowds parted just enough for him to see the top of a familiar head.

He took off after her without hesitation.

***

“Victoria! Wait a damned minute!”

She heard him barreling through the crowd behind her, but she didn’t turn to look. She just kept running.

While logically she understood she had no right to Adrian anymore, Victoria nearly lost it when that woman kissed him and he didn't do anything to stop her. But the true kick in the teeth came from what he said next.

Victoria kept her head down and tried not to cry but his heartless words kept repeating over and over in her head.

"Marriage? Family? Are you insane? I'm as single as they come and plan on staying that way, Cynthia, so if you came to see if you could be the one to change me—forget it. It's not possible."

She couldn't tell him about the baby now. Maybe not ever.

No! I can't hide something like that from Adrian. He deserves to know!

But the real question was would he ever *want* to know? Maybe their child would be a burden and a blight on his well-ordered life.

A hand closed around her arm and yanked her back. She looked up to see an infuriated Adrian glaring down at her.

The first thing she noticed about him was the fever-brightness of his eyes. They burned more green than hazel. Dimly she wondered if they'd ever looked more beautiful than right now as they blazed with rage. Next were his razor cheekbones. He was thinner than she remembered. It worried her to see him like that.

Is something wrong with him? Is he sick?

"You heard me. Why didn't you stop?"

Victoria's worry took a backseat when her temper flared. "You were busy with your date. I'm not rude enough to interrupt."

He bit off a curse. "Kit—Victoria. It's not what you think."

She winced. So did he. She took small comfort in it for a second before feeling worse. Jealousy had made her ugly and petty. She didn't like that. Victoria blew out a long breath. She fought to get her wayward emotions under control.

"You don't owe me any explanations, Adrian. We broke up a while ago. What you do in your personal life has nothing to do with me. I'm sorry I acted otherwise."

Adrian let go of her. Victoria rubbed the spot where he'd grasped her. Not because it hurt. Rather the absence of his touch hurt.

"Right. You broke up with me but the end result is the same. We don't have any ties to each other anymore."

Victoria dared to look up, to see if those words cut him as deeply as they did her. Adrian's impassive expression told her she was alone in feeling sadness at their truth.

"You're right."

He stared at her several seconds past polite. "And that's why you cried out like someone broke your heart."

As always he was too perceptive. "I was just shocked at seeing you. That's all."

She bit her trembling lip and tried her best not to throw herself at him. Victoria's heart, her body, her damned *soul* wanted Adrian. But she didn't have a right to him anymore. And he definitely wasn't waiting around for her.

How am I going to tell him about the baby? What if that's his new girlfriend? Won't it just make him resent us both?

Her answer seemed to disappoint him. He took a step back and shrugged. "Why'd you come to see me, Victoria?"

She considered spilling the truth. She then replayed part of his words to his date.

"Marriage? Family? Are you insane?"

Victoria needed to buy herself time. "I didn't come to see you."

"Bullshit." Adrian narrowed his eyes, looking over her as if disappointed.

"It's not bullshit. I was just saying goodbye. I mean, not to you, just to this part of my life. I'm moving back home and I figured I should at least look at my old stomping grounds one last time since I probably won't be back again."

Adrian let her babble without interruption. When she finally came to a breathy stop, he looked away to a distant point over her shoulder.

"So you've moved back to North Carolina?"

"Yes. I mean—"

“And you’re not coming back here?”

“No.”

Adrian smirked and shook his head. He muttered something under his breath but Victoria couldn’t catch it. “And that’s all? Finished, right?”

“Yes.”

No! I’m pregnant. I want this baby and I want you to want our baby too. I’m scared because I don’t know how to tell you and I don’t know what the right thing to do is.

Victoria damned herself for being a coward. She shouldn’t have lied to him. It wasn’t too late. She could tell him that he was right. That she really came here just to see him. That she’d been up for over twenty-four hours because she couldn’t wait to see him again. Not just because of the baby, but because it was *him*.

She couldn’t tell him that she’d harbored fantasies of him picking her up and swinging her in a circle as he peppered her face with kisses and smiles. She couldn’t share that she’d taken care with her grooming and underclothing all in the hopes that maybe, just maybe, they'd fall happily into bed.

It all seemed so hopelessly naïve in light of everything she'd heard.

"Victoria?"

"Yes?"

Adrian looked her straight in the eye. "Good."

This threw her off. "Good?"

"Yes, good. I think it's all turned out for the best, don't you think?"

"I don't...I..."

"Breaking up hurt like hell, but it was the right thing for us. You saw that when I couldn't. If we'd gotten married we'd probably be divorced within the year. I got messed up at the end there, but your levelheadedness saved us both. So thank you."

"Saved us?" Victoria asked through a growing fog of shock and dismay.

"Yes." Adrian coughed. "I just want you to know that's not how I usually act."

"Act?"

Stop repeating his words!

Adrian let out a caustic chuckle. "I don't stalk my exes if that's what you're worried about."

"I'm not worried. I never was, Adrian. I'm just..." Victoria helplessly stumbled along her words. How had their conversation turned in this direction?

"Opposites can only attract for so long before their differences tear everything apart. We're too different and ultimately wanted different things in life."

Things were tumbling out of control. "Adrian, I never wanted you to propose to me."

He held his hand up. "Let's not rehash the past, Victoria. It's not worth it to either of us."

She took a step back and hugged her waist. Cold despair settled over her. Blindly she stared at the street at the river of traffic. "I guess not."

"Good." Adrian rolled his shoulders back. He looked regal, cold even. "I guess this is it then. Do you need the use of my driver? He can take you wherever you'd like to go."

"That's not necessary."

"It would be my pleasure. You don't have to stomach my presence, if that's what you're worried about."

"That's not why I'm saying no." She shook her head. "I don't hate you, Adrian."

He arched a brow. "Really? You could've fooled me. Sorry, sorry. I shouldn't have said that." Adrian tossed her a charming grin. It still had the same effect on her, easing the crushing despair enough to let her smile back shyly.

Adrian opened his mouth and then closed it abruptly. His attention fixed back on a point over her shoulder. The loss of his stare made Victoria want to reach out and touch him so badly. She ached to trace the perfect bridge of his nose before following the kissable lines of his lips.

More than that, she wanted to know why he looked so much slimmer than when she last saw him. Victoria's nurturing side bubbled up. She wanted to make him dinner and make sure he finished at least one plate.

Maybe it really isn't too late. Maybe I can still fix this.

Hope danced nervously in her tummy. Victoria's breath came out in a shaky sigh. "I'm sorry I interrupted you back there. I didn't mean to."

"Water under the bridge. You saved me actually. I just wanted a quiet dinner out tonight. Alone."

The last word undid her courage. It was presumptuous of her to think he'd even welcome her concern after all the time, much less her cooking.

"You're welcome. I guess."

An uncomfortable silence settled between them. Even though Adrian was only a couple of feet away, it now felt more like miles. Victoria's starved gaze feasted on him in minute detail, but he was so far beyond her reach that he might as well have been on another continent.

"Umm, I'm really sorry for what Jenny said to you. She did that on her own. I mean, her intentions were in the right place, but I wish she hadn't said those things to you. I wouldn't have put a restraining order on you. I just needed time to process what had happened."

Victoria winced after saying it out loud.

Adrian shoved his hands in his coat pockets. A wall came down leaving his face blank. "No need to apologize. Like I said—I wasn't in the right frame of mind. I am now."

"I know you are. I didn't mean to imply that you're not—"

"All right then, Victoria. I better leave you to your reminiscing."

"Ah, okay."

Adrian took one step towards her and stuck his hand out. Victoria slowly placed hers in his. The contact was enough to send her body into overdrive.

This man had given her supreme happiness in a time when she didn't think she needed anything more than to survive and overcome hardship.

This man had taught her pleasure beyond compare. He had caressed and worshipped every part of her, treasuring her body in a way she never imagined.

This man had opened his life to her.

This man had *loved* her. And now this very same man was about to walk out of her life. Permanently.

“Take care of yourself, Victoria.”

She didn’t know what to say, but she didn’t want him to leave. Two words beat relentlessly in her skull.

Tell him. Tell him. Tell him.

She could make him stay. Forever even. He had loved her once. He could do it again. The next time he asked her to marry him, *if* he asked her, she would say yes. It wouldn’t matter if it was a camera-worthy proposal or one worse than the one he’d given her already, she’d say “Yes.”

It’s not too late.

“It was really good while it lasted though, wasn’t it, Victoria?”

She looked up at his beloved face. Talking about everything under the sun was what brought them together. So why couldn't she tell him? How could it go so wrong again?

Tell him. Tell him. Tell him.

Adrian's gaze searched hers. When she didn't say anything in return he let go of her hand. "It's probably your bad luck you caught me when you did. If you'd waited just one more day you wouldn't have had to see me at all."

That finally freed her from her imprisoned silence. "What do you mean?"

Adrian shrugged, looking bored all of a sudden. "I'm leaving for a month on business."

"Oh."

No!

"Good luck in North Carolina. You've got a job lined up?"

"Yes."

Tell him. Tell him. Tell him.

"I'd tell you not to work too hard, but you probably won't listen."

"No, I can't afford to take it easy. Not when I'll need time off..." Victoria's voice died. It was as good a time to tell him the truth. She couldn't have planned a perfect entrance point in fact. All she had to say was two words.

Tell. Him. Now.

She peeked up at him. Adrian didn't pick up on the end of her sentence. Instead, he was looking at his watch. A flush raced across her face.

He's already forgotten about me. Being here and talking to me is a chore, only he's too polite to tell me.

"I better get going, Adrian. I still have a few more stops to make before heading home."

"Right then." He leaned down and brushed a kiss across her warm cheek. "Goodbye, Victoria."

"Goodbye, Adrian." She watched as he turned around and walked back towards his building. Each step drove a deeper crack in her heart. Panic set in. "Adrian!"

He stopped. Victoria feared he was just going to keep going when he didn't turn around immediately. A few seconds passed before he faced her.

Victoria eased the distance between them. The time for thinking was over because the answer to her next question would determine the rest of their lives.

“Did you mean what you said back there? About being single and all?”

Adrian’s gaze blanked. “Yes. I meant it.”

She hunched her shoulders, trying desperately to get herself under control. The pavement beneath her feet could only hold her attention for so long before Victoria braved looking back at him.

“Are you happy?” Adrian frowned at her as if he didn’t understand the question. She tried again. “Is your life as you want it?”

He nodded once. “It’s as it needs to be.”

She deflated. Victoria had her answer and the lifetime burden of making the only decision she believed she could.

“I see.”

When she didn’t say anything else Adrian gave her a crooked smile. “Goodbye, Victoria.” He then turned around and walked away.

Victoria stood there until she couldn't see him anymore.

"I'm having your baby, Adrian."

The whisper came too late and there was no one to hear it or her.

***

Every step just about killed Adrian. Hollowed out, he wondered how he'd ever be able to sleep tonight when all he could think about was Victoria.

What did you think she was going to say? "I want you back, Adrian. I still love you. Forgive me for abandoning you when you needed me the most."

The pathetic truth was that he did believe and hope it was true.

Instead, he was walking away from her first before she could do it to him again.

Adrian knew himself to be colossally stupid. How could he even *imagine* that Victoria had come back to him? Why had he even considered cancelling his trip and forcing his calendar to open just so he could spend the next day with her?

Like she'd even agree to spend an hour with me much less a day.

Helpless to resist himself, Adrian had just been on the verge of asking her to dinner when she'd dismissed him in favor of making her other stops.

As a man who wasn't used to hearing "no" Adrian didn't think he could've handled hearing it from her lips. Not because he would've convinced her to dine with him anyway, but because he wouldn't.

As a man who never gave up, he had given up on the need to force, coerce, or seduce her to his will.

Adrian needed Victoria to want him as much as he wanted her. Without coercion. Without guilt. Because he loved her.

She'd just proved to him that she didn't need him at all.

While he'd been wasting away mourning her absence, Victoria obviously had gotten along just fine. She looked more beautiful than he remembered and Adrian had spent hours obsessively going over his memory of her to the minutest detail.

Tonight she'd taken his breath away. Her skin bloomed like a silken rose and her dark eyes sparkled like the desert sky.

Adrian frowned. Poetry obviously wasn't his strong suit, but what was obvious was Victoria hadn't missed him like he'd missed her. And that hurt more than words.

He blinked, finding the world around him strangely gone to water.

What am I doing?

His gaze cleared. His jaw hardened as he made a decision. Adrian had been prepared to spend the rest of his life with Victoria. He would've planned his future around her, done anything to make her happy—even at the cost of himself—and she'd tossed it back in his face without even a chance to make things better.

Tonight he learned the hard way that Victoria Montford was unforgiving and far more ruthless than himself.

Victoria could turn her back on him despite all the love they shared. She could walk away as if their time together meant nothing. As if he hadn't given her everything he had to give.

She could leave him and be perfectly okay.

No. I'm not going to do this anymore. It's time to cut ties.

Adrian could and would never say she didn't mean the world to him, but never again would he allow anyone to get so close to him. Not even her.

Never again.

FOURTEEN

Her momentous decision made, Victoria thought about catching a flight back home right after Adrian left her standing on the sidewalk. There were no stops for her to make. She could go back to the old apartment and see whoever happened to be there because she wasn't at work, but Victoria wouldn't do that to her former roommates.

She'd already burdened them with the melodrama passing as her life. How fair would it be to pop in their lives after a month and do the same thing? Maybe even worse?

All it would take was talking and Victoria knew her eyes would burst their gaskets. And what if during her crying jag one of them, most likely Jenny, took it upon herself to confront

Adrian with the truth of why Victoria had come back?

No.

Now that she had made her decision to keep Adrian in the dark, she had to get used to dealing with things on her own.

Victoria gathered her scattered thoughts in a mental net. She raised her arm up and hailed a cab. Once she arrived at her hotel, Victoria made her way up to the economy room and went through the motions of taking care of herself.

Shower, nightclothes, water, vitamins.

Still, even as she settled down for sleep with the TV low in the background and all the lights off, Victoria stared at the window, eyes wide and unblinking. Seeing Adrian tonight branded her with an unbreakable truth.

She still loved him and always would. Even though the future held no guarantees and everything solid seemed thrown up in the air, Victoria couldn't deny her feelings for Adrian Hawthorne.

Her hand settled across her still-flat stomach.

I'm so sorry, little baby, that I couldn't make this right. But I promise I will make it up to you. I'll do everything in my power and above to give you the best life ever. It will just be you and me. I promise. You won't ever have to deal with wondering if I love someone more than I love you. I won't let anyone come between us because there won't be *anyone else.*

Victoria went to sleep that night with damp eyes but an iron-resolve.

Less than a day later, Victoria crossed the threshold of her childhood home while dragging her carryon behind her. The plane trip was a hellish trial of endurance.

Victoria and Kathy had cried together over the phone when she had briefly called her with the news before checking-out of the hotel. Surprisingly, Kathy hadn't argued against keeping her pregnancy a secret or even pressed for details of what happened to make her change her mind.

That support meant more to her than she could ever put into words. It strengthened her and proved that she wouldn't have to go through this alone.

Even so, Victoria's eyes were puffy and her head pounded when she boarded the plane two hours later. Unfortunately, she couldn't sleep at all and spent her time hiding out behind a sleep mask. Victoria was glad to have left RDU behind her and had no intention of boarding a plane for the rest of the year if she could help it.

As she climbed up the stairs, Victoria was set on falling into bed and sleeping for days curled up with Cedric the cat. The rest of her life could wait until she woke up.

"Victoria, welcome back. I know this is a bad time but I have to talk to you."

She didn't see her stepmother at all when she walked through the door. Kathy must've been waiting in the living room for her to come home.

Victoria held back a sigh. She sketched a brief smile. “I’m really tired and just want to go to sleep. Can this wait?”

“I wish it could. I wouldn’t bother you at this time if it wasn’t.”

Kathy’s serious expression was enough to pierce through Victoria’s devastation and emotional fatigue. She came down two steps until she was in the foyer.

“That serious?”

“I’m afraid so.” She glanced at her watch. “I’m not due to pick up the girls for another hour so now’s the best time.”

“All right then.” Victoria walked into the formal living room. She tried not think about Adrian or what the future held for her and her child. Seeing her father and stepmother’s formal wedding picture on the wall didn’t help, but Victoria focused her attention on getting to the couch.

In other circumstances, she’d probably be dreading whatever serious news Kathy had to share. As it was, Victoria sat on the couch, crossed her legs, and waited. Her stepmother sat down next to her and jumped right in.

"Why did you and Adrian split again?"

Victoria's back stiffened. "We didn't see eye-to-eye on our future plans."

Kathy immediately picked up on her distance. "I'm not trying to pry, Victoria. Really I'm not." She let out a small sigh. "Was it about marriage?"

Victoria's leg bounced once. Was it that obvious that Adrian thought marriage to her would be such a sacrifice? Was it stamped on her forehead or something?

"How did you guess?"

Kathy deflated. She closed her eyes. "I was afraid of that."

Victoria leaned closer with concern. "What is it?"

Her stepmother reached out and linked her fingers with Victoria's. Kathy looked up to the ceiling and bit her lip. After several tense seconds, she slumped her shoulders and cleared her throat.

"I'm so sorry to have to tell you this, but I think my mother is to blame for your troubles."

"Grandma McKinnon? How?"

Kathy's blue eyes misted. "She talked to Adrian at your graduation. Apparently, she asked him about his intentions towards you and well, she left him with the impression that he needed to marry you or let you go."

Victoria's face drained of color. Her hand twitched against Kathy's. "No. That didn't happen. That couldn't have happened."

"I'm so sorry, Victoria. Mother had no right to say anything to Adrian." Kathy's speech tumbled quickly. "I want to fix this for you both. I can call him, explain that it was just my mother being her irritating self and overstepping her bounds as always. She's not being malicious about it. She really thinks she's helping. Lord knows the trouble she caused for me and your father a time or ten..."

Victoria couldn't hear anything else. She just replayed her last night at Adrian's over and over again. Now it all made horrifying sense. Victoria wanted to scream and punch a hole through the wall. Why didn't she just ask him outright *why* he thought she wanted to get married?

Because I was in shock. I couldn't think straight. I was also hurt beyond belief and feeling like my whole world was collapsing around me. I was insulted and prideful. Damn it all to hell!

"...Victoria, I'll go see him if I have to. It's not right that Mother's meddling destroyed your relationship. I can help fix this."

She snapped back to the present moment. She stared at Kathy for a bit, trying her best to process what this meant in the scheme of her life, when the stark answer came to her.

"No."

Her face crumpled. "Victoria, please."

"No, Kathy. There's nothing you can say to fix this. It can't be undone. Adrian's moved on and soon I will be too." Victoria watched in a daze as the other woman leaned forward and snatched a tissue off the coffee table.

"I was afraid you'd say that. I just hate this!"

Victoria clenched her fists. She hated it too but not for the reason her stepmother thought. She breathed in and out until the pressure on her throat eased.

It just wasn't meant to be.

"It's not your fault, Kathy."

"I know but as much as I want to wring my mother's neck—I can't. Believe it or not, she really thought she was helping. She's heartbroken that you're in this way. All she wants to do is drive up north and shoot Adrian."

A wan smile flitted across Victoria's lips. "I'd hate to have to explain to my child that his or her great-grandmother killed their father."

"It's a good thing she can't drive anymore then."

Victoria said with a catch in her voice, "Your mom just hastened the end of our relationship. Adrian isn't the kind of man who wants to settle down. He loves his freedom more than anything else and being with me was like being in a cage. Becoming a father would feel worse for him. It would be like being buried alive for him."

"Is that why you didn't tell him?"

Victoria wished she could control the rebel tears rolling down her cheeks. "I didn't get a chance to. I mean, I didn't think I should tell him after all."

"Why not?" Kathy handed her a fresh tissue.

Victoria wiped her eyes and then crushed the tissue in her hand. "I was outside of his building, where he lives, when I saw him with another woman."

"Oh no..."

"That's not the worst of it. He was talking to her. He told her how he'd never get married and having kids was the last thing in the world he wanted."

Kathy touched her on the leg. "Maybe he'll feel differently once he knows it's a reality. A lot of people say they don't want kids until they have them."

Victoria shook her head. "I can't take that chance."

"Do you think he'll do something to you?"

"Do something? You mean hurt me? No."

Relief flitted across her flushed face. "Good. I was beginning to worry. I mean, you've just been so unsure about telling him."

"Adrian was never violent to me in any way—just so we're clear. It's just I don't want my child to have a father who rejects him or her. My baby will be better off having no father than one who'll damage them that way."

"You can't know for sure that he would do that, Victoria."

She stiffened. Despair and doubt crashed into her.

Am I making the wrong decision right? Is it fair to any of us?

"Victoria?"

She coughed and cleared her throat. The world wobbled in a watery splash. "After hearing what Adrian said I just can't take that chance. Maybe it's wrong and maybe I'll look back and see this differently, but I just can't risk it."

Her stepmother remained silent for a long while before she then asked, "Are you really sure about this, Victoria? You know once you go down this road that you can't go back."

"I know."

"We'll support you no matter what, Victoria. You know that. I'm just saying that you can change it now before it's too late."

It's already too late to turn back.

Victoria made her decision and she was going to live with it. No matter what.

FIFTEEN

Four years passed from the time Adrian and Victoria left each other on a bustling sidewalk and forever altered their lives.

Adrian closed his heart off as he'd sworn. He came back from the Artic with a demeanor as unforgiving as the ice world he'd left behind. Completely focused on acquisition, Adrian took his financial empire to new heights. He worked his inner-circle relentlessly, but himself even more so.

No deal was too difficult to close if he wanted it. Money had long lost its thrill, but with very little to occupy himself outside of work—why not focus on enlarging his net worth?

After all, what else was he going to do with his time?

Relationships simply didn't happen in Adrian's world. He saw his family during the obligatory holidays for an hour or two. Romantic encounters had less of a chance to hold his attention.

Adrian did the bare minimum when it came to courting for sex. Dinner. Entertainment. A suite in a discreet hotel. No shopping trips. No jewelry. No credit cards.

No sharing of my day, no cuddles on the couch, nothing that could be mistaken for caring. It's just sex. Nothing else.

Adrian would've thought it might make satisfying his physical needs more challenging now that the lure of his affection and largesse was gone. Adrian was wrong. It made it far easier than ever before.

Despite making his intentions about relationships crystal clear, Adrian heard the whispers of past partners to temporary ones.

"You should've seen him when we were together. Adrian was all about having a good time. He was so much fun! He's so cold now. He never smiles. It's a shame. All he needs is the right woman to change him back."

Adrian didn't care to change back or change at all.

It had taken him over a year before he'd been able to sleep with anyone besides Victoria again. After it was over, Adrian sat on the edge of the bed and felt his skin crawl with betrayal and disgust. Logically he understood there was no reason for him to feel it.

That couldn't stop his primal reactions. He'd gotten up and left the woman in the anonymous hotel room without another word. It'd taken another three months after that before he tried it again with a different partner.

Eventually, Adrian found he could perform as long as he kept himself emotionally removed.

If a woman found him too self-contained to be tolerated then she was free to make an assignation with someone else. Adrian didn't make demands on a bed partner's time or faithfulness and he expected the same courtesy in return.

Going to bed with women he didn't care about in the slightest was a pale copy of the intimacy he'd shared with Victoria and Adrian made no illusions about it. He recognized how vulnerable and unhinged loving his little kitten had made him. He simply had no interest in baring himself to another person like that ever again.

Besides, the women Adrian bedded cared little for him beyond an ego-stroke and he cared even less about them. Once his physical needs were minimally satisfied, Adrian got up, arranged his pants, and left.

Truthfully, hiring escorts would be a better fit for his lifestyle. He never got naked with whoever he was sleeping with at the time and he never, ever slept with her more than once in a given time. Only the possibility of scandal kept him from seeking the illicit arrangement.

Keeping himself cut off emotionally was a lonely life. Empty. Soulless. Even so Adrian spent the majority of his limited free time alone.

While it wasn't much of a life, it was the one he was determined to live.

***

Victoria carried on as countless generations of single mothers had done before her. She watched in fascination as her body expanded to accommodate the precious baby in her womb. She went to her prenatal checkups and read all the literature she could find at the library. She constantly read aloud to her child. She also played music with the earbuds pressed right against her tummy and sang when she was in the shower.

Victoria took great care of herself, making sure she took her vitamins, ate healthy, and got as much rest as possible. Especially because she worked long hours at her job.

Thankfully, her hard work was paying off. She'd already developed a reputation of being bright, dependable, and the kind of employee who didn't need to be micromanaged. Her supervisors were mothers themselves, so they were extremely supportive of Victoria and her eventual maternity leave.

She bought a small cottage with a sweet white picket fence after her probationary period ended. Victoria paid for the home in cash and she used Adrian's money to do it.

That didn't sit completely well on her sturdy shoulders, but Kathy had been the one to defend and eventually win the case.

"Adrian left that money for you in an account solely in your name for a reason. He wanted you to have it and with you carrying his baby, you need it."

Victoria crossed her arms. "Kathy, the baby and I can make do in an apartment. I don't need any of his money. I can do this on my own."

"You won't be able to afford more than a tiny apartment in a transient neighborhood with the wage you're currently earning, Victoria. You're going to end up spending too much in gas commuting back and forth between work, daycare, and home. That doesn't even include insurance, formula, diapers, and doctor visits."

Victoria tapped her fingers on the kitchen counter. "I see what you're saying, but I can make it work. I know I can."

Her stepmother fixed Victoria with a glare that she hadn't seen since her early teen years. "You want to martyr yourself, Victoria, you can go right ahead. But you don't have just yourself to think about. There's a time for pride and then there's a time for you to swallow your pride in favor of your child. You're already going to be a single mother. Don't make your life harder than it needs to be just to make a point."

As much as Victoria would've liked to argue further—she just couldn't.

Kathy was right. Her child was already going to grow up without a father. She didn't need to suffer financially for no good reason.

Still, Victoria was Victor Montford's daughter for a reason. She may have needed to depend on Adrian's money for a few years to come, but that didn't mean she needed to siphon off her child's nest egg.

Victoria kept careful track of the money she withdrew and set up a personal repayment plan which she funded every paycheck. Besides the house, she lived on her small salary. Her car was still the same one she drove in high school. Victoria shopped thrift stores and scoured online listings for inexpensive pieces of furniture that she could update with paint, hardware, and new fabric remnants.

It was a busy but fulfilling time in Victoria's life. Still, once she settled into bed with nothing to occupy her mind, it was then that all she had lost rose up to drown her.

Victoria missed Adrian fiercely.

At least once a day she wanted to call him, to hear his voice, and tell him everything that was going on in her life. She wished she could tell him about the latest sonogram or how she felt their baby move for the first time while in line at the grocery store.

But she couldn't.

ADRIAN

It hurt but Victoria had made her decision. She had to live with the consequences and make the best of her life without the love of her life.

Eventually the fateful day arrived when she felt the first contraction and her life changed again. Victoria's labor was long. The excruciating pain was nothing that she could've prepared for.

Kathy had been by her side, holding her hand when she needed it, and Victoria had been so grateful that she hadn't had to suffer completely alone. Still, when the contractions grew so bad that she could barely remember her name, Adrian's name was the only one could sob out.

After a series of long pushes, Victoria finally was able to hold her baby. Crying, but with a wide smile on her face, she was able to look into the beloved face of her child. In that moment, Victoria's heart expanded past all barriers and pure love descended.

Just as she was named after her own father, Victoria named her little daughter after her father and began the next chapter of her life.

Victoria's only regret was that Adrian couldn't be there to share it with her.

Thank you so much for Adriana. I'll take care of her. She'll always be loved and she'll never want for anything. Even if I have to work my fingers to the bone. I promise.

Those first few months were a precious bonding time between mother and daughter. Going back to work and leaving her daughter at daycare gutted Victoria, but she had to trust that she would survive the separation.

And she did.

Showered with unconditional love, Adriana grew like the proverbial flower. Milestones were celebrated and recorded in diaries, calendars, and on film. Victoria became a scrapbook junkie with Adriana the main focus of her books.

Birthdays passed in a shower of pink, violet, and silver. Adriana's inky hair grew from an adorable cap of curls to a silky wave that reached halfway down her back. She reintroduced Victoria to the wonder of the world and her laughter had the power to make everything wrong right again.

And when the inevitable feelings of sadness came to wash over Victoria, she let herself feel it but only at night and only when Adriana was asleep in her crib and later her big-girl bed. During those long lonely nights, Victoria found writing in her journal therapeutic as well as filming her thoughts when she couldn't sit still long enough to write.

She talked to Adrian during those sessions, telling him all the little things that their daughter accomplished for the day and how proud he would be if he knew how sweet of a girl she was.

Every now and then she'd also share how much she loved him and always had. Those were usually the hardest nights to go to sleep without needing her memories of Adrian and a vibrator.

Once a week, Victoria scanned her journal pages and uploaded her footage before compiling it into an ongoing series of files chronicling Adriana's life. Even though she knew she would most likely never see Adrian again in this lifetime, something drove her to make this record. Maybe it wasn't really for his benefit or hers, but for Adriana's.

Not now when she was just a little girl who calmly accepted that families were different and that's why she only had her mommy and not her daddy. But for later when she was a grown woman who wanted to know why her father didn't know of her existence.

Victoria trembled from the thought of having to be confronted by her daughter's fury. Not telling Adrian had been a rough, but manageable, theory when Adriana was in her womb.

The reality of her silence was much different after Adriana was born. Victoria constantly questioned her decision, wondering if she hadn't tried hard enough to tell Adrian or if she had been a coward and ran away instead.

The question haunted her, but she did what she did best. She worked.

She worked tirelessly at being the best mother she could be.

ADRIAN

She worked relentlessly at being the best employee she could be.

Victoria knew that eventually it was all going to catch up to her, but she was determined to fortify her walls and keep it at bay for as long as she could.

What else could she do? This was the life she'd chosen.

SIXTEEN

Victoria looked around her as she stepped out of the cab. The city's frenetic pace hadn't changed in the four years since she'd been back. After so many years living and working at The Triangle, better known outside of North Carolina as Research Triangle Park, Victoria found the crowds to be a bit claustrophobic.

"Being in that city is like have a hundred people all trying to stand in the same spot. Madness," was what Grandma McKinnon declared when she heard that Victoria was going there for a conference.

But of course, Victoria had only heard that through her stepmother because Grandma McKinnon wouldn't dare say it to Victoria herself. The matriarch had merely smiled and patted her hand. "You be safe now and come back to us as soon as you can."

Victoria shook her head wryly just thinking about Kathy's mother. The elder McKinnon still had yet to apologize for the words that had driven a premature end to Victoria's relationship with Adrian. However, she'd always been eager to babysit with Kathy and always packed a tin full of treats every time Victoria picked up Adriana.

Thinking about her sweet daughter, Victoria suffered the tug of homesickness and wished she could feel the comforting weight of her toddler in her arms. Adriana was her entire world and everything Victoria did she did for her daughter.

Including going to a conference 400 miles away when she'd much rather sit in her daughter's cheerful playroom and craft pictures strewn with glitter, buttons, and feathers.

Victoria's mind remained on Adriana while she checked into her hotel and settled into the room. It was hard to believe that her little girl was already three. Just thinking about her put a happy smile on Victoria's face.

Adriana loved animals, the koi fish in their little pond, the quarter moon but not the half moon, peanut butter sandwiches, and The Rolling Stones. She loved her preschool and especially loved her karate class. She loved her mommy, her grammie, her aunties, and her super-grammie.

Victoria's daughter was love itself.

She was also a daily reminder of the man Victoria had loved and lost. With a headful of long, dark hair, a button-nose, and heavily-lashed hazel eyes like her father's, Adriana promised to grow into a beauty. A tall beauty at that. She was already over half Victoria's height and becoming harder for her to carry.

Even so she's still my little girl and always will be—even if she ends up topping out at over six feet by the time she's five. I'll just figure out a way to strap her to my back.

Victoria unpacked her suitcase in just a few minutes. Gathering her notepad and purse,

Victoria gave herself a quick look over and then went downstairs to the ballroom. The conference promised to be noteworthy and Victoria was ready to write away.

Hours later she emerged from the meeting space with a cramped hand. Victoria really looked forward to going to the nearest art supply store and picking up a pack of origami paper. Adriana would undoubtedly love the beautiful designs and have no problem finding a way to incorporate them into her collages.

Cheered and energized by the thought of her little girl's happiness, Victoria went back to her room to trade her heels for flats. The store was ten blocks away and she rather relished the walk after spending eight hours cooped up studying the newest regulations affecting GAAP in her field.

It wasn't quite spring so she needed a coat, but Victoria turned out to be quite comfortable during her brisk walk. As she passed familiar sights, she thought back to the naïve girl she'd been when living here. Back then she thought all she needed to do was work like a mule and that one day all her efforts would be rewarded.

Financially, that had been true.

Yet, emotionally it had been far from true.

Hard work hadn't been enough to keep her prince and hard work still wasn't enough to keep her from thinking about him.

Victoria still missed Adrian.

She missed him when she woke up in the morning. She missed him when she went to bed. It was nothing like the sharp, piercing agony that had rendered her breathless four years before. Victoria's yearning was more like an ever-present drone in background of her life of getting her daughter up in mornings, getting dressed, driving her to her preschool, going to work, and then doing it all in reverse.

It never went away.

Sometimes Victoria wondered if this fixation on a man she'd only known for less than a year was healthy. Then all she had to do was remember the happiness she'd had with Adrian.

A million memories couldn't be overshadowed by the way they ended.

Besides, how could she be blamed for missing a man who'd taught her how to love and had given her the greatest gift in the world?

It was worth it. Even though I lost him at the end, it was still all worth it.

Victoria's heart fluttered knowing he was somewhere in the city. Temptation urged her to take a walk past his building, but while she was nostalgic, she wasn't insane.

The chances of seeing Adrian in a city of millions was slim, but not impossible if she strode in front of his workplace. Or his penthouse.

No. Don't even think about it.

Victoria barely had time to deny herself when she saw a small group of sharply dressed people surrounding a towering figure swathed from head to toe in black. He turned his head and looked straight at her. The small smile on her face froze.

Time shattered. Everything came to a stop.

Victoria whispered his name, the only name that had the power to make every nerve ending come alive and tremble.

“Adrian.”

***

Adrian froze.

People swirled about, insignificant to the moment taking place right before him. Victoria stood only a few feet away. Her intense gaze sucked him in as they always had before. Attired in a wool coat that did nothing to hide her curves, Victoria managed to become even more beautiful than he remembered.

It was too much to hope she was a figment of his overworked imagination. Adrian’s mouth dried and his heart beat in staccato rhythm against his chest. Everything he thought he’d ever do when faced with her again left his mind.

His small retinue paused in confusion as Adrian remained by the limo door, unmoving and transfixed by the slip of a girl who had managed to wreck his entire world completely.

No, not a girl anymore. A woman. A woman all the more dangerous with age and time.

Victoria had brought him to his knees and she'd only been an inexperienced virgin with a sweet smile and a sweeter voice. He could only imagine what kind of power she'd wield over him now with experience and confidence.

How many lovers has she had since me? Does she think of me like I think of her?

He'd stopped all information on her the moment he'd seen her last on a similar sidewalk. The last bit had been that Victoria had closed the bank account he'd set up in her name only a few months after that night. He hadn't wanted to think to the whys before, but they pumped into his brain now.

She needed the money to pay for a new life with another man?

Adrian's jaw tightened and his flinty gaze seemed to cause Victoria to step back in nervousness. He couldn't deny the vicious thrill he felt at her response. He could still affect her even though this wasn't the kind of reaction he'd ever wanted from Victoria before.

Adrian frowned, feeling saddened by yet another piece of proof that this woman was never to be his again. He imagined she looked as shocked as he felt. The ice surrounding his heart had thawed and then refroze thicker.

He'd made his decision four years ago that he'd never let anyone close again. Even Victoria. He couldn't allow her to simply undo all the walls he'd built up since then.

She's right there. I can go to her now and find a way to talk to her again without losing my head or being a love-struck fool. Surely I can do that.

No.

It was best to pretend that he'd never seen her this evening. Even he couldn't be that much of a masochist to go back to the source of his greatest pain.

Adrian turned his head away from the woman he still wanted more than anything else in the world and entered the limousine. His staff entered right behind him. Adrian kept his gaze trained straight ahead, but he was completely aware of the sidewalk and every single person who walked past.

The limo entered traffic right when she entered his field of vision. Adrian watched her from behind the safety of tinted glass. He closed his eyes briefly when he couldn't see her anymore.

Even after she was long behind him, Adrian could picture the way her dark hair curled softly at the shoulders. Her rosebud mouth remained just as luscious as he remembered. Victoria's eyes...God, her eyes. Dark, gleaming like ebony and just as mysterious.

What had she seen these past years? Was it her past? Was it him?

He didn't dare allow himself to think that she was affected at seeing him like he was her, but Adrian hoped.

He hoped and in that hope, he feared he hadn't really changed at all. Victoria could still bring him low and if she did, how would he ever find a way to get back up again?

***

Victoria wrapped her arms around her waist. Her smile was long gone. She'd seen Adrian and he had seen her. Yet, unlike her, Adrian hadn't been affected by the encounter. He'd simply looked at Victoria as if she had been just another stranger on the street.

That hurt. That hurt more than Victoria could ever adequately put in words.

What did you think he'd do if you ever ran into him? Be your friend? Invite you out to dinner? Just because he was on friendly terms with his exes doesn't mean he thinks of you the same way.

Victoria was the one who'd turned down his first marriage proposal and left. She'd broken up with him when all he wanted was to make her and her family happy.

And how did I repay him? I had his baby and never even gave him a chance to decide if he wanted to be in our daughter's life.

She eventually made it to the art supply store but all the happiness she thought she'd have disappeared.

I deserve this. All of it.

***

Adrian and his retinue were seated for dinner within fifteen minutes of sighting Victoria. Drinks were ordered. Appetizers served. Conversation flowed, bouncing between work and weekend plans. It was normal and sane.

The direction of his thoughts were anything but.

Adrian discreetly touched his forehead. If he didn't know better he'd think he was running a low-grade fever. He wanted out of the restaurant and he wanted to go back in time to when he saw her.

Could he have imagined the glimmer of pleasure and hope in her eyes? Did he put it there himself to justify the suffocating urge to go to her?

It's done. Over.

"Excuse me." Adrian stood up and the table's conversation came to a halt. His C-Level employees looked unsure. Adrian wondered if he hadn't managed to hide the ferocious determination pounding through his veins. He summoned a casual nod. "I have to make a call."

Adrian waited until he was in relative privacy. The phone rang once before his head of security answered.

"Drop everything you're doing and find out what hotel Victoria Montford is staying at and for how long. Call me back within a half hour."

SEVENTEEN

Victoria walked through the lobby, gaze trained on skirting any possible attention from conference attendees and getting to the relative peace of the elevator. She'd spent more than she should have on the origami sheets. Victoria had no doubt as to why she'd done it.

It was undoubtedly a way to make up for the fact that Adriana didn't have a father and never would because her mother was a damned, selfish coward.

As if colorful bits of paper could ever make up for that.

Victoria really hoped that if she was selected to go to next year's conference, it'd be held somewhere far from here. Florida would be good. Alaska even better. Surely, her fate wouldn't be that cruel to have her run into Adrian in the wilderness, would it?

She made it to the elevator and punched the button with more force than necessary. What did he think when he saw her standing there? Did he think she was waiting for him? Did he think her beautiful?

Stop it. He's not thinking about you at all.

"Victoria."

Shocked out of her melancholic thoughts, Victoria jumped a step back. Two large hands settled on her shoulders and squeezed.

Please.

More than a little ashamed at the pitiful excitement stirring within, Victoria looked over her shoulder. Adrian stood right behind her. His proximity, the feel of his hands, all of it brought back memories of their first encounter.

"Adrian."

He smiled and let go of her. Victoria missed his touch keenly. She cleared her throat and tried to ignore the blush steadily growing on her face.

It was like nothing had changed. She was still a girl when it came to Adrian Hawthorne.

Except I'm not. Not really because I'm a mother. The mother of his *child.*

She licked lips gone dry. "What are you doing here?"

"Isn't it obvious?"

Victoria shook her head. Her half-smile mirrored his.

Adrian leaned a tiny bit closer. "I'm here to see you."

"Oh. I wasn't sure." When he merely stared at her, pleasant but distant expression in place, Victoria's girlish hope went into a death-spiral. "I mean, I know you saw me earlier. At least, I'm pretty sure you saw me."

"I did."

Victoria swallowed. Face-to-face with Adrian, she seemed to revert back into a clumsy young girl who didn't know what to do other than blush and mumble.

The elevator opened behind her. Adrian raised his brow but didn't say another word.

Victoria knew she could take the elevator and he wouldn't follow. It could end all over again. Right here. Right now.

Deliberately, she took one step closer to Adrian.

"I don't have to go up right now."

His gaze seemed to brighten with satisfaction, but he still didn't say anything else. The silence between them unnerved her.

Victoria licked her lips again. "Would you like to get a drink with me? My treat." She waited, stretched thin as he seemed to consider her request.

"I probably shouldn't."

Her pride took a kick to the gut. She couldn't blame him for the rebuff, especially because how things ended between them. Victoria somehow managed to say, "Okay. I understand," without blasted tears swarming in her eyes.

That will come later in the elevator.

"I don't think you do." Adrian swept one arm out. "After you, Ms. Montford."

Victoria's tummy flipped. Relief poured over her. Adrian guided her away from the bar and towards the front entrance. "You don't want to get one here?"

"No, I do not."

She didn't have anything to say to that. Silently, she walked with him to his limo. She entered it as she'd done a thousand times before. The memories of those exciting days washed over her. Victoria closed her eyes briefly and thought back to the girl she'd been by his side.

To think that fate had given her another chance to sit by him again...

"I wasn't going to see you tonight."

His words brought Victoria out of her past and into their barren present.

"Why did you then?"

Adrian shrugged. "Curiosity. I didn't think I'd ever see you again."

"Me too." She ached to trace her finger down his firm jaw. The Adrian she remembered smiled at her often. She missed that man even though she didn't have a right to complain about where they ended. Especially because of Adriana.

Maybe now is the time to tell him.

Victoria tightened her hands around the bag's handle. It wasn't even close to being the right time to tell him. Maybe it never would be.

"Is something wrong?"

She flashed him a quick smile. "No, it just feels strange. Being here again with you."

Adrian nodded. "I feel the same."

Neither of them said another word until they arrived at their destination. The driver opened up the door and Adrian exited. Victoria slid across the seat, sure that it would be the driver's hand reaching for her. Instead, Adrian held his strong hand out.

She hesitated slightly before slipping her hand in his. Just as it had always been between them, a jolt sparked through Victoria. Desire unfurled and excitement brought color to her cheeks.

Victoria was almost too affected to see if she was alone in feeling this way. Her gaze met

Adrian's and she faltered. Raw hunger darkened his eyes, making them gleam emerald. It was the same shade she'd stare into as he held himself above her, making love to her with tender thoroughness.

She wanted to go back to that time more than ever before.

Adrian didn't let go of her hand. She didn't try to let go of him. They walked into a darkened bar without saying a word. Even when they were seated at a booth, they kept their silence. It wasn't until they placed their drink orders and received them a short minute later, did Adrian finally break it.

***

"How have you been, Victoria?"

"Well—"

Adrian couldn't contain himself one second longer. "Why did you break up with me, Victoria? I mean really."

She froze, infinite sadness washing over her beautiful face. Adrian almost regretted asking the question. Almost.

Victoria smoothed her small hand over the table. “Short answer? Because I was afraid you’d resent me for proposing.”

“And that was all?”

She looked up. Her lips tightened with suppressed emotion. “Isn’t that enough?”

“No. It wasn’t.”

Victoria fiddled with her glass. Her words, when they finally came, were halting. “You pulled away from me the month before. I didn’t think you loved me anymore.”

Adrian kept his expression smooth but his insides boiled with misery and frustration. “Not love you anymore? I wanted to marry you, Victoria. I wanted to spend the rest of my life with you.”

“No, you didn’t.”

He cursed softly. “I know my own feelings, Victoria.”

“Maybe, but that wasn’t what drove you. I know why you really did it, Adrian. I know Grandma McKinnon pressured you into it and for that I’m very sorry.”

Adrian stared at her, hating the sadness that clung to her. "I still asked you because I wanted to marry you."

"But did you really? No, listen. Maybe you don't remember your proposal, but I do. You talked about marrying me as if I was holding a gun to your head. It was humiliating, but more than that—it was hurtful."

Adrian replayed those fateful minutes. He tried to see her point of view, but all he could focus on was the immense rejection she'd dealt him when she not only turned him down, but ended their relationship.

"Maybe it wasn't cinema-worthy, but it came from my heart, Victoria. Do you believe me or do you think I'm lying?"

Victoria considered him for a bit and then shook her head. "No, I believe you." She chanced touching his hand. "I'm sorry that I rejected you that way."

"As opposed to what?" Adrian hated letting his bitterness show, but it was too late.

"As opposed to not stopping to figure out why you asked me. If I had known it was because of one of my family members, I wouldn't have reacted the way I did."

"It's true that your grandmother's words pushed me in a direction I wouldn't have considered before, but nothing could've forced me to ask you if I didn't love you, Victoria. You were the first woman I had ever loved."

Shock painted her face. "I couldn't have been!"

"Why does that surprise you?" Adrian took a careful sip of his bourbon. The alcohol slid down his throat, but whatever warmth he would've normally felt paled into comparison to the fire growing steadily in his heart.

Adrian still wanted Victoria. Time hadn't been strong enough to change it. He wanted to howl with frustration. How could this one slip of a girl have the power to keep him in her chains? She wasn't the most beautiful woman he'd been with nor the most adventurous.

So why her?

Because she's perfect for me. She's perfect in a way I didn't even know I needed until I met her.

Despair crept through Adrian's façade of careful control. What would Victoria do if she knew that he ached for her every day and night since her departure? What would she do if she knew that no matter how many women he'd had since she left, none of them had been able to fill the void her absence had left?

Would she see him as devoted or pitiful?

"You're so easy to love, Adrian. I can't imagine you haven't had hundreds of women who've loved you."

Adrian didn't allow himself the luxury of avoiding her overly-bright gaze. "But I haven't loved a single one until you."

Victoria closed her eyes. Her right hand trembled slightly as it lifted her drink. He waited in agony as she took a sip before setting the glass down.

"Adrian, I have something to tell you. Something really important actually. I know it's the best setting for it but, well, you need to know."

Seeing the strain on her lovely features, Adrian sensed danger. He didn't want to hear her obvious confession.

"Can you wait?" She bit her lip and looked at him in the throes of fierce indecision. Adrian pounced. "We haven't seen each other in four years. Let's enjoy our time together and save the confessions for later. What do you say?"

Adrian schooled his features, but beneath the charming mask his nerves splintered. He didn't want to end their night just yet. He wanted to keep this precious time together, to pretend that they were the greatest of friends having a drink together instead of ex-lovers ignoring that this wasn't awkward and painful.

Victoria ran a fingertip over the glass edge. She glanced at him before quickly looking away. Pain tattooed the space over his heart. He'd seen that look a million times before.

Shy, sinfully sweet, and so much like the kitten he named her so long ago.

Adrian didn't lack anything in the world. He had money, power, prestige, and the all the doors in the world would swing open for him at his will.

Sitting there in a darkened bar, Adrian madly wished he could trade it all just so Victoria could be his kitten once again.

Why, kitten? Why did you have to run from me? All I wanted to do was love you.

Victoria nodded and said, "Okay." She gifted him a gentle smile. "I like being here with you, Adrian."

His heart squeezed. He tossed her a charming grin as if his heart wasn't breaking. "Do you now?"

"Yes. I always liked being with you, no matter where we were. Just as long as I was with you, I was happy."

Adrian casually sipped his bourbon, trying to buy time to compose his thoughts. He shoved it off and decided to go for unfiltered honesty. "It was the same for me. More so. In all these years, you're still the only one I ever wanted to come home to."

Victoria's startled gaze flew to his. Her lush mouth opened in surprise. "I would've thought you'd already replaced me ten times over."

A crack of bitter laughter pushed past his throat. "Replace you? Impossible." His hooded stare challenged. "What? You don't believe me?"

***

Victoria closed her eyes for too-short of a time. She wanted to savor his confession, to take it as an invitation back into his life. But she was afraid. Victoria was afraid that she was wrong, that even if Adrian meant every word he said, what would happen when she told him about Adriana?

How could he ever forgive her for keeping their daughter a secret?

Victoria had been so close to telling him just now, but her cowardice made it easy to accept Adrian's suggestion for later. She would tell him before she left for home.

Definitely.

It was one thing to live in her little bubble with Adriana, never seeing Adrian to justify her continued silence—even if she doubted the wisdom of her decision every day.

It was another to see him in the flesh, to be sitting within feet of him, and deny him the existence of their daughter.

Victoria looked at him, painfully intense gaze running over every inch of his beloved face. "I want to believe you."

"But?"

She responded to his barely-leashed aggression with a fatalistic shrug. "Adrian, I let you go for a reason. Don't tempt me to be selfish."

"Selfish?"

Once Victoria had been brave enough to take a chance in her feelings and leap towards him. Despite the heartbreak and sorrow that came later, she didn't regret taking her chance. Aching for the possibility, no matter how slim, of being that girl again, Victoria didn't want to hide her feelings.

Especially not when she'd already hid so much from him.

"Adrian, I never stopped wanting you. Not for one second. Not back then and not now."

He tossed back the rest of his drink and stood up. Victoria straightened, confused and worried that perhaps her words had deeply angered him. Maybe the idea of hearing she'd pined over him for years disturbed him and all he wanted was to leave Victoria to her pitiful feelings.

Adrian put on his coat. He then held out his hand, "Come."

That one word became a switch. She was instantly transported back to the countless times she was pinned beneath him as he rasped that one word in her ear.

"Come."

Victoria stood up. Excitement fluttered deep in her belly. She didn't question his command or what would happen next.

Adrian went to her side and held out her coat. She slipped her arms in and then trembled when she felt his beautiful hands rest on her shoulders.

"I want you to come home with me, Victoria. Now."

Oh God.

Victoria leaned against him and immediately felt his hardness press exquisitely against her backside. She wished they were someplace private. If they were, Victoria would bend over without hesitation for him. Already she could feel his hand clutch the base of her head, fingers entangled sweetly in her hair, as he stretched her unmercifully.

Victoria's breath came quicker.

"Will you?" Adrian pressed against her. He obviously had no doubt she could feel every hard inch of him. He wasn't ashamed and neither was she.

She leaned her head back against his chest and let out a soft moan.

"Yes."

EIGHTEEN

Adrian led her to the private elevator, one hand on the small of her back as was his custom. He managed to keep his hand there, just there in that sweet curve, when all he really wanted to do was tear off her clothes and ravish her against the paneled wall.

Victoria's cheeks remained high in color. She looked at him every so often, dark eyes gleaming with desire and unrestrained love. Adrian couldn't let himself bask in it, not yet.

He couldn't take the chance that come morning she'd regret their night. He believed his heart, frozen as it'd been without her, would simply crack into oblivion if that was the case. Adrian had spent too many years keeping himself protected to take that chance with Victoria now.

Especially with Victoria.

Yet, being so close to her, to feeling the heat of her beneath his hand...God, it was a torment too pleasurable to walk away from. If there was any possibility that this glorious woman could come back into his life, it would start with tonight.

The elevator opened. She took a couple of steps into the foyer and stopped. Adrian viewed the rooms through her eyes. Everything had changed. He had every piece of furniture replaced. The changes swept through the kitchen, the walls, and even the bathrooms.

Adrian's memories of their life together were enough to torment him. He hadn't wanted the physical reminders as well.

"It looks nice. Very masculine."

Sweet Victoria. Polite as always.

Dark wood, gray, cobalt, and spots of gold had transformed the penthouse into stylish anonymity. Adrian wondered if it pleased

Victoria or saddened her. He didn't doubt she'd correctly interpreted the changes as a way to erase her presence.

What was there to say? It was the truth.

"May I take your coat?"

She tore her gaze away from the living room, specifically the spot where the leather couch once occupied. "Thank you."

His thoughts strayed to the memories he imagined she shared.

"Kitten! I'm home!"

Did she miss those times as acutely as he did? Did she miss sitting on his lap while he unwound from his hectic and long days?

Without thought, his hands went towards her but Victoria undid the sash before he could. Adrian tried not to read too much into it or see rejection where none might've existed.

Still, he watched her intently.

He waited as she undid each button. Adrian focused on each inch that exposed her to him. Coiled, he was ready to spring and push her to the floor.

Not good. I don't have the right to do that now. I might not have the right to do it at all.

Victoria's gaze found his. Adrian's heartbeat quickened. Her hunger mirrored his. He carefully slid her coat off when all he really wanted to do was yank it off her body, along with the rest of her clothes.

Adrian's precise movements belied the urgency pounding through him. The hunger for her, denied for so long, threatened to overtake his good sense. He wanted everything, but a kiss could assuage him. Just one kiss on the nape of her neck...and then her shoulder...and her back...and the curve of her hip...

He took a deliberate step back and turned away from her. Once both their coats were hung, Adrian turned back with a pleasant, but false, expression.

"Would you like some dessert?"

Victoria inhaled, soft but deep, as she stared at his mouth. He would've smiled at her obvious thoughts, but he hurt too damned much. She lowered her gaze and answered, "Yes."

He noted the paper bag she still clutched in her hand. “You can set that down if you’d like.”

She looked about, uncertainty pulling her lush mouth into a pout. Adrian didn’t offer to help. He selfishly wanted her to come to him for it.

“Where should I put it?”

“How about in the closet with our coats?” He held out his hand and Victoria handed over the bag. Curiously, he wondered what was so important for her to have refused to let it out of her sight until now.

Once he put the bag in the closet, Adrian led her to the remodeled kitchen, one hand still on her back and closer than ever to feeling her bare flesh against his skin.

Adrian turned on the light. He wondered if the industrial-chic palette offended her feminine tastes. He couldn’t help but remember all the time she’d spent in this very kitchen. Even now Adrian still missed her cooking to an unhealthy degree.

Her cooking? Hell, I miss everything about her.

Having Victoria here was harder than he expected. Memories came at him left and right, made all the worse because seeing all the external changes proved it hadn't made a dent on the internal.

They walked to the massive island. "Have a seat, Victoria." Adrian gave into his desire to touch her. He lifted her up on the stool. He couldn't bite back a smile at seeing how far off the ground she was. "It's a long way down for you, isn't it?"

Victoria swung her legs in gentle rhythm and remarked with an impish grin, "I bet your feet stay on the floor, don't they?"

"I'm afraid so, kitten." The pet name slipped out. Her eyes misted. Adrian abruptly turned away but the feel of her hand on his arm stopped him.

"Please don't turn away from me, Adrian."

Adrian wasn't in enough control of himself to give into her plea. He had to stand there and wait.

Victoria's fingers squeezed him once. "That was one of the things I missed so much about you." She laughed. "I can't see a cat or a kitten without remembering you."

Although he held himself stiffly, Adrian wanted nothing more than to snatch her off the stool and lay her on the island. He didn't just want to make love to her. He wanted to *love* her. He wanted her to hold him in her arms like she used to, stroking his hair and making Adrian feel that for once in his life he finally had a home.

It hurt.

"Please look at me."

Adrian turned slowly. He steeled himself but her miserable expression laid him low.

Victoria licked her lips and opened herself to him further. "I can't count how many things I missed about you. There hasn't been a day that's gone by where I haven't thought of you. I just...I...I think you should know that."

Her words pierced him. His walls started crumbling and bottled up emotion seeped out.

"Then why did you leave me without you for so long, Victoria? Don't you know I've been waiting for you all these years, kitten?"

***

Victoria squeezed his arm. She found it harder to draw in a full breath of air. Why was she trying to dredge up the past? They'd broken up. It was done. Over.

But I wished it hadn't happened. I wished I'd reacted differently when he proposed.

Victoria couldn't deny her feelings. She wished that she still lived here with Adrian and their daughter. She wished the living room was filled with soft furnishings, light-colored walls, and Adriana's toys scattered about. She wished that this was still her kitchen and more than anything, she wished that she had said "Yes" to Adrian's proposal four years before.

It was foolish of her to have turned him down and walked away. All these years she had believed that setting Adrian free was the greatest act of love she could've shown him. Now she knew herself for a liar. She hadn't set him free.

She'd just run away because she was scared he didn't want her anymore.

"I'm sorry, Adrian. I didn't know."

"Why not?"

His sharp question couldn't hide the raw pain festering beneath those two words. "I never imagined I mattered that much to you."

Adrian grabbed her by the arms and pulled her to him. "How could you doubt it? You're the first woman I've ever loved, Victoria! You were the only one I really let into my life. The. Only. One."

All her sins had come home to roost. There was nowhere to hide and no way she could deny the tragedy she'd set into motion when she gave into her fear.

"I couldn't believe it because I was afraid!"

"Of what? Of me?"

"Yes!"

Fire lit his gaze bright, turning Adrian's eyes amber. "Of what, Victoria? Tell me!"

Considering how much of a liar she turned out to be, the least Victoria could do was tell him this much of the truth. “I was afraid you were cheating on me, that you got bored of me because you pulled away so much in that last month.”

“I pulled away because I was trying to figure out what our next steps should be.”

“But I didn’t know that because you didn’t talk to me.”

“You’re right. I didn’t. Then you just left.”

It was true. She just left and there wasn’t anything Victoria could do to change that course.

But she could change this moment. Right now.

“Adrian. I’m sorry.”

He closed his eyes. Victoria recognized the pain on his face because she saw it on her own every day.

Trapped in his arms as she was, Victoria couldn’t reach up and kiss his mouth. But she could touch him on his chest. She felt his heart beating strongly against her palm.

"Adrian, I'm here now and I want to be here with you."

He opened his eyes. They were bright with pain and frustration. "You want to fuck me, right?"

She dragged in a deep breath. Adrian seemed stretched to the breaking point. Victoria wanted him to break free.

"Yes. I want to fuck you. I want you to fuck me. And when all that is over, when we're no longer so angry and hungry, then I want to make love with you. I want to touch and kiss you all over. Can I do that, Adrian? Please?"

He let out a feral cry and sunk his hands deep in her hair. Adrian's firm mouth slashed across her, tongue driving deep into her open mouth. The time for talking was over.

Victoria's hands greedily snatched at any part of Adrian she could reach. He bent her over his arm and tugged her dress up. She gasped in dizzying pleasure as he suckled on her ear lobe. He gripped her jaw, gently, keeping her still for his possession and giving her no choice but to accept his pleasure.

"I need you. I've always needed you, kitten."

The words inflamed her. Victoria traced a line down his shoulder. "I've always needed you too, Adrian. It's always been you. Every time I touch myself, every time I come..."

He yanked Victoria off her feet. His lips covered her after saying, "No! The past doesn't matter...not tonight."

Victoria kissed him back as hard as he kissed her. She wrapped her legs and arms around him feeling every inch of her was on fire. Victoria just couldn't get close enough to Adrian.

He carried her out of the kitchen and into his bedroom. Adrian laid her in the middle of his platform bed, barely allowing them to stop kissing long enough for yank all their clothes off. Adrian then kneeled over her. His molten gaze appreciated every inch of her naked skin.

Victoria crossed her arms over her breasts. They were larger than when she was with Adrian. That wasn't the only difference. Everything about her was lusher. She also had a few stretch marks on her hips, belly, and thighs. Shyness descended as she wondered if Adrian would find the changes in her body lacking.

Adrian's hands slid across her thighs. "Why are you covering up, Victoria?"

Breathless and hoping his hands wouldn't stop until they reached her wet core, she answered, "I'm nervous."

"Of what?"

"Of you seeing me."

His gaze flared. "Why? You're so beautiful, kitten."

"Really? You don't find me too...round?"

He laughed softly. "If you mean perfect, then yes. I find you perfect, Victoria." Adrian skated his palm over the gentle curve of her belly. "My Victoria is all grown up now. She's a woman. A beautiful woman whose body is..." Adrian groaned in masculine appreciation when she let her arm drop. "God, your tits. I just want to suck on them all night long."

She dropped her gaze, gasping his name much to Adrian's amusement.

His mouth curled into a luscious grin. "That too crude, babe?"

"Maybe just a little."

"Still feeling shy, kitten?"

"A little."

"Hmm, is that so? I seem to remember exactly how to make your shyness go away." Adrian bent down and licked a trail from her belly up to her neck. He then kissed her neck and growled, "Cup your tits for me. Now."

Victoria hesitated for just a second. She offered them up to him, blushes staining her cheeks and excitement drumming a tattoo throughout her body.

Adrian smiled and purred, "Perfect."

***

Victoria visibly burned for him and Adrian was drunk on his power over her. Having her back in his bed was like a million wishes coming true all at once. He could barely contain the urge to pounce on her. Feeling her beneath him and touching her satin skin became its own special addiction. He wanted to be in her right this second, but the need to savor Victoria dominated everything.

Who knows how long we'll have?

Despite the darkness of his thoughts, Adrian gently took Victoria's nipple and squeezed. She inhaled sharply and arched into his hand. He did it again. "Do you like that?"

She nodded and whispered, "Yes."

He leaned down, still pinching her nipple, and flicked his tongue along the turgid point. When she reached out and brushed her hand along his rock-hard shaft, Adrian drug his teeth across her nipple in sweet punishment.

"Not yet."

Victoria moaned. "But I want you. Now."

Adrian closed his eyes and sucked her, greedily trying to fit as much of Victoria's breast into his mouth as he could. Her fingers tangled into his hair and her leg rubbed restlessly against his hip. Adrian held her tightly and switched from one nipple to the other, back and forth, while Victoria cried out his name in a sensual plea.

He eventually licked his way across her ribcage and down her belly. Victoria parted her thighs, obviously eager for what was bound to come next. Adrian wasted no time in teasing her further. He opened her delightful folds and thrust his tongue deep.

She cried out his name. Adrian growled, satisfaction filling him as fast as her honey did. He pushed her thighs open as wide as they could go and held his hands there. Adrian felt her sleek muscles strain against his palms, especially when he centered his lips over her sweet clit.

Victoria pushed herself up on her elbows. Knowing she watched him, made Adrian hurt as his cock hardened further. He looked at her, gaze heated, and sucked her gently before going harder. Adrian pulsed her this way and Victoria's belly tightened the closer she came to the edge.

He relished in watching every bit of raw emotion cross her face. She pressed the back of her hand against her mouth, as if trying to keep her loud cries contained.

Adrian released her but put one finger on either side of her clit. “Put that hand down, kitten. I want to hear everything. Everything, understand?”

Victoria shook her head.

He said her name in a low, warning purr.

“I can’t.”

“Everything, Victoria.”

Her mouth twisted in a grimace of pained pleasure. “Adrian...”

“Everything.” He didn’t move an inch until she nodded jerkily. He then bent his head back down. Adrian took her between his lips and licked her delicately. It was a test, a way to see if Victoria would do as he needed her to do. She passed beautifully.

“Oh yes...”

He gave her more and she responded louder. It became a game of give and take. Adrian gave Victoria pleasure and he took it for himself with every hitch of her breath and broken cry of his name.

The more pressure he gave on her sweet pearl, the more she gave him in return. Adrian rested his hand on her belly and redoubled his attention on her luscious folds. She whimpered and he could tell she hung on by a ragged thread.

"Don't hold back, Victoria. Come."

Her eyes widened and then bliss crashed, taking Victoria over. She yelled his name and then said the words he'd only heard until the very end.

"Oh God, I love you!"

Adrian got on his knees and snatched her up to him. With his hands buried deep in her tousled hair, and belly against her chest, he could feel the violent tremors rocketing through Victoria.

"Say it again!"

Her soft mouth parted. The words breathed into him even as her eyes filled with tears. "I love you."

Adrian bowed, taking her with him. Distantly, he felt her arms against his back. He wanted her to say it again, to tell him she'd never leave and that he could finally put his obsession to rest.

"I love you, Adrian. Then and now. I've never stopped loving you. Never."

He shuddered. She was his and he was never going to let her go.

Never.

***

Victoria's heart flew on wings. She confessed her love and not only did he not pull away, Adrian returned it a thousand-fold.

He declared it against her mouth and neck as he pulled her beneath him on the bed. He moaned it into her ear after he unrolled the condom onto his shaft and then carefully slid into her tight sheath.

"I love you, kitten. I love you so much."

Victoria let out a shaky breath when he was fully seated inside her. Despite have his child, she felt the sting of his possession as she rapidly tried to accommodate Adrian's girth.

"Am I hurting you?"

She shook her head and linked her arms around his neck. "No. Not even a little."

"Are you sure?" His hand tightened on her hip. "You're just so fucking *tight*, kitten. Tighter than I remember."

Victoria didn't want him focusing on the changes childbirth and abstinence had wrought. She arched her hips and groaned, "I need you, Adrian. Please...I want to come again with you deep inside me."

He smiled wickedly. "As my lady commands."

Adrian's first slow thrust was heaven. The time between his first and second was hell. It was too much and not enough. She kissed his chest, neck, and mouth while running her hands all over his wide back. Adrian was so wonderfully masculine and she loved feeling every hard muscle beneath her fingertips.

His hardness melted into her softness and Victoria quickly felt the delicious tremors beginning low in her belly. “God, Adrian, you make me feel so good. I’ve missed being with you so much.”

Adrian kissed her into breathy silence. He snaked his arm beneath her, making a tight seal between their bodies. Hungry and greedy for every bit of carnal sensation, Victoria desperately wound one hand at the nape of his neck and the other around his waist.

He groaned loudly in her ear. “Your pussy is squeezing the life out of me, kitten. Are you about to come?”

“Y-Yes!”

Adrian sat up and pulled her on top of him. His hands roamed across her naked back before he reached down and squeezed Victoria’s backside. “I want to watch you come. You feel so good...don’t stop moving.”

Victoria rolled her hips, feeling every inch of his glorious shaft pushing deeper and deeper inside her. When his lips fastened around

Victoria's nipple, she went crazy. Crying aloud, she dug her blunt nails into his shoulders and churned her hips harder.

Adrian's deep moans echoed in Victoria's ears along with her thundering heartbeat. On the edge, she dragged his mouth from her breast to her lips. She kissed him like fire—blisteringly hot and out of control.

He cupped her cheeks and brought his face up to hers. Adrian's gaze softened. "Beautiful."

Victoria unraveled. Adrian held her, telling her of his love in a low, passionate whisper before he stiffened beneath Victoria. They collapsed together and held each other, breathing softly in the darkness and finding there were no words except the three most important ones.

"I love you."

"I love you."

NINETEEN

They slept for an hour. Adrian woke up with Victoria's mouth kissing down his ridged belly. She sucked him, alternately fisting and laving his long, thick length with her tongue, until he barely pulled her off in time before rolling her beneath him.

Their lovemaking was familiar and different just as they now were. Adrian took immense pleasure in reacquainting himself with her curvaceous body. His lips burned a path from her luscious mouth all the way down to her tiny toes.

Adrian smiled when Victoria declared it was her time to play. She pushed him onto her back, laughing in delight as he crossed his arms behind his head and wagged his eyebrows.

"What are you going to do to me, kitten?"

"Finishing what you interrupted," she answered with an arch tone.

"By all means, Ms. Montford." Adrian then spent the next half-hour in bliss as Victoria teased, sucked, and licked him before finally letting him come in her mouth. He gripped her by the hair and bowed over her as she sucked him dry of every last drop.

When he laid back in sated exhaustion, Victoria crawled up beside him and snuggled against him with a proud smile on her lovely face. He wanted to come all over again when she said, "Yummy!"

Adrian had the pleasure of repeating it after he lifted her onto his face, holding her hips firmly in place as he licked her sweet folds, driving his tongue deep into her over and over again.

Victoria shimmied down his body and took him back into her mouth. It was hell pulling her off to reach into the nightstand, but once he was sheathed, Adrian rolled her to her tummy and took her from behind.

It was savage, primal, and thrilling, especially when Victoria rocked back against him, begging for more. Knowing he wasn't going to last as long as he'd liked, Adrian reached beneath him and rubbed her clit in frantic circles.

Victoria went crazy. She spread her legs wider and ground her pussy against him while arching her hips up to meet his frantic thrusts. Neither of them were in control and it was glorious. Soon their cries spilled together as they fell together on the bed.

"Victoria, I'm not going to let you out of this bed until you can't walk straight."

Her delighted peals of laughter rained down on him like rose petals. Adrian hugged her to him, prepared to drift back to sleep, when he felt her try to shift out from under him. His arm tightened, keeping her pinned by his side.

"Where are you going?"

"I'm hungry."

He sat up. "Hungry?" Adrian bit back a smile when he saw a look of embarrassment flash across her dewy face.

"I didn't get to eat much today and since I've expanded all this energy with you..."

"All right." Adrian got up and slipped on his pants before finding his shirt. Coming back to the bed, he commanded, "Arms out." Adrian then dressed Victoria in his shirt, making sure to leave the first buttons open and thoroughly enjoying how sexy and tousled she looked.

"You don't have to get up. I can get something for myself."

"Hush. It's purely selfish. I'm going to feed my woman so I can build up her strength for me later." Adrian picked her up and walked out of the bedroom and into the kitchen. He loved how easily she fit in his arms and back into his life.

Turning on the lights, Adrian lifted her up onto the kitchen island. "Now you just stay right here and I'm going to..."

Victoria crossed her legs and leaned into his kiss. "Going to what? Kiss me? I think that sounds good."

"I think you're right." His lips feathered across hers. "Mmm, that's sweet. I want another. And another. And another."

Victoria laughed and tilted her head back so Adrian could smother her with kisses. "Are you happy?"

"Happier than I've been in years, kitten. And you?"

"The same."

Adrian wrapped his arms around Victoria and pulled her to him. "Kitten, why were we both so stupid?" Victoria's smile faded. Sadness glittered in her tears. He immediately went to comfort her. "Kitten, I'm so sorry. I didn't mean to make you cry. Forgive me."

She covered his hand with hers. "There's nothing to forgive. Adrian, you've done *nothing* for me to forgive. Please believe that."

Adrian frowned, not liking how he sensed her words meant more than they appeared to on the surface. “Victoria, are you okay?”

She dropped her gaze and nodded. “I am now that I’m with you. I wished that I could make time stop and we could be here for as long as it takes to make everything okay again.”

Adrian didn’t admit to how much her words echoed the ones that repeated over and over again in the secret parts of his heart and soul. He’d always wanted to stop time for Victoria. He didn’t imagine that would ever really change for him.

“No crying,” he ordered gruffly while wiping her tears away with his thumbs. “It will ruin your appetite.”

Victoria let out a watery giggle. “Normally you’d be right. I’m so hungry though that I think I could still stuff my face even if I were crying a river.”

“I can’t have that, kitten. I want you happy while you’re stuffing your face.”

Only after her eyes dried up did Adrian leave her. Reluctantly. He was thankful he at least had the ingredients to make her a sandwich, but unfortunately he didn't have much else.

Victoria graciously accepted his offering with a sunny smile. Adrian, however, wasn't satisfied. With an eye on the clock, he mentally ran down the lists of what they should order for take-out.

She protested when he asked her if she wanted Thai, Chinese, or Italian. "This is enough, Adrian. Honest. Besides, it's not like I can't afford to drop a few pounds."

The frown he sent her was enough to kill the self-deprecating smirk on her face. "I'm not even going to dignify that with a response other than I love your curves and I won't have you badmouthing my tastes."

"Sorry."

"Sorry is right." Adrian took a seat and pulled her on his lap. Snuggling her close with one arm, he whispered in her ear, "Now which one tickles your fancy, kitten? I know these were your favorites once upon a time."

Victoria slid aside her half-eaten sandwich and peered at the menu. “Chinese.”

“Chinese it is. Do you still want the #9?”

Victoria swiveled her head and looked up at him. “You remembered?”

“Of course.” Adrian couldn’t resist dropping a kiss on her soft lips. “I haven’t forgotten a single thing about you.”

“Oh.”

He laughed, feeling happier than he remembered ever being—especially because he now understand all that he’d had when this darling woman had first crashed into his life.

“Adrian, do you mind ordering for me while I run to the restroom?”

Although he didn’t want to let go of her for even one second, Adrian kissed her shoulder and helped her down. “Don’t take forever.”

“I won’t.” Victoria took several steps before looking back. Adrian didn’t doubt that she’d felt his gaze on her. She blew him a little kiss and then walked out of the kitchen.

You’re getting wrapped up too fast.

He heard the warning but shrugged it off. What was the point of worrying? Victoria seemed just as crazy about him as he was about her, so her leaving would be a punishment to her too.

Adrian tried to believe his thoughts, but after making the call for their food, he found himself pacing the kitchen and watching the clock. When five minutes passed without her return, he began to get antsy. When another two minutes elapsed, Adrian poked his head out into the hallway.

Granted Victoria might need privacy, but the fear that maybe she'd decided to sneak out while he was tied up in the kitchen propelled him into action.

He checked the hallway bath and saw it was empty. He trusted she'd let familiarity dictate her actions and therefore she'd use the master bathroom. Adrian strode into his bedroom. His gaze zeroed in on the Victoria's rumpled clothes still where they'd left them.

Relief hit Adrian hard. He was about to leave the room when Victoria walked out of the bathroom with her phone in hand. She seemed to see him there.

Feeling uncomfortable that she'd think he was spying on her, when he really wasn't, Adrian shrugged and went for the blunt truth. "You were taking so long I got worried you snuck out."

Victoria shook her head. "Sorry. I was just on the phone with Kathy."

Adrian avoided her gaze, not wanting her to see the suspicion and hurt at the thought that she was talking to her lover back home. It was something he hadn't asked, hadn't been brave enough to ask actually.

It had been easier to freeze out the rest of the world and pretend tonight was all that mattered.

"You don't have to explain to me. It's none of my business who you were talking to." Adrian could hear how his voice sounded stiff and distant.

She rushed over to him. "No, it's true. See?" Victoria showed him the history. Although he tried not to look, the need for her words to be true demanded otherwise. Kathy's name was the last one dialed.

"Okay. I see." Adrian ran a hand through his hair, hating the jealousy and insecurity that driven him. "Are you, huh, upset with me for...you know?"

Victoria lunged towards him, wrapping her arms tightly around his waist. She buried her face against his chest and mumbled, "No. Never. I would've thought the same thing if it was the other way around."

Adrian wasted no time in lifting her up. She linked her arms around his neck and tightened her legs around his waist. "Kitten, I swear I'm going to end up having to put a bell on you until I get over this."

"I wouldn't mind that."

He kissed her sweetly on the mouth before murmuring, "Don't tempt me." His large hands squeezed her bare bottom. "We've got about thirty minutes before our food is delivered. Do you have an idea of what you'd like to do?"

Victoria smiled.

***

The morning sun barely streamed in through the windows when Victoria woke up. Attuned to her slightest movement, Adrian popped his tousled head. "What?"

Victoria loved hearing his sleep-roughened voice. She reached for his shadowed jaw and stroked it. "I should get up if I want to make it back in time."

Adrian groaned and plopped his head back down on the feather pillow. "Nope. Too early." Decree given, he tucked her next to him and promptly fell back asleep.

Victoria laid there for several minutes, hearing the soft sound of his breathing. From what she remembered, Adrian would've already been up and working out for almost an hour. Other than the very beginning of their relationship, he never slept in.

Now Victoria never did either. She looked at her wristwatch. Adriana was definitely up and already getting dressed for preschool by now. Sadness settled over her. She missed her daughter terribly and always did whenever they were apart for more than the workday. Lying in bed with Adriana's father made the ache worse.

As if he sensed her unhappy emotions, Adrian shifted and turned her on her side so he could wrap his arm around her waist and slide his leg between hers. Victoria relished the close contact.

Everything was going to change and maybe this would be the first and last morning she'd have with him. It would be an easy, selfish thing to pretend as she'd done all night that they could be the same people they once were.

But the truth stood before them, even if Adrian had no idea.

"Fine!"

Victoria startled. "What's wrong?"

"That's what I want to know. You keep squirming and won't lay still." Adrian yawned. "Okay, okay. Let's get up."

Already missing his arms around her, Victoria apologized and tried to get him to lie back down. "I'm sorry. You can go back to bed."

"It's too late, kitten. I'm up." Adrian twisted and kissed the top of her head before standing. "I'll be gentleman and go into the other room to take a shower."

Victoria got a perfect view of Adrian's perfectly muscled and naked backside. When he turned to the side she saw he was already hard. Victoria chewed her lip, hungering for him and all the wonderful things they could together in bed.

"Maybe I don't want you to be a gentleman."

"Maybe I don't either, but that's the way it's going to be." He laughed when Victoria couldn't quite hide her pout. "Oh, you're so cute. I should take a picture of this. Kitten, I'm leaving you so I don't make love to you for hours and end up making you late. I know how you can be about work."

Ridiculously pleased, she murmured, "Oh."

"Oh indeed." Adrian ruffled her hair and commanded, "Thank me for my kindness, kitten."

"Thank you, Adrian."

Pleased, he sauntered out of the room. Victoria was about to get out of bed and grab her phone when he poked his head back in. “You know, you can leave the door unlocked when you’re in the shower—just in case you don’t mind...you know.”

Victoria laughed. “Maybe I will, Mr. Hawthorne.”

“See that you do, Ms. Montford.”

Once she was free and clear to take her phone into the bathroom, Victoria quickly dialed home. Kathy picked up on the second ring. “Hey!”

“Hey, Kathy. How’s my girl? Is she up?”

“Right here ready to eat her sunshine pancakes. Hold on a minute, Victoria. Somebody wants to talk to you.” Kathy pulled away from the phone to address the high-pitched voice in the background saying over and over again, “Is that Mommy?”

Victoria leaned against the marble wall. Happiness melted over her as she waited for Adriana to get on the phone.

"Mommy?"

"Hi, baby pumpkin. How'd you sleep?"

"Good, Mommy. I miss you. How many sleep-agains until you come home?"

"One more, baby."

"I can't wait! Mommy?"

"Yes, baby?"

"Why are you talking so quiet?"

Guilt zinged Victoria. "I'm still a little tired."

"But it's time to be awake, Mommy. Dora is on."

"I know."

"Are you watching it?"

"No, but I knew you'd be watching. Is it good?"

Adriana quieted for a moment, gaze probably glued to the TV, before she sang, "I have to go now, Mommy. I have to eat and then get my pack-pack ready for school and the show's almost over."

Victoria smiled, wishing she could hug her little girl right then and there. "Okay, baby pumpkin. Have a good day at school, all right?"

"I will. You have a good day at your work con...conf..."

"Conference."

"Conference!"

"I will. Let me talk to Grammie, please."

"Okay! Bye, Mommy!"

"Bye, Adriana." Victoria then spent the next minute or so hearing about her daughter's upcoming day and Kathy's plans before getting off the phone. She'd been tempted to tell Kathy where she was, but when the opportunity didn't present itself Victoria chose not to push it.

She was due to fly back home tomorrow morning so there'd be plenty of time to share what she'd been up to with Kathy when she picked up Adriana after work. As much as it still surprised Victoria that she was here, Kathy probably wouldn't be surprised.

She knew and understood how much Victoria still loved Adrian. After all, Kathy still loved Victor Montford. So much so she hadn't even gone on one date in all the years Victoria's father had been gone. Strangely enough it was the loss of their men that had finally brought them close together, not as stepmother and stepdaughter, but woman to woman.

Kathy will probably be thrilled for us and be positive Adrian and I will be getting back together. If only I could be half as optimistic as her.

Victoria put her phone back in her purse. She quickly finished the first part of her bathroom routine, finding a spare, unopened toothbrush where Adrian usually kept them, and then darted in the shower before making sure to unlock the door.

Standing there under the wonderful water pressure, Victoria went over her limited options.

What's the best way to bring this up to him? Oh hey, by the way, no biggie but I had your baby and didn't tell you about it. We're cool, right?

That would obviously be the worst way. So what would be better?

The glass door opened up. Adrian stepped in, completely naked and more than ready to distract her from the increasingly unhappy thoughts crashing in her mind.

Victoria looked down at his already-sheathed shaft. “I see you’re prepared.”

Adrian’s hands slid greedily over her body. “Always.”

It was wildly erotic to feel the water falling over them while their bodies melded sweetly together. Victoria gasped his name into his mouth as she frantically came over and over again on his beautiful cock.

But what was even more beautiful was when Adrian groaned against her back, “Oh God! I fucking love you so much, Victoria! Only you. *Always* you.”

He held onto her as if he never wanted to let her go. Victoria closed her eyes and stood there for as long as he needed, but feeling that hope was all she could hold onto.

When Adrian cupped her face and kissed her, Victoria frantically traded promises with God.

Tonight. I'll tell him tonight after my workday is over. So please let me have one more day. Let me have that, okay?

Victoria did her best to go through the motions of a woman so thoroughly besotted that she had no room for other thoughts. But like a pebble in her luxurious shoe, her falseness rubbed incessantly.

She laughingly let Adrian tease her over height and even sat on the counter at his direction while she blow-dried her hair. Victoria asked for Adrian to bring in her purse and applied her makeup while he watched. She was normal. Innocent.

And lying for the last time.

Victoria went to the foot of Adrian's bed after he came out from his dressing room, looking rakishly handsome and perfect just as she remembered.

"Will I do?" Adrian asked with a wink and a smile.

"You're gorgeous as always." Victoria didn't need to straighten his black tie but she used the excuse to touch him.

"Kitten, the longer you stand there naked the more I'm going to assume you don't really want to go to your conference."

"What am I going to wear?" She picked up her dress from the floor. "It's hopelessly wrinkled and anyone who takes one look at me will know how I spent last night."

"Is that a problem?" Adrian asked with a naughty smirk on his face. His arms went around her waist and he tugged her to him.

Victoria was unable to resist feeling desire for Adrian even though they'd just made love in the shower. Cuddled against him, she was determined to get through the workday one last time before turning their world upside down.

Still, she murmured with longing, "I wish I didn't have to go back to the hotel. I wish I could stay here in bed with you all day."

"Why can't you?"

She groaned and dropped her head back. "I have Day Two of the conference and you have a busy day ahead of you too, I'm sure."

"So? We can play hooky, kitten. It'll be fun. You'll call off sick and so will I and to prove we're not complete liars, we'll stay in bed all day."

The word "liars" yanked Victoria out of the clouds and back to earth. Her clay feet returned and she feverishly thought of how she'd almost spilled to him the night before. Maybe it would've been better to get it over with than having a taste of happiness.

Although she'd been so close to telling him about Adriana over drinks last night, Victoria instead took the easy way out he'd provided.

Worse, she was grateful that Adrian seemed to have completely forgotten about the confession she'd been on the verge of giving just so she'd have more time with him.

"We haven't seen each other in four years. Let's enjoy our time together and save the confessions for later. What do you say?"

Later was going to come whether she liked it or not. Victoria knew that even with a workday postponement, she still couldn't figure out the right words to say to him tonight.

Adrian sensed her change in mood. He looked down at her with a frown. "What's wrong, kitten? You don't like the idea?"

She forced a smile to her lips. "I love the idea. Really. But, I can't miss out on the conference since it's what they sent me up here for." Victoria smoothed her hand across his chest. "Besides, knowing you'll be at work will help me concentrate on getting things done instead of dwelling on what I can't have."

The words were too close to the sadness always present in her heart. Not wanting Adrian to probe further, Victoria took a step back and asked, "Do you mind if I borrow an iron? I can probably knock out the worst of the wrinkles in no time. I just need to look presentable enough to get to my room."

Adrian's serious gaze studied her. He opened his mouth as if to challenge the forced gaiety in her tone. Instead, he shook his head slightly. “There’s no need.”

“Why not? I can try to look for it if you don’t know where it is. I’m pretty sure your housekeeper will have one tucked away somewhere.”

Adrian shook his head again. “Come with me.” He didn’t give her a chance to say anything before he took her hand and led her out in the hallway into a guestroom. Although it was clean and dust-free, Victoria’s intuition told her no one ever used this room.

Still not saying a word, Adrian led her to the other side of the room and opened up a door leading into a small walk-in closet. He reached in and turned on the light. “You can probably find something here.”

Victoria blinked in shock. It was all her clothes, grouped neatly by color and function. Even all her shoes were lined up on the wall rack by color and type. The room didn’t smell musty at all, as if it was regularly aired out or maybe that wasn't a problem when you lived in a multi-million dollar penthouse.

"Your jewelry is in the vault—if you want to wear any of it."

Adrian sounded a touch gruff, even embarrassed. Victoria turned to him, still amazed. "You kept it all?"

"Would it have been better if I threw it all away?"

He sounds defensive. Yep, he's definitely embarrassed.

"No. I'm just surprised. I would've thought you wouldn't want any reminders. I mean, you redecorated your whole place. I just assumed—"

"Yes, well, you do that a lot." Adrian walked past her and looked through her clothes until he found a charcoal pantsuit and pulled it out. "I know it's not fresh off the runway, but it's still stylish and should suffice until you get to your room."

Victoria gave the outfit little regard. Her attention was completely focused on the man holding it aloft. Adrian's shuttered gaze gave no indication to what was hiding in his thoughts, but Victoria knew.

She knew that gaze because it was the same one she showed the world every day. It was one that said she was strong and in control even when she was feeling the most vulnerable and scared.

“Thank you, Adrian.”

He shrugged. “It’s nothing.”

Victoria closed the distance between them. “No, you’re wrong. It’s everything. You saved my clothes for a reason.”

Fear streaked across his arresting features. He tried to cover it up with a lazy smile. “Maybe I did.”

“You never stopped hoping that I’d be back. You told me that last night and I was still scared to really believe you. I’m sorry, Adrian.”

He clenched his jaw and shoved the pantsuit back on the rack. Victoria took a step back, afraid that she’d offended him, and busily tried to come up with the right words to explain herself. Adrian stopped her with one hand.

"Do you believe me now?"

"Yes."

A large shudder wracked his frame. Adrian dropped his head back, his throat working crazily. "You understand what this means then?" When she didn't answer him fast enough, he snapped his attention back to Victoria. "Do you?"

"I do. I really, really do." She ran her fingertips down his clenched jaw. "You've always been so good to me. I wish I could've understood it then."

Adrian snatched her hand and kissed Victoria's palm with barely restrained fervor. "As long as you understand it now, then it doesn't matter." After he kissed her hand again, Adrian said, "I don't want this to be just one night and then we go our separate ways. I want to start over with you again. Will you see me again, kitten?"

Victoria's heart seemingly expanded with bittersweet joy. She wanted that more than anything else in the world. Being able to be with

Adrian again, every day and night, was like a dream come true.

You can't wait for tonight. You have to tell him now. He deserves to know.

She lifted her other hand and cupped Adrian's cheek while he waited for her answer. What would he do when she told him about Adriana? Would he understand or would it come too late like hers did?

What am I going to do if he hates me? How will I live with it after being back in his heart and living with his love?

Feeling the seconds ticking down, Victoria took courage and began with "Adrian, there's nothing more that I want than to start over with you. I've never stopped loving you and I love you more than ever."

The tension visibly seemed out of him. Unfortunately, Victoria put it right back when she said, "But first I want you to take me back to my hotel room. Can you do that for me?'

"Why?"

"I have something to show you."

***

The world as he'd built in less than a day disappeared from beneath his feet. Adrian sensed everything they'd experienced over the last twelve hours was about to be torn asunder. It was in the look in her eyes, the sadness that lingered like perfume. Victoria was afraid and had obviously surrendered to her secret.

No, I won't accept this.

"Tell me now."

Victoria shook her head. "I can't. I have to tell you there."

Adrian burned to yell his frustration. He felt himself shut down, to go back to his emotional default in face of Victoria's desertion.

"Please, Adrian. Just come with me."

He looked at her, gaze memorizing every inch of her face as if he hadn't remembered it a thousand times before.

"Fine. We leave in five minutes."

Adrian left her alone in the closet, unable to stand there another second all the while knowing instinctually that whatever it was she was going to show him was going to destroy their chances of going back to the way they were.

***

Victoria was glad that they were at her hotel room door. The ride over had been excruciating. Adrian refused to say a word to her and she was too jittery to try to make small talk. He gave the driver instructions to wait for them before escorting her inside.

Victoria shifted her purse and the bag containing Adriana's origami paper so she could slide the plastic card in and open the door. "Please come in."

Adrian's wary gaze took in the tiny room with one glance before stepping inside. Once she closed the door behind him he bit out, "What's so important you had to bring me here to tell me?"

She'd spent all so much of their time trying to come up with a way to tell him and now all she could was point to the small, utilitarian nightstand.

The picture sat in its silver frame. Victoria watched as Adrian walked to it. Perspiration dotted her forehead as the time for truth finally came upon her.

Nothing would ever be the same after this.

Although terror rattled inside her chest with each breath, Victoria couldn't deny the relief running through her. It was finally going to be over. She closed her eyes in prayer and hoped that Adrian would find a way to forgive her for her silence.

Adrian picked up the picture. His gaze focused on the shot of Adriana holding her kitten and smiling like Christmas had come early. His dark brows snapped into a deep frown. He turned to her and asked the one question that mattered above all others, "Who is this?"

Victoria clasped her hands and took a deep breath.

TWENTY

Victoria, who is this?" Adrian's hand tightened around the picture frame. "Tell me!"

She closed her eyes. Her skin paled, reminding Adrian of the white roses he once gave her in Paris.

"My daughter."

Adrian's breath appeared as a punch of air. She had a daughter? Victoria had borne someone's child?

Fine tremors raced through his body. Adrian couldn't stop the inferno of betrayal boiling in his gut. He knew it wasn't logical or even fair. He knew it, but that didn't stop him from feeling that Victoria had once again ripped his heart out.

Damn you, Victoria Montford. Damn you for doing this to me, for having this kind of power over me!

Adrian somehow managed to keep calm, but only by the slimmest of strings. “You have a child. I see. Now I know why you had to show me. I wouldn’t have believed it otherwise.” He carefully set the frame down on the bedside table. “It looks like you’re missing one.”

“Pardon?”

His lips quirked upwards at the prim word. “Your husband. His isn’t here. Unless, you hid him because you knew I’d make my way here. Oh wait. Maybe that’s the surprise. Well, go on. Tell me all about him.”

“Adrian, you’ve got it wrong.”

“Do I?” He ignored Victoria’s haunted expression. He leaned back against the wall and observed her through hooded lids. “Why don’t you tell me, in explicit detail please, exactly what I have wrong?”

“I’m not married.”

“No?”

“No.”

Adrian’s blood pounded through his veins in fierce relief. He’d never slept with a married woman. Adrian would’ve loathed himself to have taken part in adultery, but he would’ve loathed himself more to know it wouldn’t have taken much for Victoria to convince him to do it again.

“Are you divorced?”

“No. I’m a single mother and have been from the beginning.”

Now why did that bother him? Was it the idea that someone had abandoned her or that she’d never once come to him for help?

Idiot. Why would she do that? Victoria’s not a user and she’s definitely independent in everything she does.

“I didn’t expect that. I assumed you’d be the marrying kind.”

She shrugged. “No, it didn’t work out that way.”

“I’m happy to hear that. I know I shouldn’t be and that makes me ten kinds of a bastard for saying it, but it’s true.”

Victoria's fingers entwined at her waist. She lowered her gaze, but a shy smile eased the tenseness of her expression. "You are?"

Once again, Adrian was transported back to when he first met her. No matter how many years had passed she still seemed so innocent and shy, so much like the girl who'd easily captured his heart.

But that image wasn't real. It couldn't be. Victoria was a mother and no longer an innocent girl. Worse, she was a mother who'd failed to mention the existence of her daughter to him.

It could only mean that she had no expectation of seeing him again after today. No matter what she'd said to him just this morning.

"How old is she?"

Victoria's fingers tightened. The knuckles stood out in stark relief. Adrian frowned deeply. Why did that question worry her so much?

"She's three."

His agile mind did the math. A hateful sneer crossed his face before he could control it. Victoria hadn't wasted much time before replacing him with someone else. A someone else she cared enough about to have had his child.

You'll never learn, will you?

Adrian bitterly regretted indulging her wish for him to come to her hotel room. He should've refused her instead of giving into her wishes like a lovesick idiot.

Better yet, Adrian should've never found out where she was staying. He should've pretended that he hated her enough to never want to see her again, much less spend the whole night making love to her and thinking that maybe, just maybe, they'd had another chance to start over again.

Victoria's feelings for him had never been as strong as his for her. When was he going to learn that? How many times would he allow her to make a plaything of his heart?

Although his heart and pride were shredded beyond repair at the moment, Adrian managed to keep his thoughts steady.

It doesn't matter. She had every right to move on after their end.

Besides, hadn't he done the same in a twisted, impersonal sort of fashion?

"Congratulations, Victoria. She's beautiful and I'm sure you must be proud of her."

"I am. She's the best thing that has ever happened to me."

Her strained whisper barely made it to him. Adrian pushed off the wall. He needed to put as much distance as possible between them. Finding this out about her, he couldn't be the gentleman he needed to be. He hurt too damned much.

"Well, I've kept you long enough. I better leave you to your conference."

What else could he say? She had a life that permanently put him out of her sphere. She had a permanent bond with another man and a child as a result of it. While Adrian was many things, he wasn't the kind of man to disrespect someone else's family—even if he didn't know the first thing about being in one himself.

Goddamn her. Goddamn her for making me think that we could be more than just one night.

She has a life that doesn't belong to her or me anymore. She's a mother and she has to be there for her daughter.

I won't interfere or take her away from that responsibility.

He stalked across the small room, passing her body within inches. Adrian didn't even glance at her, afraid that if he did he would dishonor them both by losing control of his rage and calling her all kinds of names beginning with "bitch" and ending with "whore."

Adrian made it to the door when she called out in strangled panic. "Wait!"

Shameful relief netted him. Just knowing she wasn't ready to let him go eased the raw hurt a bit. He looked over his shoulder and wished he hadn't.

Victoria looked fragile, as if her entire heart had shattered at her feet and there was no way to ever fix it. Adrian clenched his jaw and bit back the words offering comfort.

"Yes?"

Victoria took a small step towards him. Her hand reached for him. “I…ah…I have something to tell you.”

He let out a sharp sigh and turned fully around. “Okay. Now what? What else could you possibly tell me now, Victoria?”

She stared at him, as if she didn’t know quite where to begin. If at all. Impatience edged his words. “Spit it out please. I really have to go.”

Adrian felt like the biggest jerk on the planet when her shoulders slumped. An apology balanced on his tongue, but he didn’t quite feel like a noble individual towards the woman who had so easily replaced him with another man and had his child.

He didn’t hate her daughter, never that, but the girl’s father—oh, yes. Adrian loathed him sight unseen. The fact that this bastard would let Victoria have his child and not step up to the responsibility of husband and father? He was absolute garbage in Adrian’s mind.

Victoria straightened up and looked him in the eye. “You didn’t ask me who the father is.”

“Frankly, I don’t want to know.”

“Well, I’m sorry but you need to know.”

“Why?” Adrian shook his head and abruptly stopped. Something akin to a sliver of wonder wrapped in disbelief slipped inside him. Why was this so important to her?

No, he had to be wrong.

“I do?”

His uncertain reaction seemed to fuel her. “Do you remember that I’m named for my father Victor?”

He jerked. It couldn’t be! Victoria couldn’t possibly...

“I carried on the tradition when I named my daughter Adriana.”

A dull roar filled his ears. He could barely make out the rest of her words.

“I named her after you. After her father.”

***

It was finally done.

She had told him.

All the years of silence, the days of watching their daughter grow and the guilt that she’d never even given Adrian a chance to be a part of it, could finally be put to rest.

God help her now.

***

"I'm her father."

"Yes." Victoria's hands fluttered before settling back down by her waist. "She's three years old and has your eyes. She's tall too, like you. She's my world and she's so beautiful, inside and out, and..."

"I have a daughter." Adrian looked about him, shocked and empty as the ramifications of what Victoria had done to him, to their little family, truly set in. "You're not joking with me?"

"I'd never joke about that, Adrian!"

He would've smiled at her indignation if the situation wasn't so serious. "There was never another man? There's no chance Adriana could someone else's?"

She colored slightly even as her features hardened. "No. We can do a DNA test if it would put your mind at ease."

He cut through the air with his hand. "She's mine? 100% no doubt about it."

"Yes. No doubts."

"So if I hadn't searched you out last night I wouldn't have known, would I? You would've never come looking for me. You would've gone back to North Carolina like nothing happened. Do I have that right?"

Kitten, don't let that be true. Please don't let that be true.

Victoria's lovely face blanched. The loss of color had the opposite effect on him.

Adrian saw red.

He exploded in the kind of rage a person felt all the way to their core. It shredded everything in its path. "You kept my child from me for three years? How the fuck could you do this to me?"

Victoria flinched. "Adrian, I'm sorry. I didn't mean for it to—"

"Shut. Up." Adrian took one step forward and she took one back. This continued until she bumped up against the wall and had nowhere else to go.

Her dark eyes, the ones that had had the power to make him believe in innocence and sweetness, filled with tears. Adrian had no mercy. He kept his voice razor-sharp even though it barely rose above a whisper.

"No, Victoria. You don't get a chance to talk, especially to say you're sorry. Sorry is for stepping on my shoe. Sorry is for spilling a drink on the floor. Sorry is even for running out on me when I needed you the most. Sorry is not the *goddamned* word to use for stealing my daughter from me."

Victoria's hand came up to her temple. It curled into a helpless fist. "I did what I thought was best for all of us. I know now I was wrong but, Adrian, I didn't know if you'd accept her. I couldn't take a chance that you'd—"

He couldn't hear the rest of her protests over the emotional agony rolling over him. Adrian wanted to destroy the room. He wanted to flip the desk on its side and rip the TV right off the wall.

All this time I had a child and I wasn't there to protect her. Anything could've happened to Adriana. Victoria could've died and then what would've happened to my daughter? Who would've taken care of her if not me?

Adrian put several feet between them. He watched as she collapsed against the wall. He raked a hand through his hair, shaken by the hatred pumping through him with every breath.

"Adrian, I never meant to hurt you. I really thought it was for the best. I didn't think you'd have room in your life for us, for her—especially after what you said to that blond woman that night."

He pinned Victoria with a look of disgust and fury. She immediately quieted, but her tears rolled down her face. He couldn't summon the slightest bit of pity for her quiet misery.

"I chased after you, Victoria. I stood there on that fucking sidewalk, hoping, waiting for you to tell me you'd come to see me. You lied to me, didn't you?"

She nodded and hiccupped. “I was going to tell you but then...” Victoria couldn’t finish.

Adrian let out yell. He knocked the chair over with one swipe of his hand. Why hadn’t he pressed her that night? Why the fuck did he let his feelings for her cloud his judgment? Why the hell had he let her walk away with his baby?

“How long did you know?” Adrian waited several tense seconds before barking the question again.

Victoria swallowed back her noisy tears. “Maybe about a month after we split up.”

“Maybe? Do better.”

“Three weeks.”

He cursed long and lewdly. “You’re telling me you knew about our baby three weeks after you left and it didn’t occur to you that I had a right to know?”

“I was wrong! Adrian, I swear to you—I didn’t plan on keeping her a secret.”

Adrian raked both hands through his hair. How could this be his life? How could the only woman he'd ever loved do something so hateful, so beneath contempt to him?

All the love he'd lived and breathed for Victoria mutated into something ugly and dangerous. Adrian walked into this room still believing in forever and was now going to leave it knowing that there was no such thing.

God, he regretted ever going down to the Sales floor that night. He should've just gotten a bottle of water. Yet, loving Victoria had resulted in the little angel staring at him from her place on the nightstand. How could he possibly regret that?

My little girl. She's mine and I don't know the first thing about her.

The stark truth of his thoughts staggered him. He'd missed everything about her. Being one of the first people to hold her, cutting her umbilical cord, changing her diapers, watching her take her first steps, hearing her first word.

Damn you!

"Who else knows about this?" he barked.

"Umm, my family."

"Who else? Did your roommates know?"

Victoria nodded miserably.

"Fuck!"

"They knew but they've never breathed a word about it."

"Obviously."

"We rarely talk now—just so you know. They're all off living their lives and well, we all sort of drifted apart."

Adrian stared her down for a long, mean minute. "I would've forgiven you anything, Victoria. All this time I've loved you and only you. And you did *this* to me. Keeping Adriana from me, never saying a word about our daughter, especially last night or even this morning when I was spilling my guts to you—to me that is unforgivable."

His words broke her into pieces. Victoria slapped a hand against her mouth and sobbed brokenly. "I wish I could take it back. I'd do anything to change it. I swear!"

Adrian's heart ached in a torturous concoction of pity, love, and loathing. Even now he wanted to take her in his arms and let her cry against his chest. A howl burned through his throat. After everything she'd done to him, Adrian still loved Victoria.

He loved her even as he hated her more than he'd ever hated anyone before.

Knowing this sickness about himself, Adrian wanted to hurt Victoria as much as she'd hurt him. And he knew exactly how to do it. Never had Adrian turned his ruthlessness towards Victoria, but she would feel it now in spades.

"Where is she?"

Victoria swallowed and then whispered, "At home with Kathy."

"That's why you called her last night?"

She nodded and bit her lip before saying, "I called her this morning too so I could talk to Adriana."

"When?"

"In the bathroom."

Adrian's rage skyrocketed. Even so, he had already thought through all the possibilities. There was only one way this was going to end.

He gave her a clipped nod and turned on his heel. Victoria played her part beautifully. She grabbed a hold of his arm before he reached the door. "Where are you going?"

"Where do you think?"

Victoria's voice became high-pitched and breathy. "Adrian, I can set things up so you can visit her. Maybe this weekend if that works for you?"

He glared at her until she released him. "You are no longer in charge here."

She faltered and then straightened her spine. "She's my daughter, Adrian. I won't let you take over."

"I am *not* asking for permission."

"What are you going to do, Adrian?"

"I'm going to get on a plane and go get my daughter."

Victoria's chest heaved, stronger and faster with each passing moment. Idly, he wondered if she was on the verge of hyperventilating.

"You can't just do that."

"Watch me."

"No! You don't have legal right, Adrian. I am the only parent she's had—"

"If I were you I wouldn't remind me of that fact. I would've been there for her, for both of you if you'd only given me half a chance. Now, I can have a team of lawyers on my side within five minutes and I won't run out of money in this lifetime. Can you say the same?"

Obvious anger tightened her mouth but terror stamped itself across her lying, beautiful features. "You know I don't. Damn you, Adrian. Don't do this."

"That's right, Victoria. I am damned. I was the damned the night you left with my child in your womb." A mirthless smile crossed his lips. "Now I'm off to catch a plane. I suggest you pack."

Pitiful hope stirred in her haunted expression. "You're taking me with you?"

"Of course, I am. I may hate you, Victoria, but I'm not a monster. Our daughter will not want to come with me if you're not there. I don't want her unhappy even if it makes me miserable.

If putting up with you is the price I have to pay to be a father to her then I'll pay it."

Victoria's small gasp reached him. "Adrian, it doesn't have to be that way. I meant every word I said to you last night and this morning. I love you."

"Pack." He lifted his arm and checked his watch. He couldn't let the words mean anything to him. "I'll give you five minutes. Anything you don't have packed by then will just have to be left behind. Go."

She stared at him for several seconds before spinning around. Victoria pulled out her phone and spoke in low tones to what he assumed was her supervisor.

"Brenda, it's Victoria. Yesterday went well, but the reason why I'm calling is that I have to get back home now. It's a family emergency. Yes. Yes. Thank you so much for your understanding. Bye."

Adrian watched as she then hurriedly rushed into the bathroom and came back out almost immediately with toiletries in her arms. Her docility should've pleased him and it did. Perversely, it also infuriated him as well.

It wasn't supposed to be this way. We weren't supposed to end up like this.

The ice around Adrian's heart hardened. This was why he'd never bothered with love before. Look at what it had done to him—he'd fallen for a girl who could rip his heart to shreds and simply move on as if nothing important had happened. This was a woman who could become pregnant with a man's child and keep it a secret from him.

The memories of their long night before raced through his brain. Not once while Victoria was nestled in his arms did she bother to breathe word of Adriana's existence.

Her kisses marked him for a fool and her words of love destroyed any chance between them. There was no way she could love him and do something this vile.

"Hurry up."

Victoria reacted to his icy command by doubling her speed. Within a minute she stood there with a laptop bag slung over her shoulder, her carryon by her side, and the store bag she'd carried the night before.

Adrian zeroed in on it. "Is that for her?"

Victoria clutched it closer, as if worried he'd take it away. "Yes. Adriana likes to make collages."

He nodded as if he knew exactly what she meant. The knowledge that he didn't know the slightest thing about his daughter infuriated him further.

"Take me there."

"Pardon?"

He bit off the words. "The store where you got the paper. We're going there so I can get her a gift as well."

Victoria nodded, brow furrowed as if trying to make sense of his demand. "Oh, okay. Sure."

Adrian turned on his heel and opened the door. As much as he would've loved letting it slam in Victoria's face, he found he couldn't completely abandon his manners. Even for her.

Adrian held the door open and waited impatiently for Victoria to walk past him. Her gaze met his before darting away. The expression was so much like the one that charmed him at the beginning. Except back then, Adrian's kitten had never been afraid of him and what he could do.

Adrian could practically scent her fear. It made him clench in disgust. It truly wasn't supposed to be like this.

He shut the door with far more force than it needed. He ignored her slight jump. Adrian walked by her, taking the carryon out of her hand without a word, and headed for the elevators.

The ride down was tense but thankfully brief. Adrian almost snarled her name when she left his side and walked over to the front desk to settle her bill. His steps weren't far behind. He reached into his coat and pulled out his wallet. Sliding the card across the counter, Adrian immediately silenced Victoria's soft protests with an icy glare. Color instantly washed her face at his highhandedness, but Adrian couldn't have cared less.

He was done with being a nice guy. Adrian was going to be taking care of her and Adriana from this moment on and she better damned well get used to it!

Once settled in his limo, Adrian engaged the tinted glass divider. Although he kept his voice soft and with the illusion of calmness, he couldn't control the razor edge dangerously scoring each of his words.

"I refuse to be a weekend parent, Victoria. I want my daughter living here in the city with me."

Adrian was primed and willing for her to argue with him. He needed to take his aggression out and the only target he wanted was her.

She deserves this.

Victoria clasped her hands in her lap. "I understand. I hope you understand that it's going to take time. I'll need to find a job first and then I'll need to give my current employer notice.

I then need to find a place to live, which might take...well, you know, some time."

Adrian smiled cruelly. He slashed his hand through the air. "You're failing to understand me. Let me make this clear. I want my daughter living with me. As in *my place*. You both will be living with me starting today."

Victoria's face paled to a sickly hue. She looked like she was about to cry. "Adrian, we can't live together. Not yet. Maybe not at all. We just saw each other again last night..."

Her voice trailed off, undoubtedly due to the same memories he had of burying his shaft deep inside her, over and over again. Adrian experienced a potent mix of lust and wrath. He hardened immediately and hated her for it.

"So? We moved in together the first time after one night. We have more cause to do it now."

"But you hate me."

He smirked. "Yes, I do. What difference does that make? Do you honestly think we'll be the first or the last couple come together for the sake of their child? Welcome to the story of my childhood."

"You never spoke about your childhood."

"Precisely. And I really should thank you for giving me yet another reason to avoid seeing my parents. I'm sure my mother is going to simply *love* knowing her first grandchild was born out of wedlock and that neither of us even knew about her existence."

She brushed away a tear. Adrian had the frustrating urge to kiss them away for her.

"I'm sorry for making things harder for you and your parents. I didn't want to force you into marriage, Adrian, because I knew how much it didn't fit into your plans."

"Don't try to turn it around on me, Victoria. I would've married you regardless."

"I know! I didn't want Adriana growing up in a house where her parents were forced to be married because of her."

"Yes, you'd much rather her grow up illegitimate and shut out of an inheritance that rightfully belongs to her instead."

"Money can't be the answer to this," she argued. Her words warbled out pitifully. "Money isn't everything."

"I agree. If it was I would've never even looked at you, much less tried to give you the world."

Victoria flinched as if he'd slapped her. "That's incredibly cruel, Adrian."

"Is it? Too bad. Kindness got me robbed of my daughter for all three years of her life. You took my kindness for weakness, Victoria. I won't make the same mistake again."

"How do you think it will make her feel to see her father treat her mother like this?"

She couldn't have played into his plans better than this. Adrian reached for her small hand. He raised it to his mouth and kissed the back of it with a gentle smile. Desire sparked in her eyes even as she gazed at him hopefully.

"I'll never show Adriana how much I despise her mother. I'll treat you with affection and respect during the day, especially in front of her.

And just in case you mistake it for something else, it's called acting, Victoria."

She tried to pull her hand away. Adrian tightened his fingers until she stopped. Victoria's mouth trembled. Her voice came out in a raw, hoarse whisper. "I understand why you're so angry, but I can't take it if you're this cruel."

"Angry? We're long past angry, Victoria. What I feel right now is something entirely foreign to me. There's simply no word for it."

"Then how can you expect us to live together if you feel this way towards me?"

Bitter poison pumped into his brain. He took immense pleasure in saying his next words.

"We're not just going to live together, Victoria. We're going to get married."

***

Victoria's stomach knotted. "You're joking!"

His mouth thinned. "What part of me do you think is in a humorous mood?"

She'd never seen this biting side of Adrian and hated it, but not nearly as much as she hated knowing he despised her. The worst part of it was Victoria knew she deserved it.

If penance was needed then Victoria would pay it. She'd pay it without complaint but this was something she just couldn't see herself being able to survive.

Married to a man who hated her? How could he even imagine this was a possibility?

Be calm. Don't let your emotions spin out of control. No matter how much this is killing you, you know Adrian isn't this kind of man. He's just hurting badly right now. You have to remember this for Adriana and for Adrian.

Victoria had to have faith that the ugliness of today would fade. They couldn't make any permanent decisions that might end up prolonging their suffering.

She tried again. "Adrian, let's be reasonable. You can't expect me to agree to this."

"I can and I will." He looked away from her as if dismissing her from his thoughts completely.

Tears filled her eyes again. She stared out the window while desperately trying to control herself. Victoria knew Adrian's reaction would be bad, and that he'd probably hate her, but never did she imagine it to be like this. Naively, she hadn't even been able to begin to imagine what Adrian's hate would really feel like.

"I'm going to want get this done as quickly as possible. I'll have my lawyers draw up the papers and have them ready to sign by tomorrow. The license won't be much longer than that. We'll be married by the close of business tomorrow."

"Papers?"

"Papers, Victoria. The prenuptial agreement in particular."

"I'm not going to sign anything without representation, Adrian."

He raised a brow. "So be it. As long as you realize that by the end of the business day you will either sign those papers or you will be saying goodbye to Adriana."

Victoria's gut felt like it had been kicked. "You just said you wouldn't separate us."

"I said I'd prefer not to do it, but if you force my hand, Victoria, I will. I will make sure that not a court in the land will give you visitation rights much less custody."

An inarticulate cry of despair erupted from her throat. Victoria lunged at him, fingers curled into talons, as she screamed, "I won't let you take her away from me, Adrian! I'll kill you first!"

He simply grabbed her wrists and pinned them behind her back. Adrian then had the audacity to laugh in her face. "Ah, kitten. I always wondered if there was a temper lurking in there behind all that sweetness. Too bad I didn't see the truth about you earlier."

Victoria bucked against him until she realized he wasn't letting her go. Glaring at him, she swore, "I'm serious, Adrian. You're not going to take my daughter away from me."

The mocking smile died from his beautiful face. "Then sign the damned papers, Victoria. Sign them and be prepared to marry me."

"Why marriage? We don't need to be married to raise our daughter together!"

"You've dictated the terms of our lives the last four years. Now it's my turn." Adrian's gaze darkened as he stared at her mouth. "Just be glad I still want to keep you after what you've done."

Victoria's rage transformed into something else. Her breathing grew choppy as she fixated on his mouth as well. "You still want me?"

"Do I still want you? Does this answer it for you?" Adrian kissed her hard. His tongue clashed with hers and Victoria sank against him, feeling boneless and weaker with each pull of his lips. He let go of her wrists and sank his fingers into her hair. Victoria's rage seeped away and soon she slid her arms around his neck.

When they parted for air, Victoria desperately whispered against his lips, "Adrian, we can fix this. Please let me fix this."

He blinked as if he'd forgotten exactly why he was so furious with her. Memory apparently came back because he pushed her away violently and bit out, "Can you undo the last four years?"

When she remained silent, Adrian snarled, “What’s wrong, kitten? Cat got your tongue?”

Wounded and wanting to lash out, Victoria deliberately wiped the back of her hand against her bruised lips. Adrian’s gaze narrowed. He yanked the same hand and pushed it crudely against his cock.

“What? You don’t like my kisses anymore, Victoria? Is this better, kitten?”

Victoria squeezed him once, unable to keep herself from responding sexually. “You’re better than this, Adrian.” She waited, stretched thin as he considered her.

Adrian abruptly let go of Victoria. He busied himself with straightening out his tie and coat, shutting her out completely.

Still, Victoria trusted that somehow, someway her words had reached him this time and maybe, just maybe, he would continue to hear her.

TWENTY-ONE

They spent the ride in his private jet in complete silence. Adrian focused on his work, effectively cutting Victoria out. If only his mind was as easy to appease. His gaze flicked to her, seeing her pale face and wondering at the thoughts surely slithering about her devious mind.

Even though it had been hours since she delivered her bombshell, Adrian still couldn't believe that Victoria had kept their child a secret from him. No matter how he many times he replayed her words, and ran them front, back, and sideways, Adrian still couldn't wrap his mind around her betrayal.

Just remembering her words of love from just this morning made him sick with fury.

How can someone say those words while knowing she's keeping this kind of secret?

No matter what Victoria said then, it still couldn't justify her lying to him by omission.

Adrian looked out the small window, seeing the clouds and blue skies. It was such a beautiful day. No one could think that there was a world of suffering below when so high in the sky. It just went to show the ugliness hiding behind beautiful illusions.

Beautiful like Victoria.

He clenched his jaw and forced the spiteful words to remain behind his teeth. They were going to be landing soon and now wasn't the time to allow his blood to remain high. If Adrian was going to start things off on the right foot with his little girl, he needed to get control of his volatile emotions.

Adrian remembered the picture of Adriana and was struck anew by how much she looked like him and her mother. Bitterness seeped in as he was once again reminded of all that he missed. Never would he have the opportunity to hold her as a newborn or witness her milestones. He'd lost so much time with his daughter and it was all because of Victoria Montford.

God, it wasn't right what she'd done! Her silence was unacceptable to him and Adrian wouldn't stand for it a second longer.

"I want a copy of all the pictures you have of Adriana."

Victoria startled at his abrupt demand. Her dark liquid gaze met his before jumping away. "Sure."

Hardly satisfied with her one word answer, Adrian prodded, "I'm surprised you're so accommodating."

She shifted in her seat. He watched as her hands tightened around the armrests. "Have I shown you otherwise since this morning?"

Mulishly, Adrian didn't like her seeming calm. He wanted her to feel as disturbed as he did. "I assume guilt has that power."

She bit her lip. "Your assumption is right. I've felt guilty about it since the night I last saw you on the sidewalk. I don't know if I'll ever stop feeling guilty."

"Good."

Victoria opened her mouth, closed it, and then dragged in a ragged breath. "I wish you could see it from my point of view, Adrian."

"I tried. Your point of view was unbelievably flawed."

"Hindsight is 20/20."

"Maybe so, but I challenge you to do the same thing for me, Victoria. See it from my point of view and tell me you'd be kind and gentle."

She finally looked at him. "I am. Why else do you think I'm letting you talk to me like this?"

Adrian closed his laptop. He had nothing further to say.

***

Victoria's stomach seemed to jump in her throat the closer they got to her childhood home. She had called Kathy after they landed, but with Adrian hovering close, Victoria had only felt comfortable enough to sketch out the bare details. She didn't doubt, however, that Kathy was probably a ball of nerves as well.

The entire ride there was a cold kind of hell. A sleek foreign sedan was waiting for them at the tarmac. Adrian chose to drive them himself. After settling Victoria in the car, he simply asked for her address and then set it into the navigation system, ensuring their communication would be kept at a minimum.

Every mile seemed like a lost opportunity to say something that could possibly repair their situation. Courage failed her each time she looked at his closed, set expression.

When they pulled up into the driveway Victoria finally turned to him and said, "I need you to let me handle this, Adrian. My daughter...our daughter...has no idea about you."

"And whose fault is that?"

"I realize that!" Victoria drew in a deep breath, fighting to calm herself and modulate her voice. "Adrian, you can't just barge your way in and force your way into her life."

Adrian's jaw tightened. His brows dropped into a glower. "Are you suggesting that we lie about who I am until a time that *you* suffice is right to tell the truth?"

"No, that's not what I'm saying." Victoria's hand hovered in indecision before she dared to touch his. She more than half expected for him to snatch it away. When he didn't, Victoria took heart in the gesture. "I'm going to tell her. Today. I'm just asking that you let me do it my way."

Adrian looked away and focused his attention on the house. He sat there for several lengthy moments before finally agreeing.

"All right. We'll do it your way." The stare he turned in her direction was void of warmth and caring. "If you're lying to me or trying to trick me, Victoria, then I promise you this will be the last time I give your thoughts and feelings any consideration. Do you understand?"

Although the threat wounded, Victoria was grateful that Adrian was still willing to take a chance on her. Especially one as big as this. "Yes.

I understand." She then unbuckled her seatbelt. "Are you ready?"

Adrian stared at her wordlessly. Victoria imagined he was trying to see if she was telling the truth.

I better get used to this if I ever plan on earning back his trust.

Adrian finally said, "Let's go." They both got out of the car and walked up the short sidewalk and onto the covered porch. Victoria always thought the pale blue Victorian farmhouse-style home was adorable. Now she wondered what it looked like from Adrian's point of view.

It must seem incredibly tiny to a billionaire used to living in some of the most expensive real estate in the world.

Victoria knew if she gave herself more than a second to think about what was going to happen next, she'd probably chicken out. So she opened up the front door and called out for her stepmother.

"Kathy! We're here!"

The older woman immediately came around the corner while wiping her hands on a towel. Her thin smile and wary gaze echoed Victoria's.

"Hello, Adrian. I hope your flight was smooth."

Victoria worried if Adrian's animosity would extend to her family. If he felt any he was able to mask it immaculately. He was all grace and civility when he answered, "It was smooth. Thank you so much for asking. I hope you and your girls have been doing well since I last saw you."

Kathy's smile became more genuine. She must've taken Adrian's politeness as an indication of his current state of mind. "Yes. They've been growing like weeds."

"I'm glad to hear of it."

Although Adrian seemed relaxed, Victoria sensed his impatience. His gaze traveled around the living room, foyer, and staircase, obviously searching for their daughter. Adriana would've run to her already if she was awake and in the den.

Victoria asked for his sake, “Is she napping?”

“She just went to sleep about an hour ago. I can get her up if you want.”

“Ah, no. I’ll…I mean…we’ll go to her room.”

Kathy’s gaze bounced between the two of them once. “Oh, okay. Can I offer you a drink first, Adrian?”

He smiled and declined.

“We’ll just be in her room then.” Victoria headed for the stairs. Adrian was right on her heels. The moment was upon them and Victoria wondered what he would do next.

She stopped right when they reached the door to Adriana’s playroom. It used to be her room once upon a time.

“What’s wrong?”

The terse whisper did little to put Victoria at ease. “I just want to warn you that it’s better if we don’t wake her up before she’s ready. Adriana is a little fussy after her nap. I mean, she’s usually very sweet all the time except when it comes to her sleep.”

“Why are you telling me this?”

She dared to look at him. "I just don't want you to judge her badly if your first experience with Adriana isn't..." Victoria's voice trailed off as she struggled to find the right words.

Adrian's face lost its hard expression for the first time alone with her since he picked up Adriana's picture that morning. "Victoria, that little girl is my daughter. There is nothing she can do that can make me not love her."

"You really mean that?"

"Of course. I already love her. I've loved her since I first heard she was mine."

Happiness lit Victoria from within. Her shoulders lost most of their tension. "I'm so glad to hear that, Adrian. You have no idea how much your words mean to me."

Adrian cleared his throat. "Well, you're welcome. I guess."

Victoria resisted the urge to throw her arms around him in a huge hug. Adrian may have thawed a tiny bit, but now was not the time to push his goodwill.

"Are you ready?"

"Absolutely."

Victoria opened the door and stepped in. Her voice dropped to a whisper when she spotted the canopied twin bed. "There she is."

***

Adrian wasn't sure if the world had stopped spinning or not. All he knew was that time had ground to a halt. He'd already taken the room in with one glance. White walls adorned with pink and turquoise stripes and gold polka dots pronounced the room as belonging to a little girl who was especially loved and adored. Artwork hung low on the walls, clipped to a string that surrounded three sides.

There was also a tiny stove in the corner and padded rocking horse adorned with a jeweled horn decorated with glittery stickers. Adrian noted a pile of tulle skirts in a large, woven basket along with a table strewn with colorful bits of paper, yarn, and glue.

But what drew his attention most of all was the small, dark head barely peeping over the top of a fuchsia comforter. It was his daughter. His and Victoria's.

Adrian found his feet seemed to be stuck to the floor. He couldn't take a step forward even though he wanted to more than anything in the world. Victoria left his side.

"Where are you going?"

She didn't answer his terse whisper. She simply picked up two little chairs and placed them by the bed. Adrian looked at them and then her. "You seriously don't expect me to sit in that, do you? I'll break it the moment I sit on it."

She smiled, genuine and carefree for the first time since they left his penthouse. The memories crowded him. He tried his best to push them away.

"They're very sturdy. I promise."

Adrian went over to it and gingerly sat down on the edge, ready at the first creak to stand up. The hard plastic held firm.

"I do this a lot," she confided in a low whisper after she sat down.

"What?"

"Watch her." Victoria leaned forward and stroked their daughter's back. "I didn't know I could love anybody more than you until I had her."

Emotion caught in his throat. Regret, sadness, and bitterness all vied to be the reigning feeling. Adrian swallowed them down. It would be obscene to voice anything ugly here in this room.

"I would've liked to have been there. I would've liked to have seen her born."

"Me too." She looked over at him for too-brief a moment. "I mean it when I say I really wish I could've done it all so differently, Adrian. It's a regret I'll carry for the rest of my life."

Adrian didn't care for the sympathetic flicker he felt for Victoria. He especially didn't care for the urge he had to hug her to him and tell her it was going to be okay. Instead, he held onto his resentment like an emotional miser.

"I don't even know her birthday."

"Adriana was born at 5:12pm on February 12. I have pictures and video…although you probably won't want a copy of that."

"I do. I want everything you have."

"Okay. I can get them for you."

"Good." Adrian kept himself from saying "Make it soon!" when he caught the silver track running down her cheek. He clenched his jaw tightly.

I have nothing to feel guilty for. Victoria brought this all on herself. If she hadn't lied to me for four years, none of this would be happening.

Victoria wiped her eyes and sniffled before regaining her composure. She didn't turn to him for comfort and he perversely hated it. His fingers itched to touch her. Adrian curled his hand into a fist before relaxing it.

She made her choices and I've made mine. Now we'll both have to live with them.

Separated by the wrongs of the past, but forever connected because of the sleeping girl, they continued to sit there, wrapped in their own thoughts, when the little bundle suddenly turned on her side and opened her eyes.

"Mommy!"

Adrian watched, transfixed, as Victoria changed right before him. Her lovely face broke into a wide, gentle smile as she stood up and crooned, "Hi, baby pumpkin."

"Hi, Mommy! You and Grammie said you'd be home in one more sleep-again. It's not the nighttime sleep-again."

"I got back early."

Adriana sprang to her feet and launched herself into Victoria's arms. "Mommy, I missed you. I drew you a picture. Do want to see?" She wiggled to get down and took one step to her table before freezing.

Adrian's heart squeezed when he looked into his daughter's eyes. Eyes that were identical his, including the long thick lashes. She had on a purple t-shirt with a fluffy, pink rabbit on it and a pair of sunshine-yellow leggings. Adriana was adorable and his.

He wanted to pick her up and hug her forever. Instead, he had to stand there and watch while she sidled away and took safety behind Victoria's legs.

"Mommy?"

Victoria reached down and put her arm around Adriana. "It's okay, pumpkin. This is someone Mommy used to know a long time ago."

Her answer seemed to put Adriana at ease. "Before I was a baby?"

"Yes. Before you were a baby."

Adrian kept still, helpless but to trust a woman who'd shown herself untrustworthy. Watching their easy and familiar interaction, he was glad Victoria was here to smooth the way. He hadn't the faintest idea of how to talk to small children.

But I'll learn.

"Why's he here, Mommy?"

"Because he wanted to meet you."

Adriana peeked around her mother's leg again. Her whisper easily carried to him. "But, Mommy, *who* is he?"

Adrian looked up towards Victoria. Her gaze asked him to stay his peace and wait. Before seeing and hearing the beautiful little angel their love had produced, Adrian might've seized control and dictated the terms of Victoria's surrender.

Now he knew without a doubt there was no way he'd risk hurting Adriana. His pride wasn't worth it. So he would wait and follow Victoria's lead. No matter what. Even if that meant delaying the news. Even if that meant temporarily setting aside his plans for vengeance against Victoria.

But I definitely won't let her know that.

Victoria picked up their daughter and sat down on the bed, keeping Adriana nestled in her arms. She smiled and began.

"Remember how we talked about families before? How people can have different families with one mommy, or one daddy, or a mommy and a daddy, or a mommy and a mommy—"

"Or a daddy and a daddy?"

"That's right. Do you remember what I told you about *your* daddy?"

Adriana's small brow furrowed. "You said he lived in a big, big city and was *very* busy working."

"That's right."

Adrian's heart took on deep, nerve-wracking thumps. Until this moment he never imagined that Adriana would've wondered about him, much less asked. For her to think even for one second that he'd been too busy to bother himself with her...

Anger at Victoria spiked dangerously high again.

"Well, baby, I saw your daddy on my trip and told him all about you."

"You did?" Adriana's grinned and leaned forward excitedly. "Did you tell him about my school and when we went on the train and the flippies I learned to do at karate?"

Victoria shook her head. "I didn't tell him those parts."

"Why not?"

"I saved it so you could tell him."

Adriana scooted closer and bounced in visible excitement. "I can tell him? I can see my daddy?"

"Yes, baby. You can tell him."

"When?"

Victoria looked at him meaningfully. Adrian's hands dampened. He swallowed, and nodded.

"How about today?" When their daughter nodded and squealed in excitement, Victoria smiled. "Good. Now let me tell you about my friend here. He's your friend too."

"He is?" Adriana peeked at Adrian, shy but curious. "But I don't know him, Mommy."

Once again, Adrian felt disbelief crowd his soul over the injustice Victoria's silence had created for them both. For Adriana to ever say those words about him, about her own father made Adrian want to cry.

As if she could sense his volatile emotions, Victoria inhaled quickly and plunged ahead.

"He's your friend too, baby, because he's your daddy."

Adriana's rosebud mouth opened. Her tiny rush of air somehow managed to fill the room.

"That's my daddy?"

Victoria's gentle voice warbled. "Yes, baby pumpkin. That's your daddy and he's flown on an airplane all this way to see you."

Adriana's smile of delight and awe faded. She looked up at her mother in worry. "Why are you crying, Mommy?"

Adrian didn't like the uncertainty on her tiny face. It made him feel even more determined that in order to keep his daughter happy, he had to keep her mother happy as well. Adrian didn't know exactly how to do that when he was still so blisteringly mad at Victoria.

But solving impossible problems is what I do best. I will solve this one too.

Victoria hugged their daughter tightly. "I'm just so happy that you can see your daddy."

Adriana squeezed her back and then asked in another loud whisper, "Can I talk to him now, Mommy? Is it okay?"

"Sure!"

Adrian stared down at their sweet girl with bated breath. This was the moment he'd been waiting for as soon as he learned of her existence.

The first words we're about to speak are extremely important. What should I say and how should I say it? Should I smile and just let her talk to me or should I start the conversation? I don't know the answer. I don't know how to talk to my own child.

Damn you, Victoria, for doing this to us both.

Adriana wiggled off Victoria's lap and scooted until she was at the edge of the bed. She looked at Adrian intently, seemingly studying his face before she said, "My name is Adriana Montford. What's yours?"

***

Victoria saw the flash of pain go through Adrian's eyes before he lowered his gaze. She winced, knowing this was just one of a thousand reminders they'd face because of her deception.

Adrian instantly covered his emotions with a beaming smile. "It's very nice to meet you, Miss Adriana Montford. My name is Adrian Hawthorne."

"That sounds like mine!"

"Did your mommy ever tell you she named you after me?"

"I think so...yes! She did. I forgot." Adriana giggled and leaned forward, her hands on her legs. "Do you like kitties?"

Adrian's gaze flicked over to Victoria before coming back to their little girl. "I love kitties."

Victoria's happiness ridiculously shot up. She wanted to believe Adrian was telling her he'd still find a way to love her after all.

Things will get better between us. Adrian won't stay mad at me forever. I have to believe that or I won't be able to make it.

"Me too! I have a kitty. I love kitties and baby dogs. I like birdies too. I saw a turtle once at the zoo. He was big and he didn't move too much, but he opened his mouth big like this." Adriana demonstrated, showing all her tiny teeth. "I liked him a lot. I want a big turtle like that. Do you have a big turtle?"

Adrian shook his head with a faint smile. "No, I don't."

"That's okay. Maybe you can have one too when I get one."

"When are you going to get one?"

"Mommy says I can have one when I grow up."

"She did?"

"Yep."

Adrian stared at her for a few seconds and Victoria could see the expression of overwhelming love in his eyes. "I have a present for you."

"You do?"

He handed the paper bag to her by the handles. “Your mommy told me you liked things like this.”

Adriana took it from him, breathless with excitement as she peeked in the bag. She let out a happy cry and turned to Victoria to chirp, “My Daddy got me pretty paper, Mommy! See?”

Victoria dutifully leaned forward and looked in the bag. “I see that! It’s very pretty.”

“Your mommy got you some too, Adriana.”

She whirled back to him. “She did? Mommy you did?”

Victoria cast Adrian a grateful glance that he’d included her too. He didn’t return her gaze. Instead, he kept his attention on Adriana. “Yes, baby, I did.”

“Can I see, Mommy?”

Victoria picked up the bag by her feet and handed it to her daughter. She listened with amusement as Adriana crowed in triumph and then began regaling them both about her grand collage plans with “Mommy and Daddy’s best and most beautiful paper.”

Adrian didn't tune her out. He sat there rapt with attention, hanging onto every word coming out their daughter's mouth. Victoria's personal grief eased back and gratefulness took the forefront.

He loves her like he said he did. No matter what happens between me and Adrian, I at least have that much to be grateful for.

Adriana abruptly stopped talking and went shy. "Can I ask you a question?"

"Anything."

"Do you have any other babies like me?"

Victoria winced at the stricken look he couldn't quite manage to hide. "No, Adriana. I don't have any other babies. You're my only little girl."

She laughed. "Good!" Adriana turned to Victoria and said in a sing-song voice, "Mommy says she's never going to have another baby but me. Maybe Daddy can have a baby sister for me so I can have one like Tracy at school."

Victoria smiled, doing her best to tamp down the spurt of pain she felt at the idea of Adrian having children with someone else. “Only mommies can have babies, pumpkin.” She chanced looking over at Adrian, expecting his expression to be as indulgent as hers. The raw hunger in his gaze consumed her on the spot.

Her mouth grew dry and her heart hammered in her chest. Victoria had to stop herself from visibly reacting, but still somehow Adrian saw his effect on her. His gaze turned calculating, as if she was a problem to solve and he’d just found the solution.

What’s he thinking about right now to make him look like that?

Victoria was almost afraid to find out.

Almost.

TWENTY-TWO

Adrian closed the door to Adriana's room and then carefully opened it again to make sure she was still asleep. Her soft steady breathing met his ears. Smiling, he made his way down the narrow hall and into the living room where Victoria awaited.

He glanced at his watch and saw it was barely past eight, but he already felt a tinge of exhaustion. Adriana hadn't taken long to warm to him and had kept him on the go. She'd shown him her playroom at Kathy's house and then insisted on sharing her lunch with him. Adrian hadn't had a peanut butter and jelly sandwich in years, but he liked it. Especially with the crust cut off.

Later Adriana made a place for him on the couch so they could watch a Disney DVD. She'd then taken him into the backyard and shown him how to draw pictures on the patio with sidewalk chalk. When he'd drawn a turtle, Adriana crowed in delight and dragged Victoria over to show her his masterpiece.

The tips of Adrian's ears warmed when she'd cooed over it. Although it had obviously been for the benefit of their girl, he'd still responded to it by wanting to kiss Victoria silly.

Those were traitorous thoughts considering he was prepared to go to war with her the next day if she didn't give into him tonight.

Eventually, the three of them took leave of Kathy's house, staying just in time to see Victoria's half-sisters before saying goodbye. Adrian had been taken aback by how big the girls were. He wondered if Adriana would grow nearly as fast and heartily hoped not. He wasn't ready to lose the little girl just yet. Preteen years could take a rain check.

Adrian found himself charmed by Victoria's home when they pulled up to the driveway. Although small, it was adorable—much like her—with its white picket fence, colorful garden, and cheerful turquoise door.

Adriana had been ecstatic to show him her cat first and then her house. She'd tugged him by the hand and shown him everything there possibly was to see while insisting he carry Charlie the orange tabby cat. Thankfully, Charlie seemed content with resting his upper body on Adrian's shoulder for the majority of the house tour.

It was bright, clean, and tidy, but homey with plush seating and hardwood floors softened by rugs. There were three bedrooms and two baths. Adriana's room was a near-duplicate of the one at Kathy's only with more toys. When she showed him the cozy home office, Adriana was proud to say her mommy was going to start school soon to be a "PCA."

Adrian helpfully asked, "You mean a CPA?"

"Yes! Mommy is smart and I'm going to be just like her when I grow up."

Adrian had been unable to resist touching the top of her head. Her hair was silky and long, reminding him of the china dolls he'd seen in is mother's cabinet while growing up. Adriana was as beautiful, but unlike them, she wasn't cold.

She was love, fire, and warmth.

"You're already so smart like Mommy, Adriana, and I know you're just going to keep getting smarter."

Adriana clapped her hands, apparently happy about being compared favorably to her mother. Adrian felt a twinge of regret in knowing he'd never felt the same about his parents.

Even though she froze me out, I can already see that Victoria is such a good mother. This little girl adores her so much. I can only hope she one day feels the same about me.

After Adriana showed him everything, including the storage closet out in carport, she sat him down on the couch with the promise of being right back. Charlie jumped up on the couch and claimed his lap, completely uncaring that Adrian's suit was getting covered in cat hair.

He would've taken the opportunity to talk to Victoria then but she seemed content with staying, or more accurately hiding, in the kitchen. Adrian refused to chase after her, deciding it was best to let her stew in her juices longer.

Adriana came running back into the living room less than a couple of minutes later. "Watch me!" Victoria took the opportunity to start dinner while he observed Adriana practice her flippies, which were forward rolls, and katas in the living room while dressed in her white *gi*.

Once he was sure Adriana wasn't going to get hurt with her tumbling, he settled down and watched her, hand resting on his chin. Sitting in Victoria's nice and cozy house, he couldn't deny nostalgia tugged him hard. He'd loved the domestic simplicity of his and Victoria's life together before and with Adriana there, it just showed him how much he missed being away from her.

It wasn't just because of her cooking or the TV running softly in the background. Besides, he could have any number of highly-decorated chefs prepare his meals, snacks, and desserts with finer ambiance.

It was because Victoria's food had been love and *she* had been his home.

No wonder he'd been so closed off after Victoria left. Adrian had lived like an exile after being banished from the only place he'd ever wanted to stay.

Adrian raised an eyebrow when the three of them later sat down at her small kitchen table. Roast chicken, mashed potatoes, gravy, stuffing, and rolls—his favorites.

After meeting his mocking gaze for a split-second, Victoria's pretty face flushed. "Like father, like daughter. It's Adriana's favorite meal too," she murmured as way of explanation.

It felt indescribable to hear her say that.

Anger and frustration aside, Adrian felt more alive in the last twenty-four hours than he had the whole four years they were apart. Even though a large part of him still wanted to curse Victoria out until he was blue in the face for what she had done, there was no way he was ever going to give up feeling this alive again.

Victoria and Adriana were *his*. Somehow, someway he was going to have to make peace with her.

That was the mantra Adrian carried with him for rest of the night. It stayed with him through dinner. He heard it in his blood when Victoria left the room to give Adriana a bath. It fired his heart when they put their daughter to bed and read her two bedtime stories. And most importantly, it imprinted on his soul when Adriana sleepily whispered, "G'night, Daddy. Stay with me until I sleep?"

Adrian entered the living room to find Victoria sitting on the couch. The TV was on, a book lay across her lap, and Charlie was sprawled out on his back next to her. Victoria looked up at him, gaze shuttered but watchful.

She had every right to be wary of him. Adrian had a lot to say and he was positive

Victoria wasn't going to like the majority, if not all of it. Still, as long as she ultimately did as he wished, he'd be satisfied.

At least for now.

"We need to talk."

Victoria sat straighter. "I'm listening."

He took a seat on the other end of the couch. Adrian was taking a gamble that she'd react the way he'd already mentally predicted. "We'll leave tomorrow afternoon. That should be enough time for you to give notice at work and withdraw Adriana from school. The sooner she gets used to her new life, the better."

Victoria's jaw clenched once. "Abrupt change isn't good for a child. She needs routine, Adrian."

"I'm not asking."

Her voice quickened, words tumbling over each other faster and faster. "Look, what difference will a few months make? She just met you today and if we move too quickly then she'll associate you with a negative change. You don't want that and neither do I."

"I'll tell you what I don't want. I don't want you both here a day longer without me than necessary." Seeing she was about to argue, Adrian held up his hand. "I haven't backed down from my demands, Victoria. I already told you how things were going to be before we ever got here."

"Yes, but I never agreed to them." She stood up and paced, careful to keep her voice low and even. Charlie jumped down, apparently irritated, and padded his way into the kitchen. "Adrian, we have a whole life here. You can't expect us to pick up and move in one day. It's not reasonable."

"Neither was you keeping my daughter's existence from me."

Score.

She dashed away an angry glitter of tears. "I'm willing to pay the price for what I've done to you. I'll do whatever it takes to make it up to you, but what I won't do is make life difficult for Adriana. She loves her life here and if you try to force us to move like this—I'll fight you every step of the way."

"Is that so?"

"Absolutely."

Adrian smiled. It took on wolfish proportions when she visibly lost her composure. "How long will you need to settle things here and move back with me?"

"Maybe a couple of months."

"No. Try again."

"A month. I can't go any lower, Adrian. I mean it."

He paused long enough for her to fidget in place. "I can accept that." Relief visibly swept through her. Adrian went in for the kill. "However, I have two conditions that must be met or this all ends and we do it my way."

"What?"

"The first is we're getting married. Tomorrow."

Victoria wrapped her arms around her waist. "We're back at this again?"

"Yes, we are."

"But *why* do you want to marry me? You're obviously still so angry with me, Adrian. You can't really want this."

"Oh, but I do." He stood up and walked to her. He carefully brushed his hand against her cheek. "You can't be trusted to run free, kitten, so I have to collar you."

"Adrian, you *can* trust me. You don't have to do this—"

"Ssh!" he admonished while laying a finger against her lush lips. "Don't say that to me, Victoria. Not yet."

She stared at him mutely. Unhappiness glittered in her liquid-black eyes.

"Now come tomorrow we will get on a plane. We will meet with my lawyers. We *will* be married, Victoria. This is non-negotiable."

Victoria laid her head against his chest. Her unconscious need of comfort from him thrilled Adrian. It was all he could do to keep from enveloping her in his arms.

Her voice came to him in delicate whisper. "Asking me to marry you is such a big decision and commitment, Adrian. This is all just moving too fast."

He knew his next words would prick her like a thousand little claws. "I asked you once before, kitten. I told you then I wouldn't do it again. I'm keeping my word because this time I'm not asking you. I'm telling you."

Victoria took a step back. He missed the heat of her body against his. He watched as her lush mouth pressed into a hard line. "What's the second condition?"

Adrian brushed the back of his fingers against her cheek. She truly was as soft as a kitten. Still, he prepared for her bite, knowing it was going to be deep.

"I want another baby. Not in a couple of years but now."

***

Shock jolted right through Victoria. She couldn't believe what he had just said. "A baby? We already have a baby."

"No, we have a little girl. I want us to have a baby."

She took a giant step away from him. Disappointed colored her tone. “Adriana isn’t a thing to replace.”

“There you go again.”

“What?”

“Making assumptions about me and then deciding on your own what we’re going to do.”

Victoria’s felt her face flush with chagrin. “I’m sorry.”

He put his hands in his pockets. “Ask me why.”

“Why?”

“Because you stole from me the opportunity to be there for Adriana. To be there for you. I didn’t get to take you to your appointments and I didn’t get to go out in the middle of the night because you craved pickles and ice cream. I didn’t get to hold your hand while you pushed our daughter out in the world. I didn’t get to protect either of you and the only way you can ever make this even *close* to okay is to let me have another chance.”

Victoria couldn't deny the trembling in her body wasn't due to outrage. Hearing his words brought out a visceral reaction that she couldn't ignore on a primal level. Remembering last night and all the nights years before that, Victoria imagined herself pinned beneath his hard sexy body, legs wide open as he filled her.

"You like the idea, don't you?" Adrian took a step towards her. His eyes glittered with open desire.

"I'm not saying that," she denied while taking a step away.

"Liar." He wagged his finger. "You've become such a little liar, kitten. It's been such a shame to see how you turned out. You were once the most honest girl I'd met."

"Don't you get tired of insulting me?"

His lips parted in a wolfish grin. "Not yet. How can I when you're so fun to poke and prod?"

Victoria bumped up against the wall. "Adrian, you already know what I'm going to say."

Adrian put his hands on either side of Victoria, essentially trapping her. "Yes, you've become tedious that way. Go ahead. Tell me anyways."

"Having another baby so soon is just madness—"

His hand covered her mouth. "Better yet, don't tell me."

Victoria's senses drank in his scent. It was a delicious mixture of expensive cologne, Adrian, and familiarity. She closed her eyes, feeling herself melt into his will.

What was she fighting for anyways? Her pride? That's what got her into this bitter tangle to begin with. She wanted Adrian, had always wanted him, and here he was giving her the means to have him on a silver platter.

I should accept his terms. I already know it's what I really want.

Besides, maybe this could bring them closer together? Maybe he wouldn't hate her as much if she just gave into his will?

I'd give anything to make this right with Adrian. I still love him that much. And this is obviously the right thing for Adriana. She already adores her daddy and he's over the moon for her. Can I let my pride come in once again and ruin this?

Things could've been so different if she'd had just opened her mouth that fateful night on the sidewalk. Why couldn't she have had the wisdom to really understand how far the consequences would reach? Kathy tried to warn her, but she didn't listen.

Oh, Adrian. I'm so sorry for all of this. Why couldn't I trust you more—especially when you'd never really given me reason not to? I should've stood there with you instead of running away because of your distance...because I was afraid. Just like I am right now. Not because I don't want these things with you, but because I'm afraid it still won't be enough.

Victoria always knew how to do things on her own, but this was torturous because she had no real control. Trust couldn't be scheduled or quantified. It had to be earned and lived.

The first step in earning Adrian's trust was understanding and giving him what he needed. Doing it this way, when he was still so understandably furious with her—it just didn't inspire a workable plan. All Victoria could do was hope for the best and in her experience—hope was rarely a good enough plan.

But being without a plan terrified her because it showed that for all her accomplishments and hard work, Victoria was still a woman who was scared that if she didn't plan every detail and control every little thing then it would all fall apart.

One tear rolled down her cheek. If she had to choose between control and Adrian again, she'd choose Adrian. All she wanted was for him to forgive her and love her again. But was she going to be stronger than her fear?

"Ssh, kitten. It's okay. You can just give into this because I'm just a bastard, hmm? I'm making you play nice with me so just agree, okay?"

"That's not it," she whispered hoarsely.

"Then what is it?"

Victoria didn't look away, even though Adrian's gaze seared her. "Maybe I don't have the right to say this to you anymore, but I still love you. I love you so much, Adrian, and maybe this makes me a weak woman..."

Her voice trailed off for so long that Adrian came closer, his mouth only a hairsbreadth away from hers. "Go on, kitten. Tell me. I want to hear everything you have to say. Good or bad." He pulled away, but stayed close enough to stroke her cheek with one finger.

Victoria's heart fluttered. She sank into his warmth, wishing he could touch her forever. Would there ever come a time when this man didn't affect her like this?

I can't put it all into words. I can't tell him everything I feel. Not yet. Not until he's really ready to hear me. Right now he'd probably just throw it back in my face or tell me I'm lying.

And yet, the way Adrian was looking at her was absolutely intoxicating. It was almost like before. Staring into his beautiful hazel gaze, Victoria felt like she could lose herself in Adrian and not ever want to be found again.

"I'm scared."

"I know."

Victoria waited for him to say something more but he just looked at her as if he had all the time in the world to wait for whatever she had to say. His finger kept stroking. High up to the top of her cheekbone, low to the curve of her chin. Over and over again.

"You're serious, Adrian? Anything I have to say? It doesn't matter? You want to hear it?"

"Anything, kitten."

Victoria took a deep breath and let the words flow. "I don't want to be one of those couples that gets divorced in a year."

"It's till death do us part for me, kitten."

"I know you said that two people can be married and hate each other."

His finger paused right at the corner of her mouth. “Yes, it’s true.”

“I don’t want that.”

Adrian gifted her a sultry smile. “I don’t want that either.”

“Why?”

He drew a line straight to her heart. “Isn’t it obvious yet? It’s because I still love you.”

Victoria reached out for him, praying that it wasn’t a game for punishment where he was going to pull the emotional rug out from under her. “That’s not what you said this morning.”

“I meant those words when I said it.”

Adrian offered nothing else as explanation so Victoria dug deeper. “And now?”

He splayed his hand across the space between her breasts. The center of his palm was over her heart. “Can’t I feel both? Can’t I hate what you’ve done and still love you?”

It stung. She couldn’t blame him though. The fact that he was holding a civil conversation with her was more than she could’ve expected when he blasted her with ice just that very morning.

"Yes, you can."

Adrian leaned down and asked, "Don't you feel the same about me?"

His feathery whisper brought a rush of emotions to the surface. "No."

"No?"

"I could never hate you, Adrian."

He kissed her earlobe. "You're such a sweet kitten, but are you sweet enough to give me the answer I want?"

It's now or never. Everything changes after this.

"I agree."

Adrian pulled back. His beautiful mouth turned up in a smirk. "You agree to what?"

"I agree to your terms."

"Which are?"

"Damnit, Adrian!" Now he was just teasing her just to get a reaction. Although she frowned and pushed at his chest, just seeing the playfulness of his expression made everything a thousand times better than before.

He shook his head and kissed her far too quickly on the mouth. “No, I don’t remember that one.”

Victoria licked her lips, trying her best to keep her voice steady. “I agree to marrying you tomorrow and I…” she trailed off.

“And you…?”

“I…ah…I…” She let out another long breath and then straightened her shoulders. She met his mocking gaze without flinching. “I agree to try to have a baby with you.”

Adrian’s triumphant expression made desire curl hard in the pit of her stomach. “Try, kitten? I don’t think we’ll have to *try* at all.” He nuzzled the base of her throat with his mouth. “I bet it won’t take more than a few times to fill you up with my come before I get you pregnant.”

Victoria’s tentatively placed her hand on his chest. The feeling of his flexing muscles caused her to press her palm harder. Carnal thoughts raced through her mind as she imagined herself overflowing.

Adrian tipped her chin with one finger. “You liked hearing that, didn’t you? You liked the idea of being filled with my come, kitten. Tell me you don’t.”

She leaned closer, curling her hand around his chiseled jaw. “I like it. I like it more than I should. Can I tell you something?”

“I’ll be upset if you don’t.”

Victoria took a chance on sharing her fantasy. “I like thinking about you on top of me, one hand in my hair, while you pound me so hard we slide across the bed. You’ll kiss me, whispering how wet I am and how hot it makes you to feel how much I want you.”

Adrian groaned, lowering his eyelids to a half-slit. “And you’ll want me more than anything or anyone, won’t you?”

“Always.”

Adrian undid Victoria’s loose ponytail. “I’m taking you to bed. Tonight.”

Giddy that a decision had been made, Victoria purred as excitement coursed through her veins. She leaned in and linked her arms around his neck. “I know. I can’t wait for it.”

“Hmm, is that so?”

“Yes.”

He fisted his hand in her hair and yanked her head back suddenly. Victoria bit back a cry and watched, mesmerized, as Adrian whispered against her mouth, “Are you on birth control?”

The jealousy and frustration in his gaze elicited a shiver. “No.”

“Good.” He teased the corner of her mouth with a brief kiss. “Then it could happen tonight.” Adrian’s hand pressed into her lower tummy. “You’re going to get round and soft with my son or daughter, Victoria. Everyone will see that you’re mine.”

“I don’t need to be pregnant to be yours, Adrian.”

He pulled back. An expression of deep sadness settled on his handsome face. “Were you ever mine, kitten?”

***

Victoria's gaze misted. Adrian let go of her hair, hating that he'd exposed himself like that. It was too soon for him to bare his innermost fears and thoughts to her.

Adrian grabbed her by the hand and walked at a fast clip towards her bedroom—the one room he hadn't been able to tour without thinking about who else might have been there before him.

"Wait! What about the lights and the TV?"

"What about them?"

"I need to turn them off."

"Screw it. It doesn't matter." Adrian pushed open the door and pulled Victoria in behind him. He closed it gently, not wanting to accidently wake up their daughter. Adrian locked it and then picked Victoria up.

She murmured his name, uncertainty rounding each syllable. Adrian opened his arms and dropped her on the bed. He instantly crouched over her, a strong thigh on either side of her, and held Victoria's wrists in his hands.

The color on her face was the same shade of pink that excited him so much in the beginning. Adrian was still as fascinated with her innocence now as he was then. The only difference was that now her innocence was an illusion.

"Let me go for a second, Adrian."

He tightened his fingers. "Why?"

She gestured at the nightstand with her chin. "I need to turn the baby monitor on. We'll be able to hear if Adriana wakes up."

Anger lit a dark, dangerous spark. "Have you had to turn it on often, kitten?" Just the idea that she'd fucked other men in this very room made him want to round them all up and beat their faces to a bloody pulp.

"What do you mean?" She tilted her head in a way that he usually found endearing. He wasn't in the mood at the moment.

"How many men have you brought here and fucked while our daughter lay asleep?"

Victoria's face whitened with shock and more than a touch of outrage. "How dare you?"

"Answer the fucking question!"

She wiggled beneath him, trying her best to buck him off. Adrian wasn't budging. "I don't have to answer anything, Adrian!" Before he could hiss out another demand, Victoria coldly asked, "How about you answer it first? Have you been faithful to me all these years, Adrian?"

His gut felt like she'd just taken a bat to it. Disgust for the soulless assignations he'd had over the years made Adrian acutely ashamed of himself. He had no right to demand anything out of her and now because of his arrogance, Adrian was going to either have to admit what he'd done or let his silence do it for him.

Silence won out.

Victoria stopped fighting him. She closed her eyes and whispered, "I don't blame you. Really, I don't. I always knew you'd move on. So why does it hurt so much to finally face it?"

Adrian let go of her and sat back on his heels. "I don't have anything to say in my defense, Victoria." When she stayed silent except for the soft sounds of her crying, Adrian clenched his hands and apologized hoarsely, "I'm sorry for being such an ass. What you did while we were apart wasn't my business. I had no right to demand that of you. I'm sorry."

Victoria shook her head and covered her eyes with the back of her hands. "No, you didn't have a right to ask, but I don't have any right to be hurt. We weren't together and it was four years. I couldn't expect a man like you to be a monk."

"A man like me?"

She dragged in a wet breath. "Yes, a man like you. A man who is so kind and handsome and so full of love. You have so much love to give, Adrian, and I know it makes me selfish to say this, but I'm so happy that you aren't married or dating anyone. Above all, I'm so glad that you still feel anything good for me after what I did to you and Adriana."

Adrian wanted to pull her to him so badly. How did he go from rage to lust to Machiavellian glee to this infinite sorrow? "I'm not that good of a person, Victoria."

"Yes, you are."

"No, I'm not." Maybe it was the darkness in the room or the fact that she still covered her eyes, but Adrian felt compelled to confess. "Now I have something to tell you. Will you listen?"

"Y-Yes."

"I fucked other women since you left me. It took me a while to do it because I was so hung up on you, but eventually I did it. I've been on clockwork once a quarter since. Never more than once and rarely the same one." He heard his voice as she must've—cold and lacking any hint of softness.

Victoria bit her lip, obviously choking back a sob. Adrian's gaze clouded. The room distorted, dipping and swirling crazily like the emotions running through him.

"I'm not telling you this to hurt you, Victoria, even though I know it is. I'm telling you this so you'll understand." He waited until she nodded once, still fighting to keep her sobs under control. "I was a bastard to them, barely knowing their names and not giving a damn whether they received pleasure or not. It never lasted more than five minutes before my body was satisfied, but each encounter left me colder. Do you know why? Look at me, Victoria. Please."

He waited, stretched thin, until she removed her hands. Adrian fell into her watery gaze, miserable that he'd put the sadness there. She stared at him, mute, but visibly wary from what he might say to her.

"I heard that I had changed from the way I was before with my exes, that I was a coldblooded bastard, but truthfully, I really hadn't changed. I've always been a coldblooded bastard. Sure I was nicer, especially with my wealth, but for all my smiles I never let anyone close enough to matter. At least this time I was honest. But I understand why it was like that."

She sniffled. "Why?"

"Victoria, kitten, they weren't *you*. I'm a billionaire and I've succeeded in changing the world through my ventures. I could have anything I wanted except for the one person I've ever loved. How could I not feel frozen? I never really knew happiness until I met you, Victoria."

Adrian bowed his head, melancholy possessing him and snuffing out the rage he'd nursed off and on since he found about Adriana.

"That night I asked you to marry me because I was so afraid of losing you. You had the guts to say no because you knew it wasn't right. But I didn't even have the guts to fight for you. I just let you slip away. Why would I ever let anyone get close to me after that? Why would I deserve it? Especially when all I wanted was you?"

Victoria shifted beneath him, getting onto her knees. Her hands cupped his face and although she still cried, her smile was full of love and understanding. "Adrian, you deserve love more than you'll ever know. You're the kindest man I've met. All the way from the first time we met."

"I was nice to you because I wanted to seduce you."

"I don't believe that. Yes, you wanted to get in my pants but I wanted to get in yours too. You weren't nice to me because of that. You were nice because it's who you are. I've met my share of wealthy people, Adrian, and you're not like them."

Adrian let out a long, shuddering breath. He buried his face against her neck. "I don't know what to say, kitten."

"Then I'll talk. You changed my world and showed me that there was more than accomplishing goals and working myself into an early grave. You gave me a daughter that I love more than life itself. You are the best thing to have ever happened to me."

Her words soothed old scars. Adrian still found himself reluctant to believe them. All his justifications over her keeping Adriana a secret from him shriveled. "You think I'm kind even though I threatened you just this morning and every chance I got since?"

"Yes."

Adrian lifted his head. "You must be the most forgiving woman I've ever met then. Even I wouldn't forgive me if I was you."

"It's a good thing you're not me then." Victoria wrapped her arms around his waist and rested her cheek beneath his beating heart. "Why shouldn't I forgive you? I kept Adriana a secret from you because I was so scared you'd reject us. I should've been braver but I wasn't. How can that ever be your fault?"

Strange how their circular conversations took on a different meaning every time they looped back to the beginning.

"Maybe it's not but it hurts like hell, kitten, to know that you were willing to let our little girl go her whole childhood without knowing me."

"I'm so sorry. I can't say it enough. Adrian, I swear I'm going to spend the rest of my life making it up to you if you'll let me. I promise."

"I'm never going to let you go again, kitten. Ever." He sank his fingers deep in her hair and bent down to capture her lips with his. Adrian kissed her with every ounce of pain and passion he contained.

Victoria moaned, tightening her arms around him as she fought to get closer to him. Her tongue thrust into his open mouth aggressively and her sharp little nails dug into his back sweetly.

Adrian brought her down on the bed and covered her body with his. Supporting himself on his arms, he stared down at her and loved what he saw. Victoria's large eyes stared back at him, lust gleaming He didn't want to wait to play with her. He wanted to fuck her raw. Not in anger. Not in punishment.

In love.

He wanted to brand her with his cock. He wanted to mark her with his come. He wanted to fill her up over and over again.

Most of all, Adrian wanted Victoria to never, ever leave him again. He was going to do everything in his power to keep her sated and happy with him. He'd avoid being ruthless as long as he could, but Adrian knew that his need for her was stronger than his need to be a gentleman.

Pained, he wondered if his mind was forever twisted or if he'd ever go back to the confident, cheerful, and laidback man he was before.

The truth whispering its secrets to him promised Adrian that he'd eventually lose her again, even if he managed to chain her by his side, if he couldn't make peace with their past. As long as he held regret for their past and let the agony continue to fester inside him, eventually Victoria would have no choice but to leave him again.

Fear, that damned emotion that Adrian hadn't acknowledged or entertained until the threat of Victoria's absence surfaced, rose up to torment him further.

"What are you thinking?"

Her whisper shook him from him dark thoughts. "I'm thinking about how good it's going to feel when I'm deep inside you."

***

Victoria knew Adrian wasn't being completely honest with her. Anger possessed him while he stared at her and it lashed her heart. She could've sworn they'd made progress in the last few minutes, but it wasn't enough.

That's okay. I'm in this for the long haul. I just need to do everything I know how to do to make him happy. And sex is the one thing we always made right.

Victoria spread her legs and brought her hips up to rub against his hard length. "I can't wait until I can come around your cock again bare again. Nothing between us."

Adrian's nostrils flared slightly. "What else can't you wait for?"

"I can't wait until I suck you deep in my mouth. I've always loved sucking you, Adrian, especially when you lick me too."

He inhaled sharply. "I love the taste of you on my tongue. It's so good, just like honey."

Victoria tugged at his belt, beyond eager to free him for her mouth. "It hasn't even been a day and I'm already hungry for you."

Adrian covered her hands with his. "Slow down, kitten. We're doing things my way, remember?"

Victoria couldn't control her pout. Thankfully, it only seemed to amuse him.

"Adrian?"

"Hmm?"

"The answer is no one."

He cocked his head, eyes bright with incomprehension until it dawned on him.

"No one?"

"No one. Ever."

Primal male satisfaction overtook Adrian. He seized Victoria and branded her with his kiss, not leaving her until she could barely think or speak. Then he crouched over her and tugged up her shirt with his teeth. Adrian kissed the exposed skin over her belly gently.

"Now, let's make a baby."

TWENTY-THREE

It was another morning but nothing like the ones proceeding it. Adrian woke up sometime after four and couldn't go back to sleep. The house was quiet and his thoughts were anything but.

Even now she might be pregnant.

Adrian put his hand on Victoria's stomach, feeling the heat of her through the thin cotton nightgown. After they'd made love for the third time, Victoria had pulled him into the shower to clean up and get dressed for bed. When he'd raised a brow and said, "We've always slept naked," she'd smiled and explained, "Sometimes Adriana likes to sleep with me late at night. I don't want her to come in and find us like this."

He heartily agreed and ended up sleeping in his dress pants and one of his old t-shirts that Victoria had pilfered when she originally left. The blush on her face was enough to keep him from teasing her into oblivion.

There were so many things he had to learn about being part of a family. Never mind the fact that he'd officially had one his whole life, Victoria's little tribe was far different from him own.

He would've never been comfortable or welcomed into his parents room. Either one since they slept in separate rooms for almost as long as he remembered. But even though he'd only been a real father for less than a day, Adrian couldn't imagine letting Adriana grow up the way he and his brother Gavin had.

That's what getting married for money and power will do to you. It makes you bitter and hard. So does staying because you feel trapped.

Sitting up in Victoria's bed, he heard the pitter-patter of feet shortly before the door eased open. Immediately, he was grateful for Victoria's foresight. Adrian smiled and whispered Adriana's name. She barely paused, so fixated was she on climbing into bed and snuggling right next to her mother. Half-asleep, Victoria shifted back towards him, easily making room for their daughter. Adriana was back to sleep within seconds and so was Victoria.

Adrian turned on his side and looked at his girls. There wasn't anything he wouldn't do for them.

Including letting them go if I need to?

Now where did that treacherous thought come from? Adrian couldn't imagine the situation that would call for it. Still, his mind worriedly circled around him and his brother's upbringing. What did he know about raising a healthy family?

I can learn. I can do anything I want as long as I put my mind to it.

The words stitched themselves to his mind when they got up together a couple of hours later. Adrian watched the controlled chaos of getting an independent three year old ready for school while getting yourself ready and making breakfast.

"Can you get her some toast and cereal?"

Adrian hopped to it, absurdly pleased to do something to help both of his precious girls. He sat on the couch next to his daughter while she watched TV and ate her breakfast. Adrian took a bite of toast when Adriana shoved it near his mouth. "Do you want some, Daddy?"

He took a bite. Satisfaction filled him when he saw how happy it made her. Adriana was so much like her mother in that way. It was always the littlest things that made his kitten so happy.

Adrian himself was also very happy with the world. He'd arranged for his calendar to be cleared for the rest of the week. Most importantly though, Adrian already had a security detail in place for Adriana. That would most likely not come as a surprise to Victoria, but he'd mention it to her make sure.

Speaking of his most beloved woman in the world, Victoria came in a few minutes later dressed and looking breathtakingly beautiful.

How did she manage to look so put together after the lusty night they spent together?

Adrian knew he wasn't going to be immaculate on the plane trip back, but he didn't mind. So what if his clothes were rumpled and every hair wasn't in place? He and Victoria were back together and they had a daughter with hopefully another sibling on the way for her. If not now, soon. And on top of all that, Adrian was getting married to the only woman he'd ever loved or ever would love.

Today was going to be the best day of his life.

The plane trip back was far different than the one yesterday. This time Victoria sat next to him, her hand held tightly in his. She kissed him more than once, but only when the steward wasn't around.

"We should be back home around six, right?"

Unable to keep from touching her, Adrian lifted her hand and kissed it. "Definitely."

"Good because I hate leaving Adriana any more than I have to. Although Kathy can keep her as long as necessary if things run over. I'll just need to call her if anything changes."

"I don't see anything changing, but I'm glad she's in good hands until then. I can't wait to see her again."

Even though they'd only dropped Adriana off at preschool a few hours before, Adrian already missed his little girl and saw significantly reduced business trips in his future as a result. The itch to acquire money and power disappeared now that he knew he had something greater and more meaningful to work for.

A happy family. A healthy, joyful daughter. A partner and lover that he could count on for the rest of his days.

Life was good and only bound to get better.

He kissed her hand again. "Are you nervous about becoming Mrs. Adrian Hawthorne?"

A sweet smile appeared on her lips for a moment. "A little."

"Don't be."

"You're not nervous?"

"Not in the slightest. I've been waiting for this, for you, my whole life."

Victoria laid her head on his shoulder and snuggled into him as much as she could. He was tempted to make use of the bedroom and show her how he really felt with his body, but they were due to land in less than ten minutes.

As usual, traffic was heavy but soon enough they were at his penthouse. After showering, shaving, and changing into a fresh suit, Adrian felt ready to take on the next step of his life. Victoria was as lovely as ever, having already gone into her closet and wearing a simple, elegant ivory dress.

She twirled for him and said, "It's not white, but I think it should do for a wedding dress."

"You look beautiful, kitten." Adrian wrapped his arm around her waist and kissed the top of her head. "We'll have another one, wherever you want, afterwards. As big as you want. I promise."

"We don't have to."

"I want to. I want everyone to know we're married and a family." Victoria couldn't hide her troubled expression fast enough. Adrian tipped her chin up. "What's wrong, kitten? Tell me."

She shook her head and ran one small hand down his bronze-colored tie. "It's just that I never thought that I'd be getting married, much less this quickly."

"I know. You know something though, kitten?"

"Hmm?"

"We've always moved this quickly. It's our way." Adrian pushed a lock of her hair behind her delicate ear. "Remember how we made love for the first time after one night? Then we moved in together just as fast? Getting married within a day after we reunited fits right in line, kitten."

Happiness brought color back to her face. "You're right." She reached up to hug him tightly. "Let's get married!"

Their enthusiasm dampened considerably once they were seated at his lawyers' conference table. Adrian's counsel weren't overtly disrespectful to Victoria, but it was there in the way they explained the paperwork and focused on the payout she'd receive if they divorced.

Elegant and restrained though they were, Peabody and Mitchell were alternately threatening and bribing her into falling in line. Adrian had seen them in action before and while he approved their methods against other opponents, he did not appreciate them against his soon-to-be wife.

Adrian discreetly looked at her and what he saw disturbed him. Victoria's lush mouth was pressed into a firm line while color remained high on her cheeks. She sat there at the edge of the leather chair, back straight, and hands folded primly in front of her.

Victoria didn't ask any questions about her financial due. The money didn't seem to matter to her at all. However, his lawyers obviously thought otherwise.

"Our client is being very, very generous with you, Ms. Montford. We want to stress that in the unfortunate event that you might challenge this agreement if your union comes to an end."

"I won't."

"Be that as it may, be aware that this agreement is airtight. You may choose to contest it at a later date, again, in the unfortunate event that you and Mr. Hawthorne no longer suit. If you do, know that you will incur significant legal cost and still not be able to break this agreement. Do you understand the words I have spoken to you?"

Adrian abruptly stood up, beyond annoyed with their tone. "Gentleman, give us the room."

His lawyers nodded and left without another word, obviously aware they had offended their biggest client. Adrian then turned to Victoria and held her hand. It was cold and damp. "Are you all right?"

She gave him a shaky smile. "Not really, but I'll be okay. We just need to get this part done so we can go before the judge and make this official, right?"

"Kitten, tell me what I can do to make this better."

Victoria kissed his knuckles. "It's okay. I'm just not used to dealing with people who think I'm gold digger—at least I haven't had to deal with it for a while."

His brows snapped together. "What do you mean?"

"It's nothing."

"Victoria..."

She opened her mouth and then abruptly closed it before starting again. "It's just that I had deal with the occasional snide comment or two when we were together."

"Why didn't you tell me?"

"Because I didn't want to make you worry or cause you trouble."

Anger made his tone blunt. "Victoria, you can always come to me if anyone gives you shit. Understand? I'm serious. I want to know."

She shrugged, giving him a sad little smile. "It's the price I have to pay to be with someone like you, Adrian. It's always been like that and probably will, but I love you enough to stomach it."

***

The devastated look on his face immediately told her she'd said the right thing the wrong way.

"Adrian, I'm sorry. I didn't mean for it to come off bad. I just meant—"

He cut her off. "What do you mean 'stomach it,' Victoria?"

"It was just a bad turn of phrase. I just mean that I love you so much that I'll do whatever it takes to be with you." Victoria saw that her words didn't calm his bad reaction. It only seemed to make it worse.

"I don't want that from you, kitten. I don't want being with me to be a trial you have to endure." Adrian stood up. Victoria missed his touch, especially because she didn't understand what had gotten him so upset.

He started pacing, raking a hand through his hair and cursed softly.

Victoria desperately tried to fix what had gone wrong. "Adrian, you're not a trial. I'm with you because I want to be."

He abruptly stopped. A look of indescribable sadness came over his beautiful face. "Or because I threatened to take Adriana away from you and made you come here less than a day later. I finally understand why you left me. You were setting me free because you loved me that much, didn't you?"

Coldness slinked about her, eliciting a shiver she couldn't contain. "Yes, but what does that have to do with us now?

Adrian put his hands in his pockets. "You can go."

Victoria sat there, pained bewilderment rooting her in place. "What did you say?"

"You can go, kitten. I don't want to keep you here by force anymore." Obvious sadness twisted his lips. "You deserve better than that."

"No. Stop." Heart pounding with dread, Victoria went to him. "Now you listen here, Adrian Hawthorne. Yes, you threatened me yesterday and I threatened you. But if you think for one moment that the only reason I'm here today is to keep my daughter, well, then you don't know who I really am. I love you, Adrian, and I'm marrying you today because I love you. I do what I want to do and that especially refers to you."

Adrian kept quiet, but his attention remained fixed on her.

"Talk to me and tell me what's really going on. Are you scared to get married?"

"Hell no!"

"Then what is it?"

He raked another hand through his hair and looked away out the window. "My mother used to always say she had to stomach being married to my father. Hearing you say the same words just took me back to that."

"Adrian, I'm so sorry. I didn't know." Victoria hugged his big body to her, taking solace when he didn't remain stiff in her arms, but seemingly melted against her.

"How would you? I never talked to you about my family before."

I can tell him anything. It'll be okay.

ADRIAN

"Do you know I used to think the reason why you didn't talk about them or had me meet them was because you didn't see me as marriage-material. That's probably another reason why I reacted so badly when you did propose."

"I'm sorry, kitten. It wasn't like that. Honest. I barely could stand seeing them. I definitely didn't want to inflict them on you. Besides that, I just didn't like talking about them."

"Why not?"

His arms tightened around her and then he took a step back. Adrian kept both of her hands in his. "There's not much to say. We see each other about once or twice a year. We're not close and I don't see that changing."

"What about your brother?"

Adrian shrugged. "Gavin? He's got his own life."

"You know I didn't even know you had a brother until I..." Victoria's voice trailed off, reluctant to admit to her internet snooping. "I read that he's your adopted brother."

"Yes, well, Gavin...he..."

The last time she heard Adrian stumble so badly was when he was proposing. Now that she knew better, Victoria understood that whatever it was he was going to say meant the world to him. She waited patiently.

"Gavin isn't...he's my half-brother. My father had an affair which resulted in Gavin's birth. We only found about him when he was seven. His mother dropped him off in front of our building and left him there with a note. Gavin didn't speak for two years."

"Oh, that's so awful!"

"No one knows that he's my half-brother. Officially, my parents adopted him and that's the story we've kept."

There was so much left unsaid that Victoria didn't wonder anymore why Adrian was distant from his family. She squeezed his hands. "I did the same thing to you in a way by keeping Adriana a secret, didn't I?"

Adrian blinked, gaze unfocused as if he was thinking of the past. "I guess you did. I didn't put the two together, but yes."

She bent her head down and kissed his knuckles. “Forgive me, Adrian.”

He suddenly cupped her face in his hands and kissed her passionately and thoroughly. Victoria surrendered to the sultry pull of his lips and tongue. When he pulled back, she leaned against him limp and breathless.

Adrian smoothed his thumbs across her warm cheeks. His gaze glittered like emerald glass. “Yesterday I was angrier than I ever remember being. It’d been so long since I let myself feel much of anything that I exploded in a way I shouldn’t have. I said things I shouldn’t have.”

“It’s okay. I understand.”

The look he gave her was so full of love. “I also forgive you. I know you, Victoria, and now that I’m not furious and hurt anymore I know you wouldn’t have done it if you didn’t feel like you had to. I’m just sorry that I made you feel that way. You were my kitten and all I ever wanted to do was protect you and make you happy.”

"You did, Adrian." Victoria's tears coursed down her cheeks. She didn't bother to wipe them away. "Do you really forgive me?"

"Yes."

She rested her head against his chest and let out a quivering breath. "I'm sorry I didn't talk to you when I needed to. I just kept everything inside, pretending things weren't bothering me when they were."

"Kitten, you're not the only one guilty of that. For all that talking brought us together, you and I didn't talk when we most needed to. And that's why I have say this." Adrian gestured to the conference table. "We're not ready for marriage yet."

Victoria took in the neat stacks with one glance. Although she'd hated how his lawyers practically painted her with a money-hungry brush, she was willing to deal with it and sign practically anything to make Adrian feel secure and to be his wife. Still, she knew he was right.

Because of that Victoria tried not to let her mouth wobble from disappointment. “I guess we’re not.”

“Both times I tried to force our marriage to fit and both times have been wrong.”

She arched on tip-toe until Adrian leaned down close enough for her to kiss him sweetly. “Not wrong. Marrying you would never be wrong.”

“Oh, yeah?”

“Yeah.”

“Ms. Montford, be warned that I am taking your statement as a pre-engagement of sorts.”

“Really?” Victoria found a way to smile despite the heaviness in her heart.

“Only if you’re okay with it.”

Victoria kissed him again. “I’m more than okay with it, Mr. Hawthorne.”

True there was disappointment but there was also hope. Because of her hope, Victoria knew that one day the time would be right. There wouldn’t be the need for threats, secrets, coercion, or fear.

Even now the fear she'd carried for so long that she couldn't measure up or that one day Adrian would tire of her and see she really wasn't so special, slowly disappeared.

Adrian gestured to the window. "Want to grab a chair and talk?"

"What about your lawyers? Won't they be needing to come in?"

He shrugged. "They can wait."

Victoria laughed. A beat passed before Adrian joined her. Their shared tension and sorry seemingly melted together, leaving them fresh and clean.

"I would love to talk." He pulled two leather armchairs over to the window. Once they sat down she reached out for his hand. Adrian entwined his fingers with hers. "So what would you like to talk about?"

"Anything. Everything."

EPILOGUE

Three Years Later

Adrian slowly walked back and forth, careful to keep his sleeping son from rousing. Victoria poked her head in the door. “How’s he doing?”

“Fine. Just fine.”

She padded over to him on slipper feet. “I can take him.”

“Not a chance, Mrs. Hawthorne. This is me and Victor’s bonding time.” Adrian shot her a concerned frown. “Besides, what are you doing out of bed? You’re supposed to be resting.”

Victoria stroked the back of their baby’s head. “I missed this little one too much to stay in bed.”

"You shouldn't be up, kitten. You only gave birth four days ago."

"Yes, but I feel fine. Really, Adrian. Thank you for caring though." Victoria reached up and ran the backs of her fingers along his stubble cheek. "How are you doing, Daddy?"

Adrian closed his eyes in bliss. "Better than fine. Perfect."

He thought through all the twists and turns he and Victoria had taken before getting here. All the things said and unsaid until they finally reached a point where they could trust in one another's words and trust in the place in each other's hearts.

They'd had a long pre-engagement where they'd learned how to be a couple and a couple in a family. Balancing that along with being parents was a challenge, but one he'd loved undertaking. Eventually, Adrian had stepped down from his rigorous career and appointed a CEO to run things.

The visit with his parents went a smidgen better than expected but not nearly good enough for Adrian. They had coldly berated him the night before he brought Victoria and Adriana over. Only the fact that the subject of their ire wasn't in having Adriana, but rather not knowing he had a child made it better.

They were polite to Victoria and quite a few degrees warmer to Adriana. Odd that they didn't seem to care enough to foster a good relationship with him and Gavin, but definitely wanted one with Adriana.

"Sometimes it easier for people to be grandparents than parents. They need the time and distance to see their mistakes. At least, that's what Kathy says about her mother."

Adrian bought a huge estate in North Carolina with plenty of acreage for privacy, but not so far away from the Triangle that Victoria's commute was going to be soul-sucking. When he told her he planned on being a work-at-home Dad, Victoria hadn't batted an eye.

She understood that he needed the bonding time with his daughter and just as he had been solely focused on his business ventures, he wanted to be just as focused on his family.

Although they'd went back to practicing safe sex after leaving the lawyers' office, they both felt disappointed when Victoria hadn't gotten pregnant after all. Still, he and Victoria agreed it was for the best. Especially after she'd given him a box containing her scrapbooks and a thumb drive containing Adriana's birth along with her video journal.

Hearing everything Victoria had gone through, all her fears and worries about their daughter, about her relationship with him, brought Adrian to tears. Especially when he watched her giving birth. Victoria calling for him forced him to his knees.

Adrian nuzzled Victor's soft, downy head. "He's so tiny, kitten. I can hardly believe that one day he'll grow and be as big as me."

Victoria gently rubbed her newborn's back. "I know. They grow up so fast. That's why it's important to take lots of pictures and video."

Victor let out a tiny mewl before settling back down into the curve of Adrian's neck.

"Ssh, little one. Daddy's got you."

He proposed to Victoria a year after they'd moved in together, when they were on vacation. Adrian and Victoria rented a huge beach house on the Outer Banks and invited her family over. They were slated to come closer to the end of the week, leaving Adrian just enough time to present Victoria a ring after they'd made love late into the night and were on the deck hearing the ocean and watching the stars.

Victoria had laughed and cried before launching herself into his arms. "Yes, yes, yes!"

The third time was indeed the charm.

Grandma McKinnon approached Adrian at the reception, shoulders square and expression stern. He expected her to lecture him and say something to the effect of "It's about time!" Instead, she surprised Adrian.

"I apologize for what I said to you at Victoria's graduation. It wasn't my place. You're a good man, Adrian, and I should've never questioned it. I apologize."

Their honeymoon was short but sweet. Then married life began. It was a time of kindergarten, homework, holidays, and finding time to kiss and say "I love you."

Before he knew it, Victoria gave him a little wrapped box with a set of baby booties. "Does this mean what I think it means?"

"Yes!"

"Daddy, I'm going to finally have a brother or a sister. Isn't it wonderful?"

Adrian had swept both of his girls in his arms and whooped in joy. For the next seven months he'd become a mother hen, fussing over Victoria and making sure she didn't overwork herself. She'd the patience of a saint, even though she was in graduate school and studying for her CPA exam.

Victoria's water broke in the middle of the night. After a long afternoon of walking the halls and sucking on ice cubes, their son finally made his appearance at 5:12pm at 7lbs. 8oz. with a full set of lungs.

"What should we name him?" Victoria asked while nursing their son.

"Since you named our daughter after me, it's only fair that I name our son after you."

And now here they were.

Life was good and only bound to get better.

"What are you thinking about, Adrian?"

He smiled, feeling his love for Victoria and the life they were creating together overflow.

"Everything." Adrian leaned down to kiss her gently. "I love you."

"I love you too."

THE END

OTHER TITLES

Mad, Bad, & Dangerous to Love Series

Mad for You

First Night (A Mad for You Short)

First Lines (A Mad for You Short)

Bad for You

Dangerous for You

All to Love You

Rebecca and Trevor

Being Trevor's – A Novella

My Love Series

My Love Forgive

Marcus's Mercy (A Dark Romance Serial)

Marcus's Mercy #1

Marcus's Mercy #2

Marcus's Mercy #3

ABOUT ANNA ANTONIA

Anna is a lover of all things dark and passionate. Living in the Southeastern United States, she enjoys antiquing, DIY thrift store finds, sedate hiking along trails, and spending time with her family and menagerie of pets. Being the only girl in a household full of men makes it hard to always be a lady, but she gives it a good old college try.

Printed in Great Britain
by Amazon